UNRAPTURED: AURORA

By

Joel Kreger

UNRAPTURED: AURORA

By

Joel Kreger

Text copyright © 2019 Joel W. Kreger

ISBN   978-1-733709-1-0

Dedication

To those who dream of a better world,
and to those who work to make it so.

PREFACE

The northern lights were beyond spectacular on this warm spring evening. There are few words to describe the magnificence of the pulsating colors of the aurora borealis that filled the night sky. Scientists may have developed their explanations for how electrically charged particles from a solar flare entering the earth's atmosphere cause such a display and how that may sometimes cause electrical disruptions in our modern day world, but such explanations can not fully explain what caused the events of that early May night - and the time that followed.

PART 1 - AURORA

Chapter 1 - Let There Be Light

Aurora Cortez-Smith had just walked out of the school building late that evening upon the completion of her favorite event, the "Festival of Nations" in which her students shared with the community the research and art displays they had constructed to communicate their knowledge about the people and cultures of the world.

She was standing by her car, one of the few remaining in the parking lot since she had stayed to help clean up after the event. As she stood transfixed by the stupendous display of the northern lights undulating across the sky, she suddenly realized that the lights that normally illuminated the parking lot were dark. Turning around she noticed that there were no lights in the school, nor in any of the surrounding buildings of the small town. The ever-changing lights of the aurora were amazingly bright and were illuminating the parking lot as brightly as if the streetlights were still on. Then she realized there was an absence of sounds. The air was still and quiet, except for the multiplying sounds of dogs barking and people shouting in the distance.

She pulled the key fob out of her purse and pushed the button to open her car door, but nothing clicked. She grabbed the handle and tried to open it, but it was still locked. Quickly she slipped the manual emergency key from the key fob and unlocked the door. When she opened the door, none of the interior lights went on. Sitting down in the driver's seat, she pulled her cell phone from her purse and tried to turn it on. Nothing. It was as if someone had turned a switch and all the lights and power in the world had been turned off.

"Damn," she said softly to herself and wondered what she was to do. No lights. No car. No phone.

"Hey! Aurora!" a voice shouted out from near the school.

It was Maggie, the Math teacher, and as she nervously and quickly walked toward Aurora, she blurted out, "Are you okay?"

"I'm fine, but nothing seems to be working."

"I know! I'm really freaking out! I was standing there talking with Tom. Suddenly, all the lights went out, and he was gone."

Stepping out of her car and standing to meet Maggie, Aurora questioned, "You mean he just disappeared? Poof? Just like that?"

"Well, not with a poof! He had just said that he was going to go finish sweeping the cafeteria. He turned away from me, and then the lights went off - and he was gone!"

"I'll go back in with you. We'll find him."

"No, we won't. He is gone. There was still enough light from the skylights for me to see. He just vanished. Right before my eyes. I called his name, but he was gone."

"That's crazy. He has to be here."

"I know! But he's not, I tell you! What the heck is happening?"

They stood in stunned silence for a moment and then the loud voices from across the parking lot drew their attention. In the eerie glow of the flickering skies, they could see that some people had come out of the houses across the street from the parking lot. They were talking loudly and gesturing frantically.

Oakwood was a small midwestern town. The teachers were well known in the community, and in return, they knew most of the people and the families who lived in the community. The school grounds bordered a well kept up neighborhood of those old-fashioned two-story houses with the porch on the front and the detached garage in the back. Stately oaks towered over the front yards where the people were gathering. Quickly, the two women teachers decided to join the group. They could hear the loud voices saying things similar to what they had just shared between themselves moments earlier. One of them, the husband of a secretary in the school office, was the loudest.

"What the hell is going on? She just disappeared! We were sitting and watching the TV when BAM! The lights go out, and she is just gone. The kids, too. No one is left in the house but me."

"Now, Pete, settle down," reassured his neighbor, Jim, who stood there with his wife, "I'm sure there must be some explanation. People don't just disappear like that."

"The hell they don't! It just happened!"

"Okay, okay, calm down. I'm sure we'll find out what is going on. Let me grab a flashlight and see if we can find 'em."

"It won't work. Nothing will. I tried every flashlight in my house. None of them work!"

"Okay, then let me get my kerosene lantern lit, and we'll go look."

By this time, Aurora and Maggie had made their way across the parking lot and street to the Peterson's front yard and joined them. While Jim went to get his lantern from the garage, they shared their stories with Pete and with Jim's wife, Carol.

Jim returned carrying his kerosene lantern which gave a soft and steady glow. Together the five of them walked to Pete's house. An inspection of the home revealed no one else present except for the family dog and the gerbils in the son's bedroom.

Pete was still visibly upset by the absence of his wife and children but had shifted into a mood of despondency. He took one of his wife's candle decorations from the mantle display, lit its candle, and dejectedly declared, "You folks might as well go on home. I don't see as if there is anything more you can do here. They're gone."

Carol patted him on the arm and said, "Are you sure? You know you can come and stay the night with us."

"Naw, that's okay. There's nothing you can do. I'll be

okay here. I just can't figure out what is going on. Who knows, maybe it's that damn rapture thing Karen was always going on about."

Maggie, who made no secret of herself being an agnostic, gave a snort, while Aurora attempted to politely comfort him, "I don't know, Pete, but maybe things will be clearer in the morning."

He gave no reply, but slumped into his recliner and stared off into space. The others quietly left his house, closing the door behind themselves. As they stepped off the front porch, Carol said, "You ladies can stay with us tonight. None of us know what is happening, and even if we don't have power, I wouldn't want you venturing out in the night not knowing what is going on."

Maggie's first reaction was to decline, "I know Mike will be looking for me to come home, and if I don't show up, he'll come to get me."

Shaking his head Jim spoke up, "I know you folks are self-sufficient, and maybe Mike will head on into town, but if all the power is out here and none of us can get our cars or trucks started here, I doubt that he'll be driving into town tonight. Even if he started walking right now and left the kids at home alone, it would be a couple of hours before he would get here. I still think it'd be best for you to stay here overnight. Tell you what, I'll write up a note, take it over to the school, and tape it to the door telling him where to find you. Just in case he does show up."

With a glance at Aurora, Maggie sighed and said, "I think you are probably right. It probably is best. Moreover, Aurora, you definitely have to stay too. There is no way you can go home tonight."

"Yeah, you're right. It doesn't look like I will be making the half hour drive to my apartment, and I'll feel better staying with someone I know.

With those words of agreement, they went into the Peterson's home where Carol lit some candles, and they sat down in the family living room while Jim left to take the note over to the school and tape it to the door. All three of them were obviously troubled and confused about what had happened. Maggie was drumming her fingers on the coffee table as she sat, leaning forward on the sofa. Aurora, sitting next to her was nervously pulling her shoulder-length hair and tying it up in a ponytail. Carol was chattering about how they could sleep in the guest room and that everything would be okay in the morning. After a few minutes, Jim re-joined them.

"I didn't see anyone else over by the school."

"We were the last ones there," said Aurora, "Well, except for Tom, and Maggie said he disappeared, too."

"I wonder," said Carol, "maybe Pete was on to something. Karen certainly did talk about the rapture often enough. I remember her trying to convince me to join her church so that when the rapture happened, I would go to heaven with her. I know Karen and the kids believed it, and that she was frustrated that Pete would never go to church with her. Also, you said Tom disappeared too. I know he was active in his church. Jim and I, however, we have our beliefs and our doubts, but we aren't fanatics about pushing anything on other people. You, Maggie, everyone in town knows you don't believe in any god. What about you, Aurora? You're pretty new here, and we don't know that much about you because you're not from here and have only been teaching here just a couple of years. What is it you believe?"

Aurora hesitated before she responded, "I am spiritual, I do have beliefs, and I was raised a Christian; but my beliefs go beyond that. I think there are many truths in other religions."

Jim blurted out at that, "Well, that means you sure ain't one of those fundies," and in a joking manner added, "Guess that means no rapture for you!"

"Jim, you stop that," admonished Carol, "this isn't something to joke about."

"Maybe not, but I think we may be on to something. We'll have to check it out in the morning. Let's try and get some rest. Maybe the power will come on in the morning, and maybe it won't. In any case, I think it is going to be an interesting day."

Chapter 2 - And there was morning, the first day . . .

As the morning light started to bring the new day, Aurora began to stir in the Peterson's guest bedroom. They had tried to sleep, but it had been a restless night. The warm spring night had prompted them to keep the window open a few inches, and they had heard shouts and strange noises throughout the night. Maggie had finally fallen asleep, and Aurora had lain there for some time before drifting off to sleep herself. Now she quietly lifted herself from the bed and stood in front of the dresser mirror looking at herself in the dim light. She saw a young woman in mid-twenties, petite, with soft, wavy, shoulder length black hair that was tied back into a ponytail. She had inherited her looks from her mother, who was of Hispanic heritage. Her mother had also insisted she be named Aurora, in honor of her Mexican grandmother. She loosened her hair and began brushing with the brush that was sitting on the dresser.

As she ran the brush through her hair, she heard Maggie's voice, "When you are done with that, how about combing out this tangle of mine?"

Aurora glanced over at the bed and saw Maggie sitting up, her naturally red and curly hair wildly askew. With a soft chuckle, she responded, "That looks like more than what I am up for this morning. I think you'll have to handle that one yourself."

They heard a gentle rap at the door, and Carol's voice softly asking, "Are you ladies awake yet?"

"We're awake. Come on in," replied Aurora.

Carol opened the door and said, "The power still hasn't come on, and Jim doesn't think that it will anytime soon. The water pressure is low. I expect the town water tank is getting pretty low, so it might be all gone soon. We ran our tub full of water so we'd have some water if the power doesn't come back on. Also, I left a pitcher of water on the sink in the bathroom if you want to wash up. Come on downstairs when you are ready. Jim has been talking with some of the neighbors, and there are some things we should probably talk about."

Aurora and Maggie gave each other some wide-eyed looks and then Maggie said, "Okay, Carol, give us a few minutes, and we'll be right down."

After freshening up, though without the shower each of them would have enjoyed, they made their way downstairs to the kitchen where they found Jim and Carol sitting at the table. Jim had paper and pen in front of him and was making a list.

"Well ladies," he said, "I'd say 'good morning' to you, but I'm not so sure that it is all that good."

Carol sighed, "Jim, just tell them what you know. Or what you think you know."

"All right. Here goes. Those northern lights we saw last night were the brightest ones that anyone around here has ever seen. Even the folks who used to live hours north of here have never seen anything like it in their lives. There must have been one of the biggest solar flares of all time that caused it. It looks like all electric stuff is burned out. We haven't found anything electrical that works. Another weird thing is that guns don't work either. A few people tried shooting some guns last night, but nothing fired. Everything was a dud. I don't see how a solar flare would cause that, but in addition to the loss of electricity, our guns don't work. There's been no vehicle traffic either. No one has driven into our community since it happened."

Aurora, listening intently and with a slight frown on her face said, "Wow, but what about the people. The people who went missing. Did anyone figure out what happened to them?"

"That's the bizarre thing. We may have been right last night. It seems that all the really fundamentalist conservative type religious folks are gone. Near as I can guess at this point, I'd say that one out of every two or three people in town is missing."

"Really? So it was the rapture?"

"I don't know that I would call it that. However, they are the ones that are gone. Maybe their god didn't want us and just left us here to fend for ourselves."

By this time, Carol had decided that they were going to need something to eat so she had gotten up to get them some breakfast. She said, "We might as well eat some of the things from the fridge. If we don't get power back on soon, some of that stuff won't last long."

As they started to eat some of the items that Carol pulled from the refrigerator, Jim continued to tell them some more what some of the other neighbors had experienced and what they thought it might mean.

Several minutes into that conversation they heard a knocking on the front door. When they opened the door, they saw Mike, Maggie's husband, standing there with their two children. The family's two workhorses were tied to the oak tree in the front yard. Maggie nearly flew out the door and lept into Mike's arms, hugging him and the children, and then trying to explain what had happened.

In short order, Carol had ushered the family into the house and was feeding the children. Max was a growing boy of twelve and Siobhan was a vivacious young girl of ten with flaming red hair like her mother. When Carol placed food in front of them, they didn't hesitate, but dove right in. Soon after, the adults started giving Mike the rundown of what had transpired in the last twelve hours. Mike shared the awe that he and the kids had felt while laying out and watching the northern lights, and the dread they started feeling when Maggie never came home, which multiplied when they went inside and found that nothing electrical was working. Mike had held the youngsters in his arms on the couch in front of the fireplace. They made plans that as soon as the rising sun would begin to brighten the sky, they would take their team of workhorses, which Mike used to compete in draft horse competitions, and ride to town to see what had happened to Maggie.

Aurora just sat there while most of the storytelling was going on. She didn't say much, but she was deep in thought. She was trying to figure out what her options might be. It had become apparent that, at least for the short term, she was committed to this community and her friends here. She wasn't a local. She didn't even live here. This was her first teaching job out of college, and when she accepted it, she decided not to live in Oakwood because it was so small. Instead, she had rented an apartment in a larger community thirty miles away because it was closer to her parents, who had lived another thirty miles beyond that point. Sadly, they had been killed in a car accident more than a year ago. She had felt no need to change apartments, so she still lived in that community, even though she knew only a few people there. Without a vehicle, and as a single woman, she knew she wouldn't be taking the risk of traveling to her apartment until she knew more of what might be going on. She had no real reason to get to her place, and what's more, she had people she knew and friends here in Oakwood.

She had some decisions to make. Although no one had yet said anything to her about what she was going to do, she just knew what Maggie was going to offer - she could come out to their farm in the hills. She also knew that Jim and Carol would probably be saying something about staying with them. In addition, there were perhaps other staff members from the school that would also welcome her into their homes. However, she wasn't one who wanted others to take care of her. She was an independent and strong woman and would take care of herself. She would pull her own weight wherever she was.

14

Chapter 3 - It is not good to be alone

Knowing that, immediately she wanted to let others know that she would be making her own decisions, Aurora spoke up during a pause in the conversation.

"Maggie, Mike, you know I've been out to your place before. I'm wondering if I could come out and stay with your family for a little bit. I promise I won't be a burden. I'll pull my own weight. At this time of year, I expect you'll be needing extra help with that big garden of yours. One thing I know is that I don't want to try to travel to my apartment right now. There is no one there for me to try and go back to."

With nothing but a glance to Mike, Maggie responded, "Well, you don't even need to ask. Of course, you can. I should have offered. I'm sure we'll be able to use plenty of help. I think we'll be putting in a much larger garden than usual this year."

Carol, who had been busy serving the children as much breakfast as she could lay her hands on, said, "Well, you could stay here too if you want to. We sure won't mind."

"No that's okay. I appreciate the offer, but I think that Maggie and Mike's would be a good place for me to help out for a while. If they'll have me, that is."

Maggie smiled. "Of course, Aurora. It will be great to have your help. I don't know what the school plans to do about its future, but I doubt we will have any classes to teach for some time. The world has changed around us. I don't know how long it will be this way, but the practical side of me tells me that it might stay this way and that we better make our best choices for survival as soon as we can."

Jim and Mike had been sitting quietly and listening to the women. Mike turned to Jim, then slowly said, "Jim, I think my wife is right. The world has changed. Maybe it would be best if you and Carol come with us, too. We have enough room in our house for you. You might be safer coming with us."

"Safer?" questioned Carol. "What do you mean safer?"

Jim held up a hand to forestall anyone else speaking before he had a chance. As a retired teacher, he knew how important it was to have his listeners' attention before speaking.

"Mike has a legitimate point. Perhaps a third, to a half, of our town's population disappeared last night. It's a rough estimate, and we'd have to take a local census, but suffice it to say that many of the people of our community are gone. Many of them were good reliable folk. I also know that some of those who remain could cause problems in town. With no electricity, and with no one coming to help us, I'm afraid for our community. Unless there is an authority in our community that takes control, it will quickly become a matter of whoever is strongest dominating the others."

Carol interrupted, "What about the mayor and town council? Surely they'll take charge."

Jim shook his head with resignation. "No, they won't. The mayor is one of those who disappeared, along with half the council."

"What about the school board?" asked Carol.

Jim shrugged as he replied, "I don't know. Most of them live out in the countryside. They might, or might not still be with us. Besides, they have their own places they'll be worried about."

"And our local cop?"

"Jeff is sixty-some and out of shape. Without a working gun, I don't expect anyone will pay him much attention."

"All the more reason for you to come with us," Mike asserted, "It might not be safe for long here."

Jim pursed his lips and hesitated before responding, "If good-hearted people run away, only the sour ones will remain. I think we need to stay. Oakwood will need to assemble a group of level headed people to organize affairs here. I think I have a responsibility to be one of those people. Don't get me wrong, I think you are right to go back to your property and manage it the best you can, but I think we are needed here."

Carol solemnly nodded her silent consent.

The others murmured comments of acceptance, and then Maggie declared, "Well then, that's settled. Let's get packed up and start heading back to the farm. As the old saying goes - we're burning daylight!"

Chapter 4 - Darkness was over the face of the deep

Jackson Stewart was on the road to the family cabin in the north woods when his car just died as dusk was deepening on that beautiful spring day. He had been driving north, transporting the small parcel of his father's ashes to be scattered in his beloved wilderness of the north, and he had been mesmerized by the stunning display of the northern lights that were dancing in the sky. Then, without warning, the engine shut off. The headlights, radio, dashboard lights, and everything else electrical in the car just shut down. Fortunately, he knew to slip the car's gear shift into neutral so that the steering would not lock up. He safely guided his car coasting it to the side of the road. He looked ahead of his car down the road. No lights. He looked behind his vehicle. No lights. No one was coming. Reaching his hand into the glove compartment of his car, it closed around his flashlight. He pushed the switch to turn it on. Nothing. The batteries must be dead, he thought. He pulled his cell phone out of his pocket. Nothing.

After a few moments, he opened the car door and stepped out into the night. The stunning aurora pulsated through the sky. Sounds of the spring night reverberated loudly from the creatures inhabiting the nearby wetlands and woods on the sides of the road. It was one of the few times since certain situations in his military experience that he heard the pure sounds of the night unmuffled by any sounds of mechanical or electrical activity. For a few moments, he allowed himself to soak in the pure sweetness of the night.

But then his mind clicked into a more analytical mode. He began by orienting himself. In memory of his father, he had veered off the state highways and unto county highways that led to the small town of Oakwood. His father had spent the early years of his teaching career at Oakwood High School, and it had seemed fitting that his ashes would pass through Oakwood on the way to his final resting place. Recalling the final curves in the road that he had navigated before his car died and comparing it to the mental image of the online map he had checked before beginning his drive, he estimated that he was still several miles south of Oakwood.

He deliberated for several moments, considering whether it would be wiser to stay with his vehicle or begin hoofing it to the town. The northern lights continued to brighten the landscape making it more visible by the moment as his vision adjusted to a view without the illumination of car headlights. He considered that it was late enough that there would be infrequent travel on this rural road. It was unlikely that there would be any cars passing by. His military training gave him cause to consider that there might have been some sort of electromagnetic pulse (EMP) that had been detonated. Alternatively, perhaps there had been a massive solar flare. In either case, the condition of his car indicated that everything electrical was fried. He doubted there would be any other cars moving on this road tonight. He glanced at his watch and realized that it no longer worked. It was a battery-driven digital watch. Reality sank in a little deeper as he realized that not even the smallest electrical item he carried with him still functioned.

He decided that he would rest for a couple of hours in the car. Then in the morning, he would repack his backpack with the best items of survival gear in his car. When daylight dawned, he would leave his car and would begin the trek north toward Oakwood.

The aurora continued to flare throughout the night, and Jack's rest was fitful. While the sky swirled above him, his mind swirled with thoughts and plans for the coming day. When, at last, the sky began to brighten from the rising sun, he started to rummage through every section of the car. He wanted to know what might be in every cranny and corner of his vehicle before he repacked his backpack and deserted his vehicle.

He was pleasantly surprised by some of the small tools and items he found, including the Swiss Army pocket knife from his youth and his Grandpa's old hand-winding pocket watch. He carefully tucked each item of importance into his pack, including the package of his father's ashes. The ashes weren't survival gear, but Jack felt he couldn't part with them by leaving them with the car. He thought about scattering them in the woods along the road because his father always said he wanted his ashes to be scattered in the woods, but Jack felt there must be a better place. He felt compelled to carry his father's package onward.

One of the prized items that he always carried with him when he made the trip to the family cabin was his compound hunting bow. His father had taught him as a youth to hunt with a traditional recurve bow. When Jack left the military, he had purchased this expensive bow as a sort of "discharge gift" to himself. He valued his time alone while hunting in the woods, and this bow was a tool that gave him pleasure as he honed his hunting skills. There was no way he was going to leave this weapon with the car. Fortunately, he transported it in a lightweight protective case. He considered taking it out of the case and carrying it at the ready position but decided against it. If he met anyone on the road, he would appear more threatening with it exposed.

He tried to start the car one last time, but the result was the same. Nothing. After a final glance at his phone - still dead - he stuffed it in his pack. There wasn't much use for it in this condition, but maybe there would be in the future - who knew? Then he leaned over, grabbed his backpack by the straps and flipped it over his head as he slipped his arms through the straps.

He adjusted the pack's belt around his waist and fastened it securely. Slinging the bow case over one shoulder, he looked both ways down the county road and then started walking north toward Oakwood.

Chapter 5 - And there was morning

He had walked over a mile down the road when he passed out of the woods into open farmland on both sides of the road. He could see a farmhouse a half mile further ahead. He hadn't encountered anyone on the way, though he had played a couple of scenarios over in his mind about what he might say if the situation developed. The situation of a farmhouse, likely occupied, was one that he had considered. He hoped he might find help there.

He continued walking down the road and as he approached the driveway to the farmstead a dog began barking. Jack stopped at the end of the driveway. The name on the mailbox read simply - Grady. He could see the black lab standing on the large front porch barking at him. The front door opened and a teenage boy stepped into view, closing the screen door behind himself.

"Hey, mister!" The boy shouted, "Where'd you come from?"

Jack pointed down the road from the direction he had come.

"My car died on me while I was driving last night. I'm walking to Oakwood to see if I can get some help. Do you have a working phone on your farm I could use?"

The boy hesitated. Jack noticed some movement through the screen door, and then the boy yelled back. "If you're walking for help, why are you carrying that big pack on your back?"

Jack smiled to himself, thinking that the boy didn't answer the question about the phone while probing him for more information. Whoever was behind that screen door was prompting him. Smart people are wary of strangers while at the same time being open to them. He considered what his reply should be before he answered. He decided that complete honesty was best.

"Nothing electrical in my car worked. Not even my cell phone. I was traveling north to my family's cabin, and I didn't want to leave my valuables in the car." He paused and then added, "Is it okay if I come up the driveway a little bit, so we don't have to shout at each other? You have a nice looking dog, but he won't attack me, will he?"

Without hesitation, the boy replied, "Naw, he's friendly ..."

The boy hesitated mid-sentence as his head jerked to the side, apparently listening to a voice behind him.

Jack went on, "I won't come any closer unless you say it is okay. I just don't want to be yelling at you. Some dogs don't like that. If I'm yelling towards you, he might think I am attacking you."

Again the boy hesitated before answering. Finally, he said, "Drop your gear where you are and come on up to the house. I won't let the dog attack you."

Jack smiled as he thought to himself that he wasn't actually afraid of any dog, but if the boy thought he was - that was fine with him. Slowly he shed his bow case and backpack and gently set them down in the grass by the edge of the road. He made his way up the driveway towards the house. As he walked forward, he noticed two cars and a truck parked in the driveway. The farm appeared to be a "hobby farm" because while the farmhouse was a large, old, and well-kept-up farmhouse; the outlying buildings looked weathered with age and somewhat neglected. There were a couple of horses in the paddock by the old barn, but there were no other animals present, and there was a noticeable lack of large-scale farming equipment. It made sense that folks would hobby farm here. This area was a region of hills and hollows, suitable for old-fashioned small scale farming, but with little of the productive flat land that was a necessity for a modern industrial scale farm operation.

When Jack reached the bottom of the front porch steps, the boy said, "That's far enough."

Jack could see there was movement behind the screen door, but he couldn't see any details. He started the conversation.

"As I was telling you, my car died as I was driving down the road. I can't get it started again. My cell phone doesn't work either. Do you suppose I could use your phone?"

The boy (Jack estimated him to be about sixteen) sighed, "Sorry. Our phone isn't working. The power has been out since late last night."

"Hmmm," came the reply from Jack, and he allowed an expression of puzzlement to show on his face. "Did you notice the northern lights when you lost power?"

"Couldn't miss 'em. What of it?"

"I think it might have been a solar flare. Fried everything electronic. None of my battery operated stuff works either."

The teenager shook his head. "I don't think so. A solar flare or coronal mass ejection could certainly cause an aurora borealis, and it could mess with the electrical grid, but it shouldn't have any effect on battery operated gadgets."

"Stop it, Dylan. Don't be such a geek," a voice from inside the house interrupted them, and the screen door opened. A young woman, college-age by Jack's estimate, stepped through the door and joined her brother on the porch. Her blonde hair was tied back into a ponytail, and she wore jeans and a t-shirt. She looked Jack over with a careful appraising eye and then took over the conversation. She directed her next comment to Jack.

"My brother's right, you know. A solar event couldn't cause everything that has happened. People are missing, too."

Jack couldn't mask his surprise. "Missing? What do you mean people are missing?"

"I mean that people are missing. People who should be here, have disappeared."

Jack was truly puzzled.

"Who? And how did they disappear?"

The young woman looked him over for several seconds as she considered what to say. Having made a decision, she took a deep breath and gave him an invitation.

"You might as well come up and sit on the porch with us, and rest a bit, while I tell you what happened." She turned to Dylan. "Go get our guest a glass of water."

"Mandy, we don't have any tap water - the pump is electrical, and we don't have power."

She sighed, "Of course. Might as well grab something from the fridge. That stuff won't stay cold forever." She turned to Jack, who was walking up the porch steps. "What'll you have, mister? Milk, ice tea, apple juice?"

Jack smiled. "My name is Jack. I'll have some apple juice, thank you." He motioned toward one of the rockers on the expansive farmhouse porch. "May I sit?"

"Be my guest. I'm Mandy, and my brother is Dylan."

They settled themselves into the porch rockers. Dylan returned with the glass of apple juice for Jack and joined them. Jack took a long and satisfying drink before asking Mandy, "Now, what is this about people disappearing?"

Mandy launched into her explanation. She had driven back to the family farm after her final college class of the semester yesterday. She had spent a couple of hours with her younger sister, riding and caring for their horses. Then after supper, the whole family (Mom, Dad, Dylan, and the two girls) had sat around the kitchen table late into the night playing games. Suddenly, at 10:21 p.m. to be exact, for that is when the kitchen clock stopped, the lights went out - and her mom, dad, and sister were gone. There had been enough light from the powerful northern lights that they could faintly make out each other's forms as their eyes adjusted to the diminished light. Their eyes were still adjusting when their mom, dad, and sister simply vanished. She tried to use her phone as a flashlight, but it was dead. Mandy and Dylan had searched around for flashlights, but when they found them, they didn't work. Finally, they found some candles and lit them. There was no sign of the rest of the family members - only the chairs where they had been sitting. In the hours that followed, they had searched the farm, and while they couldn't find their loved ones, they discovered that nothing that was electrical was in working condition. They had no explanation for it. They had watched for traffic on the road, but there had been absolutely no traffic on the road since the event. When they saw Jack come hiking down the road, they had a hopeful sense of relief that help might be on the way, but also an apprehension that he might be a harbinger of danger.

Jack listened intently to their story. It meshed with elements of what had happened to him, but he was as baffled about the disappearance of their family members as they were. "I don't have any answers for you," he lamented, "there might be an explanation, but I don't know it."

Mandy sighed with resignation, "Yeah, well I guess that's just the way it is. I'm not sure what we are going to do here. Without electricity, and with our back-up generator not working, our refrigerated and frozen food will soon spoil."

Dylan added, "Mom does have some canned food from last summer in the pantry, but not much, and without power, we can't draw water from the well. The cattle tank is filled with water for the horses, but when that is gone, we won't have any way to get water to them."

Jack thought for a moment and then asked, "How far is it to Oakwood? Isn't there a small river that runs through it?"

Mandy responded, "Town is only five miles away, and the

Strange River goes right through it. The river comes in this direction, but at its closest, it is about three miles from here. Then it turns west. I don't think we can get our water from there."

"So, in the long term, you can't stay here."

"What are you suggesting?"

"Why don't you saddle up your horses and walk with me to Oakwood? Let's see if anyone there has any answers."

Mandy was hesitant about leaving the farm and glanced at Dylan.

"Ahhh, maybe we should just wait here and see what happens."

Jack shrugged. "The choice is yours. However, I'm going to be heading on into town. You're welcome to join me if you want. If you stay, you might want to be careful about any visitors. I'm harmless enough, but what if someone who wants to take advantage of your situation shows up. If you have any guns, you might want to have them handy to protect yourself."

Dylan snorted. "It wouldn't help."

Again, the surprise was evident on Jack's face.

"What do you mean?"

"Our guns don't work. With all the weird things happening, I was worried and checked them out. The ammo doesn't fire. I tried early this morning. It's like they're all duds. And then there is the gasoline. . ."

"What about it?"

"It doesn't combust as it should. Oh, it still burns, but slowly. There is no explosive combustion like there should be."

Jack wrinkled his brow in thought. "I don't see the connections between all of these events. It is as if somehow the world got turned upside down."

Mandy sighed, "Completely torn apart, I'd say, with family being taken away from us."

Jack thought for a few moments before making his next suggestion.

"I really think you should come with me. Pack up the gear and supplies you want on your horses and then walk with me to town. I do have my hunting bow with me, in my gear by the road; that'll give us a weapon of protection if we need it."

Mandy and Dylan briefly discussed Jack's suggestion before agreeing to it. While they went about their tasks of preparing their horses and getting their gear assembled, Jack went back out to the road and retrieved his pack and bow. He then sat on the porch and examined the firearms and ammunition that Dylan couldn't get to work. He went through a process of carefully examining each gun and its ammo. Then he attempted to test fire them, but his result was the same as Dylan's - nothing worked. Even with his military knowledge of weapons, the situation made no sense to him. This gear was in good condition and should work. His best explanation was that some element of the ammunition was faulty, but even if so, it was unlikely that ALL of the ammo would be so affected. Before they left, they locked all the guns securely in their cabinet. They took with them the hunting knives owned by the family, as well as the hatchet and ax that the family stored in the barn. Also accompanying them was the family's black lab, Raven, who by this time had openly accepted Jack as a friend.

Mandy and Dylan had saddled the horses and fastened their supply packs to them. They let the horses carry their gear while they walked and conversed with Jack. The skies were clear of clouds and the day warmed rapidly. They traveled for a couple of miles and were nearing a crossroads where an east/west gravel road bisected the tar road they were on. A pair of horses and several people had rounded a bend in the road from the northern direction of Oakwood and were coming towards the crossroads.

28

Soon Mandy and Dylan recognized them and began waving to them. When the groups approached to within shouting distance, they started yelling greetings. They had encountered Maggie, Mike, their kids, and Aurora.

Chapter 6 - Crossroads

Mandy was a recent graduate of Oakwood High School, and Dylan was a current student who had both Maggie and Aurora as his teachers. Both groups quickly told the rudiments of their stories, and when Mandy told them about the disappearance of her parents and sister, she noticed Maggie give Mike a knowing glance.

"What?" questioned Mandy.

"Well, I don't know how to say this, or ask this, but it seemed to me that your parents were very religious. Am I right?"

"Yes, they faithfully went to church every Sunday. They are true believers, for sure."

Maggie explained. "Well, it seems that all those in town that were what you call "true believers" disappeared at the same time last night." She hesitated and then asked Mandy, "But why are you still here. I thought you went to church with your folks. Aren't you one of the believers?"

Mandy shook her head, "I stopped believing everything they did a couple of years ago when I went off to college. So, you think this is the rapture they were talking about in church? You think they were taken to their heaven?"

"It's the best answer that we have been able to come up with so far. What about you, Dylan? And you, Jack?"

Dylan shook his head, "I just never believed that church stuff. I guess I just couldn't. It didn't seem right to me."

They all turned to Jack.

"You could call me an agnostic. I'm not sure. I don't know. I've seen a lot of good and a lot of bad in my life that can't be ignored or explained. But the traditional church explanation doesn't seem to be the answer for me."

Maggie gave a thoughtful and caring response. "Well then, the three of you fit in with the rest of us who are left." She again glanced at Mike, searching for his approval even though she knew he would give it, and then continued, "Would the three of you like to join us? We're heading back to our farm. We have a feeling we're going to be doing without modern conveniences for quite some time. Come to think of it, there might be some safety and strength in numbers. You're welcome to head on into town, but I think that they're going to be having their own struggles." She smiled and added, "Why don't you join our little clan - the Nelsons - and we'll start our own little village in our valley."

Mike added, "You know how we've tried to keep some of the "old-fashioned" ways alive at our home. You folks could be a big help to us because it looks like we will have to expand our operation. I won't hide the fact that your horses would be of help to us. Another team of horses, even if they aren't draft horses, would certainly help to do some of the work we're going to have to do."

Jack could sense the relief that was coming from Mandy and Dylan. He realized that the opportunity to be with people that the youngsters knew and respected would give them a sense of security. He could see that Maggie was watching him and was trying to gauge his reaction. Mandy and Dylan were nodding their heads in acceptance, and as they did so, they turned to see Jack's decision.

Jack deliberated for a moment more, looked north up the road, and then he made his decision.

"I was driving north to my family's cabin, but that is a couple of hundred miles north of here. In this present situation, it doesn't seem as though it would be a wise decision to make that trek. If it is truly okay with you, I will accept your offer and come to your farm, at least temporarily. I'm not afraid of hard work, and I promise I will pull my own weight."

Mike thrust out his arm for a handshake. "It's a deal. Now let's get moving. As we walk the road, you can tell us your story,

31

and we'll tell you ours."

They talked as they traversed the winding, dusty gravel road. It made its way through small fields and tree-lined hills, and then crossed a small river. On the far side of the river, they left the gravel road and entered a driveway that followed up the side of a small creek as it plunged through a narrow gorge. The gorge widened as it wound its way into an open valley surrounded by wooded hills on all sides.

Chapter 7 - Spring Hill

As they rounded a bend in the tree-lined driveway and passed an old storage shed, they could see the valley open before them, and the farm buildings come into view. A couple of hundred yards up the driveway was an old farmstead that had been restored and added to in the last few years.

"Welcome to Spring Hill," said Maggie as she waved her hand expansively, "it is our humble home. It may not be much, but we are proud of it."

Jack looked it over critically. He thought that there was much to be proud of. There was an old farmhouse with a detached garage sitting under a canopy of tall trees, but the centerpiece of the farmstead was a newly constructed home that was impressive in its large size and distinctive handcrafted style. Near the old house stood an old barn. Its bright red color suggested that it had been recently restored. To its side stood a modern metal storage shed of considerable size. There was also a couple of larger wooden sheds of some sort further up the valley, nestled beneath the edge of the trees. He noticed a handful of goats in a small pen near the barn, and further up the valley observed a couple of grazing dairy cattle. This farm was apparently the only farm in the small valley and had probably been initially settled when people first came to this region. He estimated the total open acreage in the valley that could be tilled was in the range of 150 to 200 acres. Some of it had been cultivated this spring, but much of it was lying fallow. Jack had noticed a couple of farmsteads on the roads before they had crossed the river and came up the valley, but none of them appeared to be actively farming anymore. The landowners probably rented the land out to the remaining active farmers in the area.

"This is a fine looking place that you have here Mr. and

Mrs. Nelson," complimented Jack.

"Oh, stop right there!" exclaimed Maggie, "I won't have you calling us Mister and Misses. Our names are Maggie and Mike. You are here as a friend and comrade, so I expect you to call us by our names. And unless you have some objection, or want to be called by some strange name, we'll be calling you Jack. Understand?"

Jack chuckled out loud, and then he smiled and said, "I hear you, and I understand you," and then he added, "Maggie."

Mike joked, "Of course, there might be times you'll call her 'Boss,' I sometimes do."

The light-hearted teasing and conversation continued as they made their way up the long driveway. The family dogs, a couple of black labs came running to greet them and give them a welcome homecoming long before they reached the buildings. The dogs greeted the Grady's dog (a littermate of theirs) with yelps and wagging tails.

Maggie suggested, "I'll take Aurora, and we'll go put something together for lunch. Why don't the rest of you take care of the horses and then come on up to the house? We'll have lunch and make a plan for what we are going to do."

Jack was impressed when he saw what the Nelsons had done with the barn and then was doubly impressed when they entered the house for lunch. The barn was a traditional Midwestern gambrel barn with a double-sloped roof on each side. By the look of its foundation stones, it appeared to have been built in the early 20th century. The lower level of the barn housed the horses and dairy cattle that the Nelson had, and the upper floor was the hayloft. There was a dirt ramp sloped up to the center of the far side of the barn that allowed easy access to the hayloft from the outside. On one side of the barn stood a small cement silo. Although the exterior wood siding of the barn had obviously been restored and painted a traditional bright barn red, Jack expected to see an old-fashioned interior. However, what he experienced was a pleasant surprise. While Mike had kept the atmosphere of the lower level by refinishing the ceiling beam work and walls, he had removed all the old equipment and flooring and redone it with modern cement work and furnishings. There was ample room to stable the additional horses that they had brought with them. Mike's pride was evident as he showed off the water system that he had installed in the barn. He had laid an underground tile below the frost line from the creek further up the valley, close to where the spring-fed stream bubbled from the ground, and run the line to the barn and house. There were also several pieces of old farm equipment near the barn. They could either be pulled by a team of horses or by the small tractor (unworkable now) that sat next to them.

The house was handcrafted almost entirely by Mike. It was an open floor plan with a center fireplace. Jack was the only one who had not been in the house previously. Aurora had been there as a part of some faculty gathering, and both Mandy and Dylan had been there as a part of student activities that Maggie had hosted. Mike pointed out a couple of the unique features that he had built into the house: a wood-fired oven, a hypocaust heating system, composting toilets, and a solar power electrical system that allowed them to live off the grid. Unfortunately, since the northern lights event, the electrical system was no longer functioning.

Maggie and Aurora soon placed a number of the refrigerated items onto the large oaken trestle table.

With an infectious laugh Maggie declared, "It looks as though, at least temporarily, the Nelson clan has doubled in size! Let's eat!"

The food was heartily appreciated and enjoyed, and the conversation started out light-hearted, but it soon turned serious as they began discussing what tasks needed to be done. Food was not an immediate problem because the Nelson's pantry was still filled with a sizable number of canned items from the previous harvest, but without replenishment from the modern food chain distribution system, they would soon find themselves without many everyday items.

It was fortunate that the Nelsons were involved in an heirloom seed project and that their current year's shipment of heirloom seeds was already in their storage shed and waiting to be planted.

"Why are you planting heirloom seeds?" asked Jack.

Mike and Maggie looked at each other, and Maggie was the one to answer.

"Some people around here refer to us as 'crazy tree-huggers,' and I guess we are, but there is more to it than that. There is a huge developing market for non-GMO and healthy organic foods. We believe they are the healthiest for us, and we also see an opportunity to make an income from it as well. I suppose now we'll have to hope we have enough to survive on. Maybe things will turn around, and the lights will come back on again. If so, we can sell what we produce. But for now, I think we had better work hard to plant and harvest all we can. Our survival may depend upon it."

They continued to discuss aspects of immediate tasks, as well as some longer-term plans, until Mike said, "I think we had better get some more land plowed. The soil will warm faster if it is turned over. We've got seeds to get planted soon, and we can't be wasting time. None of our tractors will work, so, if it is alright with the rest of you, I like to hitch up our team of workhorses and show our newcomers how I work with a team of horses. Mandy and Dylan, I know that you two are comfortable around horses, but I'd like to get Jack and Aurora exposed to them. Even if they aren't going to be driving the team, they should know how to manage them."

Maggie nodded. "And I'll take the kids and get some organizing done in the house and the old farmhouse. If we're going to be expanding the size of our clan, then I think we better be reorganizing our living space."

They went about their tasks for the afternoon. A long afternoon of plowing with the horses, and teaching the newcomers how to manage the team, resulted in about a half of an acre of the land being tilled. While they were cooling down and tending to the team of horses, Mike declared that in the morning they would try to hitch the other horses (even though they were not draft horses that the Gradys had brought with them) to the plow and teach them how to pull the farm equipment. Mike had an old harness set that could be adjusted to fit the smaller size and girth of the saddle horses. They wouldn't be able to do the amount of work that the team of draft horses could, but their horsepower could be useful.

At supper, Maggie informed them that the children had helped her to straighten up the old farmhouse and prepare a couple of rooms that could be used as bedrooms. There was no longer running water in the building and obviously no electricity, but there would be more privacy than if they were all in the main house together. There was also an old, but usable, outhouse behind the old farmhouse that could be used for their toilet. Immediately, Aurora and Mandy offered to take the one bedroom, and then Jack and Dylan looked at each other and agreed to take the other.

Chapter 8 - The First Week

The spring weather cooperated for the next couple of weeks and using both teams of horses the Spring Hill Clan were able to open up a couple more acres of land that had been lying fallow. They had both teams out in the fields again (one team plowing and the other team smoothing the soil with a harrow) when the dogs announced the arrival of a group of people walking up the long driveway.

Mike half-expected to see Jim and Carol Peterson leading a group of people from the town. He felt Jim was being overly optimistic when the couple had stayed in Oakwood to help the town organize and deal with this crisis. In Mike's opinion, there were a few bad apples in Oakwood that would cause trouble for the others. However, Jim and Carol were not leading the rag-tag group; instead, it was folks from some of the homes on the road between Oakwood and Spring Hill. Some of them were walking bikes they had brought with them, and a couple of them pulled small wagons and utility carts that were fully loaded.

Mike handed the reins of his plowing team over to Mandy and walked over to greet the new arrivals. Jack had been chopping wood by the barn, but at the warning of the dogs, he had stopped and stood to watch the action happening down the driveway. Maggie, Aurora, and the children were planting seeds in an area up the hill from the barn that had been fully prepared for planting.

Mike talked briefly with the leaders of the group and then escorted them up the driveway to the buildings where Jack and Maggie joined them. After brief greetings, for these folks were no strangers to Maggie, and then introductions to Jack, they told their story. They no longer felt safe in their own homes and hoped that they might find safety at Spring Hill since it was further away from Oakwood. The group consisted of four family units that lived in houses scattered along the road heading south from Oakwood.

Yesterday a group of men and boys had come out from Oakwood and taken food and other supplies from them. There were too many of them to fight off, so these poor folks had no choice but to let them take what they wanted. After the raiders had left the families had gotten together and discussed what to do. They knew they couldn't stay because they knew the thieves would return in the future; and then who knew what might happen. The raiders might not stop with taking supplies, they might molest the people as well.

Jack could see Maggie's fury growing as she became incensed at the telling of these events. Finally, she blurted out, "Who is behind this?"

One of the young mothers in the group rolled her eyes. "Andy Miller and the rest of the Miller gang. You know it is a large family, they're related to half the town. When a bunch of them get together, they pretty much can do whatever they please. And who can stop them now!"

"Jim and Carol Peterson said they were going to try and organize the town. They wouldn't let this happen."

"I don't know anything about the Petersons, or what is happening in town, but folks from the Miller clan are scattered throughout the town and countryside," she paused and then sarcastically added, "I doubt that they asked permission from anyone to steal from us."

Maggie gave a snort of frustration and a sigh. "Oh, I know Andy well enough. We were in high school together. He was a real jerk back then. When I came back here to teach, I ran into him at a ball game. He's still a jerk."

Even though there were men among the refugees, the young woman continued speaking for the group, "We knew you had this place in the valley and saw you passing our houses the first day. Being further from town, we think that they might not come out this far. We were hoping we could throw our lot in with you. All of us are willing to work on your farm, and together there might be enough of us to stand up to the Miller's if they do come out here."

Jack was silently watching and listening as this conversation took place. In his mind, he was adding up the numbers. This group had four women, three men, two teens, and six younger children. If they were added to the Spring Hill community, the numbers would total five men, seven women, three teens, and eight children. That would be twenty-three mouths to feed. It would be a challenge to produce that much food, but with all of them working, it could be done.

As if deliberating, Jack asked, "How many raiders did you say were in the Miller gang?"

"There were five of them when they were at our place," answered the woman while the others nodded in agreement - then she added. "But they have a lot of relatives, and there could be more next time."

Jack sighed heavily, "And they might well come out here if they know you have come here. But then again, since they live in this community, I'm sure they already know about this place." Turning to Mike and Maggie, he went on, "Twenty three people to feed is a large number, but the more we have here, the better we can defend ourselves."

Maggie was sadly shaking her head. "Jack, we are peaceful folks."

Jack pursed his lips before replying, "Maggie, I can see that you are peaceful and generous, yet the truth of our situation is that we may have to defend ourselves. We can't let the bullies of the world run over us."

Mike stepped into the discussion, "You are right, of course, Jack. We have to stand up to those who would abuse us, but I don't know much about fighting when it comes down to it."

A resigned expression crossed Jack's face. "But I do. My time in the Marines isn't a time I really like to talk about, but I do know how to fight. I'll teach you how to defend yourselves."

Mike nodded in acquiescence, and they both turned to look at Maggie.

"It looks like the old farmhouse, will turn into even more of a bunkhouse," said Maggie, "welcome to Spring Hill, friends. Mike, what should we do for a meal tonight? Should we butcher a goat or some chickens to feed this crew?"

Before Mike could answer, Jack replied, "We better be careful with the livestock we have, and in the next days we may have to foray out of the valley to see if we can get more, but for today, let me take my bow, and I will head up the hill into the woods. I've noticed a lot of deer tracks, and I think I can be back in a few hours with some fresh venison."

So while the newcomers were welcomed and getting settled into their new lodgings at Spring Hill, Jack took his bow and headed up the valley into the woods.

Chapter 9 - Hempstead

Within a few minutes of stepping under the eaves of the woods, Jack came upon a game trail. He followed the path and was surprised to find that the trail, after first rising slowly up the hill, then followed a sideways pass through the hills and soon began descending into a forest on the other side of the hills. He thought that this must be the county forestland that Mike had told him lay beyond the ridges of Spring Hill Valley. He followed the trail for several minutes and then his ears started to pick up the sound of a rhythmic clanging.

Jack tried to stay alert for signs of recent deer activity, but his curiosity was piqued by the sound. As he followed the trail, the noise grew louder and louder. He felt himself being drawn to it. Eventually, he came to a place where he could see an assortment of buildings in a clearing ahead of him. He worked his way to the edge of the woods where the buildings were.

For several moments he stood in the undergrowth and surveyed the scene. He could see a small cabin and several buildings of considerable age, yet apparently still usable. The cabin had an attached one-car garage that had been added on to it at a later date. The side-swinging doors of the old garage were swung open, and Jack could tell that the sounds were coming from within the garage. However, from his current vantage point, he couldn't see what was causing the noise. He carefully made his way across the open space to the buildings and peered into the garage.

It was a scene he did not expect to see at a small cabin in the woods. The garage was empty of vehicles and in the center of the garage stood a husky man of medium height, with his back to the door, in front of a blazing forge. The garage vibrated with the sound of him pounding a piece of metal with a hammer. The man plunged the strip of metal back into the fire and then, without turning around, spoke.

"Well, are you going to stand there all day watching me, or are you going to step in and introduce yourself?"

After speaking, the man slowly turned to face his visitor.

Jack was caught slightly off guard, but he quickly recovered and replied, "Yes sir. My name is Jack Stewart. Sorry if I startled you."

The man chuckled and said, "First of all, don't call me 'sir' - I work for a living. Second, you didn't really surprise me, I saw you in the mirror." He motioned to a mirror on the far wall. "Now, tell me what is a marine doing standing in my door?"

Jack was puzzled. "What? How did you know I was a marine?"

"You have that look about you, but the Semper Fi tattoo on your arm is pretty much a giveaway. In my younger days, I did my stint as a grunt for Army intelligence." The man chuckled again and added, "I know that's quite an oxymoron - imagine 'army' and 'intelligence' used in the same phrase. Oh, and my name is William Hempstead, but most folks just call me Bill."

Bill stepped forward and extended his arm in greeting. Jack responded by also stepping forward and grasping the burly man's hand in a firm handshake.

Bill asked, "Now, what can I do for you?"

Sheepishly, Jack held out his bow. "I was out deer hunting for the people at Spring Hill, but then the sound of your forge caught my interest. I guess it's deer hunting I want to do. I don't suppose you could help me with that.

"Deer hunting? For the Nelsons? At this time of year? Isn't that poaching? That doesn't sound like something the Nelsons would approve of."

"There are two dozen of us at Spring Hill now. A bunch

more came in today, and we have to find some meat to feed them. And given the events of the past week, I'm not sure that any rules about poaching still apply."

"Ah, so folks are gathering at Spring Hill. Anyone figure out if it was an EMP pulse, a solar flare, or something else that fried everything electronic?"

"No, sir. I mean, Bill. It affected things like gunpowder too. An EMP or solar flare wouldn't do that. And a bunch of people went missing - the fundamentalist religious believers, if I understand those things correctly."

"Whooo," said Bill as his eyes went wide, "they had their rapture! Well, how about that."

Jack shrugged and shook his head. "I don't know if that is what happened, but what I do know is that the rest of us are struggling to survive in this changed world, and we have a couple of dozen people to feed at Spring Hill now."

Bill grabbed a towel from a hook on the wall and started wiping the sweat from his face and arms. He glanced at his forge and then shifted his gaze to a small freezer placed along the wall. Then he nodded his head in an indication that he had made a decision.

"Jack, now isn't the best time of day to be out deer hunting. Mind you, I'm not questioning your skill, but I have a better alternative for you."

"What do you have in mind?"

"I love a good steak, and I've got a small freezer full of thawing meat here. I'd hate to see it go to waste. Give me a few minutes to close down my forge and put my tools away, and I'll help you pack as much of it as we can over to Spring Hill. You can go deer hunting some other day."

"That sounds good to me, Bill. Do you have any backpacks that we could use to carry the meat, or will I have to improvise something?"

Bill smiled. "I've got a few backpacks I've used on camping expeditions over the years. Never could seem to throw them away. Looks like they will come in handy now."

He walked over to the edge of the garage and lifted a step-ladder off its hook, set it up near the far wall and then climbed up a couple of steps to reach into the rafters. After rummaging around a few moments, he grabbed a couple of items and tossed them over to Jack.

Jack nodded. "These will work fine. I'll pack them up while you straighten up your shop and grab some gear. I imagine you'll want to spend the night at Spring Hill, rather than hike back here in the dark. How much can you carry?"

Bill laughed out loud. "Split it evenly into the packs. Unless you don't think you can handle it and want to put a little extra in mine."

A half hour later, after Bill had cleaned up the shop and gone into the house to get some stuff, he returned to the garage. He had a scabbard and sword strapped to his waist, a pistol-style crossbow in his hand, and a satchel that held a chihuahua slung across his chest.

Jack took a long look at him before saying, "I'd say that, except for the dog, we look as though we're heading back to medieval times."

"We may well be. Bows, swords, and all the rest." He patted his sword. "Hand-forged in this very shop." Then he waved his pistol crossbow. "Crafted by my hand." Finally, he put his hand on his dog. "And this is Maximus. He's a small dog with a huge personality and a beautiful soul. He is in his final days I fear. I won't leave him by himself. Not even for a night."

Jack shrugged. "You pack it, you carry it - that's my motto. If you want to carry him with you, that's no business of mine."

"Well said," replied Bill, "now let's saddle up and get

moving."

Bill hefted his pack and slung it over his shoulders, and then he grabbed a hand-crafted walking staff from near the door. Jack stood looking at the strange sight. A fifty-some-year-old man with a massive pack on his back, a small dog strapped to his chest, sword on his hip, with a pistol crossbow in one hand and a wooden staff in the other.

"Marine, what are you gawking at? Get your gear in place and let's get moving."

Jake made a motion to pick up his pack but then stopped to ask, "Aren't you going to lock up your place?"

"Naw. I'll come back tomorrow. I do have the gate to the road chained shut. That's a good mile down the road. And if any ill-intentioned folks are determined enough to walk up here through the woods to ransack the place, a few locked doors won't stop them. I've got a few valuables stashed away in secure places that thieves wouldn't be able to find. It is best to leave the place open, so they don't wreck the doors or windows."

Bill made a final check of his forge, and then the men adjusted their packs and made their way into the woods where they stepped onto the deer path. As they made their way uphill toward the hidden pass through the hills to Spring Valley, they shared information and stories. When Jack shared that his full name was Jackson Stewart and that his father had spent the first years of his teaching career at Oakwood High School, Bill made him stop.

"Are you saying that your father is Greg Stewart?"

"Yes. Though 'was' is a more apt description. Dad passed away this past winter. I was making my way to our family cabin up north so that I could scatter his ashes around the woods he loved."

"You have my condolences. Greg was a good man. We started our teaching careers in the same year at Oakwood. He was only here a few years before he moved on. Did he ever tell you much about Oakwood?"

"Not much. I know I was born during his time here, but we moved away shortly after his third year, so I was too young to remember anything. He never brought me back here, but he did mention he enjoyed his time here. That's why I was heading north on these country roads when the event happened. I thought it would be a nice gesture to pass through Oakwood since it was a part of his life. Little did I know that I would become stranded here."

"We had some good times together. I was sad to see him leave but glad of the opportunity for him. When we started teaching, I never thought either of us would end up being 'lifers' in this school. He left, but I ended up staying. I can see a bit of him in your features, now that I'm looking for it - and some of your mannerisms, too. I hope you have the same sense of humor. As I recall, his humor was usually pretty dry, and he was sometimes sarcastic - even cynical, but he always enjoyed life."

"That describes him well enough. Hey, shouldn't we get moving? We can talk as we walk."

Bill chuckled as he began walking up the trail. "Of course. Let's go."

They continued their trek up the trail and through the narrow pass in the hills to the Spring Hill farm. During their walk, Jack learned that Bill had retired from Oakwood High School a year ago at age fifty-five. The cabin in the woods was Bill's retirement home. He had purchased the property, which was surrounded by the County Forest Reserve, nearly ten years ago in anticipation of such retirement. Bill had spent his years at the school teaching the social sciences. His classroom had been next door to Maggie's, and he was good friends with her. Outside of his school responsibilities, he had a broad range of interests and hobbies. As Bill told Jack about his wide variety of activities,

Jack thought that Bill sounded like the perfect description of a modern renaissance man. Then his mind registered the practical notation to this observation that the advice of such a person might be very beneficial in this changed world.

Chapter 10 - Evening Council

The contingent of Spring Hill folks was excited to see the two men emerge from the woods. All of them immediately recognized Bill. One cannot teach in a small school district for a lifetime and remain a stranger. People who move into small rural communities are forever considered "outsiders," but at least Bill was a respected outsider. The sight of Bill attired with sword, crossbow, and dog was startling, but the excitement over their arrival with food soon washed that away. The folks immediately began discussing plans for grilling the meat the men had returned with.

Mike looked at the packs and commented, "That's a lot of meat. Why don't we grill some of it, use some of it for a 'perpetual' stew tomorrow, and then make some jerky from the rest of it?"

Maggie's reply was immediate, "Great idea. I have a recipe for Native American pemmican that I have been dying to try."

Jill, the most verbal of the young mothers that had just joined the group, said, "Wait a minute. Pemmican? Perpetual stew? You are going to have to explain those to me."

Bill, ever the teacher, replied with almost encyclopedia-like definitions, "Perpetual stew, which is also known as hunter's pot or hunter's stew, is a stew where almost anything that is edible is added and then cooked. It is kept cooking over the fire and is never, or rarely, emptied all the way. Ingredients and liquids are replenished as necessary. Pemmican is a traditional Native American food. It consists of a mixture of dried and ground up meat and dried fruit and berries. Both the stew and the pemmican can be quite tasty."

After the evening meal, and after the younger ones had gone to bed, the older members of the community sat around the campfire ring that the Nelson's had constructed. Their conversation focused on future plans for the community, both the immediate future and long-term.

Both Bill and Jack expressed their perspective that Spring Valley was a naturally defensible position, but that some essential fortifications should be added. A gated wall at the opening of the valley to the surrounding countryside would be advisable. Also, some training in archery and archaic weapons would be necessary. They also recommended that they increase the size of the community, adding productive members to their group would increase the number of preparations they could make for the coming winter.

Jack raised a concern, "I've been to parts of the world where I have seen resources become scarce, and the law disappear. Society descends into anarchy. That could happen here. Protection is vital. We need numbers, and we need weapons."

Mike and Aurora voiced their concerns that more significant numbers of people meant larger accommodations would need to be built, including practical considerations like a latrine that could handle a growing population.

Maggie, that kind and generous soul, expressed her worries about the people outside the valley and the people in the town of Oakwood. How could they be helped?

Round and round the fire they went sharing their thoughts and concerns. Finally, the conversation slowed and their eyes turned to their most elder member, Bill Hempstead. He took a long time looking at the people seated around the fire. They were his colleagues, former students, and friends. They trusted and respected him.

"Folks, we need to make some decisions, and you're looking to me for leadership. I'm not the guy to be the boss of this operation. I'll give you whatever advice and help I can, but that's all I want to be. It's not in my bones to be a dictator."

Maggie interrupted him, "Bill, we all know you aren't that kind of guy, but you are organized, and you know how to get things done. Could we have a democracy and vote for you to at least temporarily be the chief of our group?"

Bill shook his head. "Spring Hill is your home. You, or Mike, should be our leader."

Maggie could see Mike's eye widen as he shook his head. She knew what he was thinking - that he was a craftsman and no leader.

Aurora spoke up, "Maggie, Bill's right. I've worked with both of you. Bill is organized and talented, but this is your place, and you are a natural leader. Others may have impressive skills," she hesitated briefly and glanced coyly at Jack, "like Jack with his military skill, but the people of this community know you as well as they know Bill. Better, maybe, after all, you were born here and grew up as a member of this community. You are the one to be the head of our Spring Hill community."

Bill quickly said, "All in favor as electing Maggie as our leader, raise your hand."

Then Bill raised his hand high and the others rapidly followed suit.

Bill declared, "That decides it. Maggie, you are the boss. What title would you have us call you? Boss? President? Leader? Madam Chairperson?"

Before Maggie could answer, Aurora offered, "We aren't all related, but we are becoming sort of like a clan here. How about Clan Chieftain? Or just Chief?"

Maggie sighed, "I guess Chief is okay if you need to give me a title, but I would rather you just call me 'Maggie.'

Bill smiled. "I intend to return to my cabin in the morning and grab a few supplies that might help us, but I could use a couple of strong backs to be my porters. What's your order,

Chief? Can you send a few of your crew with me?"

Maggie sighed with feigned exasperation, "Of course, Bill. Take as many as you need, but leave Mike enough workers to help in the fields. We need to get the crops in."

"I was hoping you'd also let me take a packhorse with me, too."

Maggie looked at Mike and raised an eyebrow in question.

Mike shook his head. "I'd prefer not to send either of my workhorses. I want to keep them in the field. How about the team that Mandy and Dylan brought in with them. They can't get as much done in the field as my team can, but they're solid mounts."

Maggie nodded and turned to Bill. "Will they be sufficient for you, Bill?"

"We won't be riding them. They'll do for what I want them to carry. Thanks, Chief. You won't regret it."

Chapter 11 - Armed and Dangerous

Early the next morning, Bill made his way over the hills and back to his cabin. Accompanying him was Jack, two of the men that had joined the Spring Hill community the day before, and Mandy leading the two horses. The morning was sunny, yet the air was still crisp, and the dew was heavy on the ground. They walked through the woods in single file, and they were silent, immersed in their individual thoughts as the sound of songbirds and the rhythmic beat of the horses plodding on the woodland turf gave them a sense of calm.

When they reached Bill's cabin, he assigned them tasks. He directed Jack and the two men to disassemble the small wood-fired forge and blower, gather his tools and some stock of iron, and then to find a way to pack them and the anvil in a balanced manner on the horses. He took Mandy into the house with him. There he went from room to room opening secret hiding spaces in cabinets, walls, and floors where he had hidden items he considered valuable. As he handed her the items, she carried them out to the garage and returned for more. After several trips, Bill followed her out of the house, and they surveyed the pile of goods they had assembled.

Bill opened the larger bags and containers so that the others could see his treasures. There were comments of surprise and admiration. Bill's hoard included several swords, daggers, bows, arrows, other weapons, as well as numerous smaller miscellaneous items.

Jack exclaimed, "Whoa, there, Bill. What were you going to? Arm a medieval army?"

Bill chuckled. "Forging the blades is a hobby. Since I am a history teacher, or at least I was, I was interested in medieval weaponry and armor. I guess I just put two of my interests together. It was my intention to start selling some of them online to see if I could make any money with them, but that's not going to happen now."

"No, I think our online days our past. But those babies sure will come in handy as we arm and train our people to defend Spring Hill."

"That was my thought, and that's why I wanted to get my forge over there. I think we will require even more of such in the days to come." Bill took a moment to look at each one of the others. "Have any of you ever handled a sword before?"

Jack nodded, but the others all shook their heads.

Bill muttered, "Well, I do know that all of you have at least touched a knife since you are all deer hunters so . . ." his voice trailed off as he sorted through his armory. "I'll give each of you a dagger for now, and when you are ready to handle a sword, then you can have one of these. Jack, I figure you're ready for a sword now, so you can have what I consider my finest of this bunch."

The two men, Steve and Dan, hefted the blades admiringly and thanked Bill. Jack pulled the sword from its sheath and thoughtfully scrutinized it before he replied.

"This appears to be expert craftsmanship. Apparently, you have a real talent for this, Bill."

"Thank you. It is something I enjoy doing. I'm glad you appreciate it." Bill then turned to Mandy, who was staring at her blade. "Mandy, what are you thinking?"

She pulled her gaze from the dagger Bill had handed her and looked questioningly at Bill with her bright blue eyes wide open, "Do you really think I will need this."

Before Bill could answer, Jack said, "I hope you never need to use it. But, yes you should have it. In today's world, you had better be ready to defend yourself. If nothing else, having it with you might deter someone from attacking you. I would feel better if you wore it."

Bill gave Jack a thoughtful look but said nothing.

Mandy smiled slightly and replied, "Okay, if you think I should."

They went about getting the horse packs settled and gathering as much of Bill's food stores from the house and other supplies as they could. Once they had arranged their loads, they began their return journey to Spring Hill. Bill was the final person to enter the woods, as he was trying to cover their tracks the best he could. He gave one last wistful look at his cabin. Just as his teaching career had come to an end, now his solitary life at the cabin the woods was drawing to a close. Resolutely, he turned and followed the rest.

Chapter 12 - Building a Community

The next several days brought numerous changes and additions to the emerging Spring Hill Community.

First, an expedition was sent to the homes of the four families that had fled their homes after the Miller clan raid. The houses had been ransacked, they assumed by the same group of Miller's, but there were still many items that they found useful - including a snowmobile trailer. They pulled the now useless machines off of the trailer, rigged a way to hitch it to the horses they had brought with them, and loaded it with supplies to carry back to Spring Hill.

Second, Jack strongly felt that they needed to have a defensive presence at the opening of the Spring Hill Valley, so he persuaded Maggie and the others to use the old driveway shed near the gravel road as a sort of outpost. There they could station people to keep a watch at the entrance to the valley and to give a warning to the rest of the community if a threat presented itself. More work would need to be done to make the shed a livable building in the winter, but for now, it could be adapted to provide a place for a guard crew.

Third, they sent an exhibition back to Mandy's home to pick up gear and supplies for their horses, as well as taking what household supplies and tools they could gather. The trip went without incident.

Next, they sent an expedition westward on the gravel road that passed their driveway. For a while, the gravel road paralleled the river as it twisted its way between hills and skirted the southern ridges of the Spring Hill Valley and the county forest. That road went for a couple of miles before it connected with a paved county road that ran north/south along the western edge of the county forest. Just south of the junction of the gravel road with the paved highway lived a couple of families that Maggie knew. She felt that if they were still there, they should be invited come to Spring Hill and join the fledgling community. One of the families was the family of a teacher that Maggie worked with, the other was an active farm family with children.

When the offer was extended to Maggie's friend, Holly, and her husband, Thad, they were quick to accept. With them came their high school senior son, Caleb, and their college-age children, Megan and Cody.

The Arnold farm family was another matter. They hesitated to leave their farm. It had been in their family for generations. They had sold off the dairy operation several years ago, yet had continued to farm the land and to raise 4-H animals with the children. They had two milk-producing cows with a couple of young calves, several sheep, two llamas, and a couple of cages of rabbits. After being persuaded that there was no possible way they could continue to farm without modern equipment and that the safest course for the immediate future, would be to go to Spring Hill, they reluctantly agreed. The family and their whole menagerie moved to Spring Hill, and on that day the number of the fledgling community rose to three dozen.

Maggie soon realized that providing food for such a population on a daily basis was certain to be challenging. Until their crops started coming in, they were reliant on the remains of her previous year's pantry (which was rapidly being depleted), whatever game they could hunt, and whatever supplies they could glean from the neighboring countryside. The excursions to the homes of the recently joined members were helpful, for they were able to bring some foodstuffs with them, but those would only carry them through the next few weeks. She considered sending people into Oakwood, but with the number of people who still lived there, probably more than a hundred, she doubted they would have any extra food to be shared. A couple of residents made mention of the bison herd on the Rudd farm north of Oakwood, but she deemed that too far away and too risky for several reasons.

Finally, she decided to send a delegation to the Bartels farm, which lay about four miles to the east. She knew that they raised some beef cattle in addition to the crop farm operation they had. Perhaps they would negotiate the sale of some of their herd. Maggie wasn't on the best of terms with either Sandy or Derrick Bartels, because there had been some disagreements with them over school issues, but Maggie was willing to give it a shot.

With major trepidation and minor hope, Maggie set out early in the morning. Holly was at her side, followed by Jack, Thad, and Cody. As she was leaving, she said to Bill, "You're in charge while I am gone. If anything happens to me, I know you'll watch over the others."

The trek over to the Bartels farm was uneventful, although the number of deer openly roaming the fields was noticeable. Perhaps an increase in the harvesting of venison could alleviate the food supply issue for a couple of months. The way that the spring growth was growing unchecked in the fields probably accounted for the deer herd, and the presence of a couple of hay fields only a mile from the valley entrance presented the possibility of putting Mike's old-fashioned horse-drawn sickle hay mower to good use.

The Bartels' dogs, a couple of collies, started barking loudly as the party neared the Bartels Farm. When they turned off of the road and began walking up the driveway, a voice shouted out at them, "Stop right where you are! I've got my hunting bow here, and I'm not afraid to use it!"

The Spring Hill contingent immediately stopped. The dogs continued their barking, but they stayed near the house.

Maggie recognized the voice as belonging to one of her

high school students. She glanced around and then loudly announced, "We mean no harm. We just want to talk to your folks."

"What do you mean - you mean no harm? We can see your swords and bows. Stay together on the road and talk from where you are."

Maggie looked at Holly. Holly shrugged, but Jack whispered, "Get us closer, so we can dive for cover behind that wagon if we have to."

Maggie raised her voice so it would carry over the dogs barking, "Listen, Kyle, this is really hard to shout. Can we at least take a few steps closer, so we don't have to shout over to barking dogs? And it would be helpful if you could get them to stop."

There was no response from the house for a few moments, then the voice called out, "Okay, walk up to near that flower bed and then stop."

As they quietly and slowly walked forward, Jack whispered softly to the others, "Don't look but be aware that someone is circling around us to our left. He must have come out of the back door of the house."

When they reached the flowerbed, they stopped. The dogs remained near the house, and they heard Kyle ordering the dogs to stop barking.

Holly called out in a friendly voice, "Hi, Kyle. This is Mrs.Henderson. I'm here with Thad and Cody. I hope everything is okay for you folks. Can we help with anything?"

"I recognize all of you except that guy with the sword and the bow. Who is he? And what is he doing with you?"

Jack, who had been standing behind the women who were the spokespeople for the group, took a step forward.

"My name is Jackson Stewart. I was driving through the area when the power went out and my car stalled, stranding me here. These folks were kind enough to befriend me. I came along with them to protect them from anyone who might want to hurt them. By the way, you may want to suggest to whoever left the house and is going behind the barn to circle behind us, that they should be careful. I'd hate to see anyone accidentally get hurt."

"What are you talking about?"

"I don't want any of my new friends hurt, but I don't want anyone else hurt either if that can be avoided."

The was a short pause, and then the screen door opened. A young man stepped out holding a hunting bow. He glanced toward the barn and yelled. "Tony! Don't do anything stupid! Step out where we can see you."

All eyes turned toward the barn. Slowly, from the far edge of the barn, a young man stepped into the open. He was holding hunting bow, and he had an arrow at the ready.

Maggie seized the opportunity. "Whew!" she tried to lighten the mood by joking, "I was getting nervous. I didn't want to see arrows flying. One of them might have hit me."

Tony asked, "What are you doing here?" What do you want?"

"As I said - we are here to talk. It is hot standing here in the sun. Can we sit on the porch and talk? And can you ask your folks to come out? I'd really like to visit with them."

Tony lowered his bow and waved them forward. "Yeah. Let's sit down. But forget about talking to mom and dad. They aren't here. They're gone."

Maggie and Holly gave each other knowing glances.

The old two-story farmhouse had a large screened in porch with several chairs and a porch swing. It was obviously well used as a place of social gathering and relaxation. When they were seated, Maggie started the conversation by expressing concern for the young men's welfare. Tony, who was older than Kyle and had been a classmate of Cody's, shared that they had done alright for several days after their parents disappeared.

However, when Andy Miller and several of his crew showed up things had taken a turn for the worse. Miller had invited them to join him, but when they refused, he ordered his followers to take the herd of beef cattle from the pen by the barn. Tony and Kyle had moved to stop them, but the gang had beaten them up and left them lying on the ground. Miller then had his gang drive the herd of two dozen cattle down the road toward Oakwood. His final actions had been to laugh at them and to call them wimps, and then walk away.

Kyle added, "That's why we had our hunting bows ready - we weren't going to let anyone steal from us and beat us up again."

Holly could see the sympathy and anger welling up in her own son's eyes, as they listened to his friends' story. "Kyle, Tony, this invitation is really Maggie's to make, but a number of us have moved to her place at Spring Hill and are trying to help each other make a go of it there. I'm sure you would be welcome there." She turned her eyes to Maggie, "Right, Maggie?"

"Of course. You don't even need to ask," directing her next words to the young men, Maggie added, "We all know that over the years I had some disagreements with your folks. But I have no hard feelings about that. Certainly not toward the two of you. I hope you can join us. Please consider it."

The young men looked briefly at each other and glanced at Cody, who was nodding his approval and agreed to come. Then Tony smirked at Kyle and chuckled.

"I guess we can have the last laugh on that blowhard Miller. He thought he took all our cattle, but he didn't realize we had moved some livestock to a back pasture a few days before that. Could you folks use a dozen beef and some horses at Spring Hill?"

Maggie's eyes lit up. "That's one reason we came here. We were going to ask to see if we could buy, or bargain, a few of the cattle from you. We'd love to have you bring your herd with you."

Holly quickly added, "I'm one of the more recent additions to the Spring Hill community, so I want to make sure you understand. If you bring your livestock to the community, they will belong to the community. Other than the clothes on our backs and a few personal items, we are basically sharing whatever with have with everybody else. We are in this together."

Both Kyle and Tony voiced their agreement. Kyle took the dogs and went to go and get the cattle while Tony worked with them to assemble some of the farm supplies to carry back to Spring Hill. Fortunately, the family had a couple of wagons that could easily be pulled by the horses that were with the cattle. They loaded the wagons to take as many supplies from the farm to Spring Hill as they could. It was a long day's work, and the sun was setting by the time the horse-drawn wagons, followed by the small herd of cattle, came up the driveway into Spring Hill.

Chapter 13 - Plans

Jack had assigned himself guard duty at the driveway shack that night. He had Mandy's lab, Raven, and two men of the community with him. He sat on a boulder by the small creek that flowed down the valley alongside the driveway. It was well after the light of day had vanished and the world was awash in the light of a nearly full moon and the flickering aurora, when Bill ambled down the driveway, staff in hand and sword on hip. When Bill neared the shed, Raven trotted out to greet him. Jack whistled for Raven, who then led Bill to his position.

For a few moments, they sat together in silence and appreciated the sounds of the night and the soothing sound of the waters in the stream. Then Bill broached the subject that had brought him to Jack.

"I know Andy Miller. He was a student of mine at Oakwood High School. Andy was a troublemaker to be sure, and was never one to be trusted. To put it bluntly - he was a bully and still is. I don't doubt that he will be paying us a visit soon. If he hasn't heard of the growing Spring Hill Community, he will on his own soon figure out that there might be something worthwhile in this little valley, because he knows that this is where the Nelsons live. We need to be ready for him."

"What do you suggest, Bill? I would love to have a gated wall here at the entrance of the valley, but we don't."

"So would I, and I intend to use my iron forging skills to help us build one. But there's a real likelihood that we can't complete that project before he pays his first visit to our little valley. To begin with, I think we need to have plans for attacks that might come at day, and for those that would be at night. I suspect he, and other folks of his ilk, might not know the strength of our numbers. Probably they would come during the day the first time so they can see the layout and see what they want to take. However, we should expect that if we repulse them, then they would probably think that they could return at night and attack us under the cover of darkness."

"Right. So I will make and implement a couple of plans to use our strength to confront any attack during the day and also to have an alarm that we might respond to any of those who are attacking at night. We have people I have been training in the use of the swords you brought us, but I would like you to make more. We also have several bows that folks had for deer-hunting, but we could use more. Are you able to craft bows, or must we look elsewhere?"

"I might be able to if I had the equipment and time. Maybe one of the others has such a skill. Ask Maggie tomorrow. She might know."

"We really do need to work on a wall. It would be nice to be able to use the river as a moat and have a wall along the river bank. We could then have a protective gate at the bridge. However, that would be a large wall and as the river flows it would only protect us from the east. We would still be exposed from the gravel road to the west. Ideally, that is where we should have an outer defensive perimeter. For now, I think we should work at constructing a wall of stone and timber across the narrowest point of the driveway gorge."

In the semi-darkness, Jack could see Bill nodding his head in agreement. Then Bill said, "I noticed that one of the abandoned homes nearby has a couple of old cattle gates. I will go tomorrow and salvage those and bring them back here. I can use them to fashion a gate that will slow down any uninvited guests."

They continued their conversation for the next couple of hours, but finally, Bill said it was time for him to get some sleep, so he bade his young friend good-night and walked up the driveway leaving Jack to his thoughts. The one thought that Jack kept returning to over and over again - was the one thing that was becoming a certainty in his mind. It was a certainty that at some point in the future there was going to be some kind of confrontation with the neighborhood bully - the infamous Andy Miller.

Chapter 14 - More Plans

The days since the aurora burst upon them had flown by as those who were left struggled to cope and survive in the changed world. During the closing days of May, the people of Oakwood would typically be holding high school graduation parties and celebrating the Memorial Day weekend. There were no graduation parties to be held this year and the idea of celebrating a national memorial day seemed strikingly out of place. However, the leaders of the Spring Hill community decided that some sort of celebration should be held.

The initial idea for a community observance came from Aurora. She was the art teacher in the high school, but she also had a college minor in anthropology, and she knew the importance of a group of people building a shared sense of belonging if they were to flourish. Bill and Maggie quickly supported the idea and plans were developed to hold the event on the Monday that would have traditionally been Memorial Day.

Aurora suggested to the other leaders that there were three things which could legitimately be the center of a festival: a celebration of the crops being planted, the remembrance of those who had been raptured, and a ceremony which would mark the formal establishment of Spring Hill as a unified clan of people.

Bill nixed the idea of a rapture recognition, even though it fit into a traditional remembrance theme of the Memorial weekend because he felt that if they decided to recognize such an event, then it should be held on the anniversary of the day of the event. He also spoke against the celebration of the completion of the planting as the key ingredient. Seasonal agricultural festivals would undoubtedly become a part of the tradition of Spring Hill if they survived. But those could wait. He felt it was more important to mark a formal establishment of Spring Hill. They could write up a rudimentary compact for the community, much as the earliest colonists in the Americas had done for their settlements. In the first days of their community the residents of Spring Hill had informally appointed Maggie as their Chief, this compact would formalize that action. In addition, a formal compact would give the newer members a sense of belonging and chance to declare their loyalty to the group.

Bill's logic swayed the group, and they agreed to hold a "Founding Day" to formally mark the establishment of the Spring Hill Clan. Aurora was designated to plan the events of the day, and Bill was commissioned to come up with a draft of a written compact for the other leaders to consider.

Bill also raised some questions about religion that he wanted them to reflect on: Since the original inhabitants of Spring Hill, Maggie and Mike, were openly agnostic, was that going to mean that no religious observances would take place in the community? Had "the rapture" changed people's attitudes about religion? Show there be freedom of, or from, religion? No answers to these questions were agreed upon, but at least a discussion was openly begun.

After the decision was made to make plans and preparations for Founding Day, Mike mentioned that the hayfield which was outside of the valley and down the gravel road towards the crossroad junction was now long enough to mow and harvest its first crop. Putting up the crop would be necessary to maintain Spring Hill's herd of livestock in the winter to come. After it was cut, he would need a crew to gather it in and transport it to the barn. He also mentioned that he would like the community to begin building a more substantial root cellar. The Nelson family had experimented with a small root cellar in the last couple of years, but it was not large enough for the needs of the present community.

Immediately after Mike put in his requests for workers,

Jack raised the issue of defense. He insisted they need to allow time each day for the members of the community to learn basic skills for their personal and communal protection. He also expressed the firm opinion that the gate wall at the entrance needed to be completed as soon as possible.

Then Holly, who had lived and taught in the community for nearly as long as Bill, voiced her opinion that they should soon be sending a party to Oakwood to check on conditions there. Perhaps the Petersons had been able to pull the community together in a positive way. Maybe the stories about Andy Miller reflected that he was only conducting his misdeeds outside of the organized town.

The assignment of people to the simple, everyday survival tasks had fallen to Maggie as the chief of the clan. Although it was a taxing responsibility, Maggie relished few things more than a "good spreadsheet." The consideration and delegation of such tasks gave her pleasure. However, decisions concerning the major projects that had implications and consequences on other projects were decisions she didn't want to make alone. She encouraged her group of councilors to discuss all of these proposals thoroughly. Maggie knew she would have the responsibility as the arbiter of any final decision, but she wanted to be sure she had fully heard their concerns and recommendations. She realized that all of their requests were necessary. It was a matter of prioritizing them.

Chapter 15 - Visitors

It happened shortly after breakfast on the following day. Mike had removed the sickle bar from the hay mower and given it to Bill to sharpen in the shop that Bill had set up in one of the old sheds on the property. The old foot-pedaled grinding stone was rapidly spinning, and the sparks were flying. Jack and two of the men were standing nearby holding their axes, waiting for Bill to sharpen their tools so they could work on chopping down and trimming trees for the planned entrance wall. Some of the children and women, wielding hoes, had moved into the fields to do the work of weeding - a never-ending task. A couple of the young men had their hunting bows in hand as they prepared to go on a deer hunting expedition. Maggie and some of the women were in the middle of a discussion near the barn. Every individual had a task for the day and was either moving toward it or had already begun their work.

Suddenly, the clanging of the alarm bell at the guard shed punctuated the air. Normal activity stopped. Eyes turned toward the driveway. The clanging abruptly ended and within moments six men appeared striding up the driveway. The community dogs were barking at the strangers, but sensing their threat, keeping distant from them.

Kyle Bartels, one of those with a hunting bow in hand, hissed, "It's Miller!"

Jack gave quick orders to those who stood nearby. The men with axes stepped forward with him to the center of the driveway, and those with bows moved several yards to the sides and held their bows to the ready.

The men coming up the driveway were led by a portly man who strutted forward with a display of self-assurance. The men all walked with tall staffs, that upon closer observation were spears fashioned by blades that were hand-fastened to tool

69

handles.

They were a good ten yards away from Jack when Jack held up his hand and said, "That's far enough."

The men stopped.

Andy Miller looked around. "Who are you? Who is in charge here? Ain't this the Nelson place? You come in here and start bossing them around?"

Jack stood silent as Maggie stepped up to his side and spoke.

"Andy Miller, well, well, well. You have a lot of nerve just marching in here and spewing out a bunch of questions. Nobody has been bossing any of us around, and nobody, including you, is going to start now."

Andy opened his mouth to make a quick retort but then hesitated as he glanced to the sides because his peripheral vision caught sight of some of the bowmen shifting their weapons.

At that moment several people noticed Caleb, Holly's son, in the distance. He was limping up the driveway and rubbing his arm. Some of the folks, who were already in the fields where running to give him assistance, They pulled him to the edge of the driveway and made him lie down on the grass. There was whispering and pointing. Soon everyone, even Miller's men had turned to look at the youth.

Eyes aflame, Holly came hustling from the barn to stand by Maggie's side. "What did you do to my son?"

"Heck," spat out Miller, "it was was nothing. He was clanging that stupid bell. We just knocked him to the side. If he's hurt, it's his own fault for getting in the way."

Maggie was steaming, but she held her anger in check as she said with steel in her voice, "You, and your gang of thugs, are not welcome here."

"You think you can tell me what to do? You always did consider yourself the high and mighty one. I remember when you were just a scrawny kid and teacher's pet. They aren't around to protect you now. You stupid bitch."

There was a loud banging sound from the shadows of the tool shed. Andy stopped and peered toward the shed. Bill slowly emerged as he strolled out of the shed with his crossbow pistol cradled in his arms.

"Hello, Andy. I don't see the logic of you staying here and spewing nonsense. It would be wise of you to turn around and march on out of here before you, or any of your followers, get hurt."

"Hempstead!" Andy almost spat the name out. "You old fart. So you are the one running this operation. I should have known."

"There are numerous things you should have known, Andy. However, I 'running this operation' is not one of them. I'm not in charge here, I'm only helping out. She's the one you have to answer to." Bill pointed to Maggie. "I would suggest that you apologize to her and then be on your way, but I don't think you're man enough to do that, so I suggest you just clear out. You are slightly outnumbered."

Andy looked around as if calculating the odds. "Bah. We could take you down if we wanted to. But you're not worth it. Let's go, boys."

They turned and started walking back down the driveway. As the Miller crew passed Caleb and the group tending him, they laughed and sneered at the youth, ignoring the defiant glares of Caleb and the women. Before they reached the shed and departed from the view of the gathered crowd, they stopped momentarily.

Andy turned and yelled, "Don't think you've seen the last of me."

Back by the buildings, Maggie snorted in derision and muttered, "As if we should be so lucky."

71

With all seriousness, Jack said, "He will be back. Someday, he will be back. I doubt that it will be during the light of day. His type is more likely to return under cover of darkness to attack. Whenever we go outside this valley, and even when we are in the valley, we should keep weapons close to hand as we work. And now, more than ever, it is important we get to work on that defensive wall and gate."

Bill added, "And I think that it would also be prudent for us to send a surveillance team to Oakwood to determine what the situation is there. Andy may be in charge, or he may just be doing this on his own, it's hard to tell. Jack, do you think you could select a team and slip into Oakwood to reconnoiter?"

"Yes, but we better do it at night, so we can avoid any Miller sentries if he has them."

Maggie declared, "Both of you are right. Make your plans. Now let's get back to work. As Mike would say - we're burning daylight!"

Chapter 16 - Oakwood by Night

During his time in the Marines, Jack had pulled a couple of tours of duty in the Mideast. He was trained and experienced in making nighttime patrols - although this current excursion would be without the type of gear that he was accustomed to using. He discussed with Bill what kind of information he should seek, where he should go, and who should he take on his scout team. Bill gave his recommendations and offered to go, although he indicated he thought it would be better to take younger people who would know the terrain, and who could move quickly if need. Jack choose as his team a couple of young people who would know the area and the people. Cody, with his hunting skills, and Mandy, who was developing serious self-defense skills under Jack's tutelage, were his logical choices. Both of them were recent graduates of the high school and knew the terrain and inhabitants of the community.

The walled gate at the entrance of the valley was not complete, even though they had worked feverishly on it that day. Under Bill's command, a strong, well-armed crew was positioned there for the night. They would take turns sleeping but could be roused at a moment's notice if called upon.

Shortly after sunset, the three scouts slipped past the defensive fortifications and stepped out of the valley. By the time they reached Oakwood all light from the sun would have vanished. The partial moon would not be rising until after midnight; however, the Northern Lights still brightened the sky. The intensity of the aurora had slightly diminished since the beginning of the event weeks ago, but every night their pulsating beauty continued to brighten the night sky.

The scout team was lightly armed. The manner and purpose of their excursion was stealth and intelligence gathering. They had no intention of initiating any conflict but needed to defend themselves if called upon. All of them carried daggers forged by Bill, and both Jack and Cody carried their bows. They also carried walking staffs which easily doubled as quarterstaffs in a fight. For the first part of their journey they walked the road, but as they approached the town, they slipped off the main road and walked along the tree line that edged the Strange River. Away from town, the fields that lay between the road and the trees had been tilled before the event, but nothing had been planted in them, and they were becoming overgrown with weeds. As they neared the town, they could see that some portions of the fields near Oakwood were planted and being tilled. They could see that on the far side of the cultivated ground, and beyond the paved road, a small fire flickered in front of the high school.

They stopped and sat concealed in the shadows of the trees and carefully observed the scene. They could make out that figures were coming and going from around the campfire, and they could see occasional flickers of light from with the school.

Before leaving Spring Hill, both Maggie and Bill had suggested that they try to contact Jim and Carol Peterson - the couple that took in Maggie and Aurora that first night of the event. If a positive group were in charge, then it probably would include them. On the walk to Oakwood, Mandy and Cody discussed a couple of people they might try to contact, and Jack agreed that since he was a stranger in the community, it would be best if the two locals made the first contact.

Sitting in the shadows of the trees, they discussed what they saw and what they should do next. Mandy pointed out the Peterson's house on the far side of the northern school parking lot. No lights or activity were noticeable. Jack was hesitant to approach the school openly since it would be difficult to do so unobserved.

Suddenly the fire in front of the school flared.

Cody whispered, "That's Miller. I'm sure of it."

Jack replied, "That decides it. We avoid the school for now. We could try sneaking around to the back of Peterson's house, but my intuition tells me that they wouldn't be near Miller's group. Is there any other place where it would be logical for people to gather? And what about the friends you mentioned we might contact? Where do Amber and Evan live?"

"Evan's place is on the other side of town, but Amber lives by the river, near the community center. If we stick near the river, we can get fairly close to it."

"Okay, then we head for Amber and the community center area."

Stealthy, they moved north along the tree-lined river. Soon they reached a point where they encountered family dwellings on the river shore. Amber's home was the third house, and the community center lay one block to the east of it.

"Mandy, do you know if any of the families along the river have dogs?"

"I think both houses used to, but I know Amber doesn't. She's allergic to cats and dogs."

"Okay. Let's stay as close to the river as we can, and hope that the dogs are inside. Be as quiet as you can."

They carefully made their way to the back of Amber's house. It was considered a large rambler but was actually a bi-level home since it was built near the river and had a lower level entrance door in the rear. No dogs gave warning. Jack carefully turned the knob of the back door. It was locked.

Mandy whispered, "Amber's bedroom is on this level. The window to the left is her window."

Jack instructed, "Go to the window and gently tap on it. We don't have a light so she might not be able to make you out in the darkness. Whisper your name as well."

Mandy followed the directions. She tapped and

whispered. Then tapped on the window and whispered again.

They heard the slight slide of a double-hung window opening.

"Mandy? Is that you?"

"Yes. It's me. Are you alone?"

"In my room, yes. But Mom, and my step-dad, Steve, are upstairs."

"I've got a couple of friends with me. Can you let us in?"

"Sure. Should I tell my folks?"

"If you can you trust them to be quiet."

"Of course. I'll unlock the door, and then go get my folks."

Within moments the door clicked. Mandy opened the door led Cody and Jack into the downstairs family room. Amber quickly moved to embrace Mandy and then left to get her parents.

Shortly after that, Amber returned leading her parents downstairs. Her mother carried a candle that offered some illumination to the room. Amber, Sue, and Steve had wide-eyed expressions as they saw their visitors armed with bows, daggers, and staffs. Mandy reassured them and made introductions.

Jack took over asking questions about the situation in the town. It soon became apparent that there were two factions of survivors in town. One faction was lead by Jim Peterson, and the other was the Millers. The Peterson faction considered themselves the "legitimate" governing organization of the town since it included what members of the town council who remained as well as other community leaders that had been appointed to the new council. Jim Peterson was the newly appointed mayor.

"We reconnoitered the Peterson house when we came into town but didn't see any activity there," commented Jack.

"That's a sad story, "sighed Sue, "Carol passed away. She was diabetic. When she ran out of insulin, she went into diabetic shock and died. Jim was devastated, but he forced himself to snap out of it for the good of the community. He moved out of his house and is one of those staying in the community center."

They went on to detail several aspects of the Peterson faction, and then Jack asked them if it might be possible to have Steve go over to the community center and request Jim to come and meet with them. Steve agreed and left, promising to return with Jim. Then Jack asked about the Millers.

Amber's disgust was evident as she remarked, "That bunch is scum. They do whatever they want and don't give a damn about anyone else. And Andy is the worst of the bunch. He's a lecherous pig."

Mandy was concerned by the tone in her friend's voice, "Amber, did he do anything to you?"

"He tried. But others stopped him. Don't go near him."

By asking a series of questions, Jack guided the conversation into finding out intelligence details that might give them essential knowledge. Oakwood was a town that lay in a valley along the east side of the Strange River. To the west of the river, forested hills and bluffs ran from a mile north of the town to a few miles south of the town. About a mile east of the river more hills and bluffs limited access to the community from the east. The primary ways into and out of the town were the country roads that ran to the north and to the south. Oakwood, which previously had about 400 residents, now had nearly half that number in its environs. In the days immediately following the event the population was placed at less than 200, but in the ensuing weeks, people from the surrounding countryside had straggled into town. It was a small town without many industries. There were a couple of gas stations, a couple of bars, and a couple of churches. The largest employers had been the local school, a nursing home, and a small lumberyard. The lumberyard could be a good source of resources for future construction products. The nursing home provided an interesting opportunity. It was a large building, nearly deserted, but now beginning to be used. When the "rapture event" happened, twenty of the twenty-three residents suddenly disappeared. In the days that followed, the remaining residents passed away due to medical conditions. Now the building was being used to house refugees coming from rural areas to the north.

They heard the sound of the upper front door opening and soon Steve, followed by Jim Peterson, came down the stairs. Jim was slightly taken aback by the weaponry that the scouts carried, even though they considered themselves lightly armed. Recognizing Mandy and Cody, he listened carefully to their introduction of Jack and their description of events that had occurred at Spring Hill, then he started telling them about the situation in Oakwood.

The Miller clan was worrisome. Zeke Miller was the clan's patriarch. He was in his sixties and owned the "Hometown Bar" near the south end of town. He was a crude opinionated SOB. Most of the more educated residents who had moved into the community over the last couple of decades disliked the man, but because many of the locals were his relatives and followed his lead, they often had to defer to him. During the initial days following the event, his establishment had been the center of activity for his relatives and cronies. Because Zeke was overweight and in poor health, he didn't venture far beyond his bar (he lived in an apartment behind it), but his son, Andy, did. Andy was the old man's alter-ego. In this time of crisis, the clan had turned to Zeke and Andy to give them direction. Andy (with Zeke's encouragement) decided that the school would be a suitable headquarters for his clan. Because the administrators and many of the teachers lived out of town, there was no one to stand in his way when Andy and his boys took possession of the school. The City Council didn't care for the idea, but they didn't have the power to stop him.

Once the beer ran out at the Hometown Bar, the center of the Miller clan activities shifted to Andy's headquarters at the school. Nominally, the Millers claimed to be supporting the Mayor and City Council at the Community Center, but practically speaking they did what they wanted. Mayor Peterson knew that the Millers were sending foraging groups out into the countryside south of Oakwood and that they were bringing goods back to town, but he was unaware of the methods that the Millers were employing. One example of this was when the Millers brought the Bartels cattle herd to town, Andy claimed the Bartels had sent them because they wanted to help the town, and there had been no evidence to disprove him.

Jim was concerned about what was happening at the school because he had no valid information - only rumors. Whenever someone from the city council went to the school, they were denied entrance by one of Miller's men. Rumors were that Miller was holding some prisoners there, that he was hoarding supplies from the rest of the community, that he was conducting strange rituals, that he was recruiting people from the countryside to join him, that he was training his own police force, that he was conducting bizarre experiments in the school's science lab, that he was pillaging homes to the south, etc.

Some of these rumors seemed outlandish, but in this changed world it felt as though anything could be possible. Jim did think that the Millers must be doing something with the people who lived south of the town because numerous people had come into the town from the north, but he knew of none that had come from the south. The news of the Miller attacks on the families directly south of town, the Bartels farm, and then the altercation at Spring Hill distressed him. Most of the people in the Oakwood seemed supportive of the leadership that he and the city council were providing, but he wasn't confident they would follow him in a direct confrontation with the Millers.

Jack informed Mayor Peterson that Spring Hill was constructing defensive fortifications and was concerned that if the conditions of the event continued, then a couple of situations might develop. One was that people from the cities to the south might start fleeing urban situations that were becoming dangerous, thereby posing a threat to rural areas. A second was that local people, such as Andy Miller, might try to become small scale warlords. He encouraged the Mayor to consider developing defensive forces for the Oakwood community and to be extremely wary of the Andy Miller faction.

When the scout team left Oakwood that night, they felt both reassured and apprehensive. Oakwood was in good hands under the compassionate and competent leadership of Mayor Peterson and the Council. However, the threat of the Millers appeared to be real and growing.

Chapter 17 - Making Hay

The sky was beginning to brighten when the scout team returned to Spring Hill and presented themselves to the guards posted at the barrier to the valley. The scouts were physically exhausted, yet they immediately met with Maggie and the others and shared their report.

The rest of the community was stirring to activity. Today was to be the day of gathering the hay. After Andy Miller's threatening visit, Mike had taken his horse-drawn sickle mower to the hay field outside the valley and cut about ten acres. The hay had been left to try in the sun and was ready to be gathered in.

Mike hitched his team to the rake and hitched another team to a wagon. He would rake the hay into rows and then people would lift the hay with forks on to the wagon to be transported to the hayloft of the barn in Spring Hill. Wary of a return by the Millers, the crew was well armed with swords and bows. They did have to lay their weapons to the side while they were working, but they kept them close at hand. They also posted watchful guards on the road and at the perimeters of the field. In addition, Jack and his scout crew, though tired from the previous night's adventure, had accompanied them and dozed under the shade of a neighboring grove of trees.

It was late afternoon, and most of the crop had been gathered, when an alarm went up. People were approaching on the road from the south where the gravel road had its junction with the paved county road. At the sound of the alarm, the hay-gathers dropped their tools and picked up their weapons. Meanwhile, Jack and his scouts came hustling out from their rest under the shade tree.

The approaching group stopped when they saw the

weapons in the hands of the Spring Hill people. The refugees looked ragged and tired. There were about a dozen adult men and women and a similar number of youth and children. They huddled together briefly, and then one man and one woman stepped forward and walked toward where Jack and his people had positioned themselves on the road.

They stopped when they got within a couple of paces, and the man spoke.

"We're refugees from Bluffton. Folks are starving and sick there. Other folks are abusive. We are trying to find a better place."

"Sick?" asked Jack, "Are any of your party sick?"

The woman answered, "Only weak from lack of food. I'm a doctor, and I don't think any of us are carrying diseases like cholera, typhus, or dysentery. I was afraid we would get infected if we stayed. I can't promise you that we aren't carriers, but I don't think so. We need food. I thought a rural town, away from the main roads, might be a place of safety and food. Oakwood came to mind. According to the map, we are only a few miles from there. We saw your people working in the field and hoped you might help us. Are you from there?"

Jack was slightly surprised by the woman's openness. He was sympathetic to their plight, but he was reluctant to welcome them into Spring Hill quickly.

Mandy was one of those who had come out of the valley with Jack. She stepped up to him and whispered, "We can't let them go on to Oakwood. Miller would grab them."

Jack grimaced. He knew she was right. They would be a large group for Spring Hill to assimilate and might put a strain on the community's resources, but their skills and labor would be of benefit. Besides, there was no way he could in good conscience allow them to proceed to Oakwood and to fall under the control of Andy Miller. He leaned over and whispered a few words to

Mandy, instructing her to run to Maggie and inform her of the situation, and that he was bringing the group to the entrance gate. The final decision about whether or not to accept them was the responsibility of the Clan Chief. Jack didn't doubt that she would admit them, but they didn't know that.

After Mandy ran off, Jack turned back to the couple. "I'm in charge of protection for our group, and I can't promise you that our Chief will admit you, but I'll take you to our settlement. You can make your case there. Go, gather your people and follow me. It isn't far."

The refugee leaders walked back to their group, and the Spring Hill hay-gatherers went back to their task. Soon the refugees returned to Jack, and he led them down the gravel road toward Spring Hill. When they reached the driveway, Jack encouraged them to refresh themselves in the waters of the Strange River while they waited for the Chief to come down the driveway. Jack left refugees under the watchful eyes of the Spring Hill guards and walked up the driveway to share his information and impressions with the others.

It wasn't a long wait. In fact, as soon as Mandy had alerted Maggie that there were refugees on the way, the Chief and her primary advisors, (Bill, Holly, and Aurora) left their tasks and hurried to the valley entrance. Once there, they had taken up positions where they could unobtrusively observe the newcomers for a few minutes prior to meeting them.

The refugees, while relatively large in numbers compared to the Spring Hill community, were not very intimidating. The only weapons they carried were walking staffs.

Aurora leaned close to Maggie and whispered to her. "I know that woman nearest the bridge. That's Doctor Westin. She's my doctor in Bluffton. I like her."

Maggie nodded that she heard, and then turned to Jack. "You conversed with them on the way here. What do you think?"

"I think they are good folk and we should consider bringing them in. Their leader did raise an important issue for us to consider in the future. Will refugees be disease carriers?"

"Do you think we need to quarantine these folks for a few days?"

"Not since the Doctor vouched for them. But I do think we should be prepared to do so in the future. Maybe we should have a spot down the river valley where refugees can camp a few days before entering our gate."

"Good idea." She turned to the others. "Any objections to letting these folks in right now?"

They all shook their heads. Holly commented, "No. Food might be tight for a bit, but I don't see that we really have a choice."

Bill added, "Actually, I think we should start sending recruiting teams into the countryside and contact anyone in the area that is trying to make a go of it. Perhaps they want to join us, move closer, or perhaps they want to align with us. There is greater safety with a strength of numbers."

Holly agreed with him. "I think there will be a number of people who are interested in that. They may not want to live in the valley, but they might want the security of belonging to our group."

Jack nodded thoughtfully and added, "I think it would be wise to post a surveillance team near the crossroads, both to catch any refugees that might be headed up the road toward Miller, and to warn us if Miller is out and about. If it is alright with you, I'll train some of the youngsters to be on such a 'watch duty' for us."

Maggie smiled. "Alright then! Let's go meet our new friends!"

Chapter 18 - Founding Day

A couple of days later, on the Monday that would have been Memorial Day, the Spring Hill community held their Founding Day. The day started cool and cloudy, as the final days of May often will be. After breakfast, the crowd gathered on the driveway in front of the Nelsons house - which people were beginning to call 'The Chief's Hall.'

Bill stood before them and read the Compact of Association for Spring Hill. It detailed some of the particulars of their commitment to live together as a community. Ascribing to the compact gave each individual the opportunity to choose to belong to the group. They offered a public declaration of their commitment to the group, and in so doing received the group's public commitment to them. From the oldest to the youngest, each person present was given the opportunity to sign the document. Maggie and her family went first, which seemed proper since they were giving to the community the land, to which they had held title before the event.

All the members, even the most recent ones from Bluffton, signed the document, then the gathering held an election for the position of Clan Chief. It was more of a public acclamation than an election because Maggie was already accepted by the residents of the community as their leader. This process simply formalized what was already an accepted reality. Bill had persuaded Maggie that the time would come when they would probably need to establish a more formal procedure for the determination of leadership, but at this point, a public acclamation would be enough to give official legitimacy to the community leadership.

Maggie stepped forward to speak. The applause slowly subsided. She spoke in heartfelt and straightforward words of her hope for the future of the community.

"Fellow citizens of Spring Hill. A changed world has brought us together in this place. What we make of our new world is up to us. We have a chance to build a world that is compassionate and caring. It will take hard work and dedication to build such a world. We will need to defend the ideals we live by, and we may need to physically defend ourselves against those who might seek to destroy us and what we build. I promise you that I will do my best to serve this community. I seek to make life better for all of us."

Maggie when on to briefly acknowledge her chief advisors and their roles: Mike, Jack, Bill, Aurora, and Holly. She concluded by promising that she would listen to any concern that an individual might bring to her, from the oldest to the youngest. Then she asked each of her advisors to say a few words about their current situation and some of the projects on which the community would need to be working. This was important because, while the longtime residents of the Oakwood area knew Maggie and her advisors, the refugees from the south did not.

After the speeches, Aurora led them through a series of "ice-breakers" to help the people learn about each other, and "team-building activities" to help promote a sense of camaraderie and ownership among the members of the community.

As Jack participated in the activities, he watched Aurora with admiration and appreciation. She had people skills. She knew how to connect with people. In addition, she had a natural beauty that was magnified by her energy. Jack smiled when he realized that he was growing quite fond of her. Suddenly he noticed that Mandy was standing by his side.

"What are you smiling at, boss?"

Although Mandy had no military training, she was a fast learner and was becoming a favorite aide to Jack. He turned his attention to her, and it suddenly struck him that he enjoyed her at his side. Jack suddenly realized that he was also growing quite fond of her. He momentarily struggled to find words to respond to her.

"I'm just thinking that we are building an interesting life here. Several weeks ago, I didn't know any of these people. Here I am today, feeling like I belong to them. They are relatives, in a manner of speaking. I care about them. I care about you."

"You do?" she replied with a slight coyness in her voice.

He stammered, "Why, uh, of course. I, uh . . ."

Jack was saved by the action of Bill motioning for him to come over to him.

With relief, Jack said, "It looks like Bill needs me. Let's see what he wants."

Jack led the way to Bill. Mandy walked by his side, and a smile was evident on her face.

When they reached Bill, he looked as though he was going to ask Jack a question, but then he stopped and looked at Mandy before addressing a question to her.

"What are you grinning about?"

"Just enjoying the day, Mr. Hempstead."

Bill gave her a look, glanced at Jack, and then looked back to her.

"It certainly is a fine day to enjoy, Mandy." After a moment's pause, he directed his next comment to Jack. "There's much to appreciate, isn't there Jack?"

Jack gave him a quizzical look. He had gotten to know Bill extremely well since their first meeting at Bill's cabin several weeks ago. They had spent time working together and relaxing together. Their conversations, both public and private, had been complex and revealing to each other. Now Jack wondered just how much Bill was reading his thoughts at this moment.

Bill flashed an enigmatic smile before going on.

"I know all these activities are important, and Aurora is doing a wonderful job leading them, but I think we had better get to work on the gate. I finished the final iron workings for the gate, and I think we are ready to assemble it. That will probably take several hours, but the sooner we get it up, the sooner I think we will all feel safer. Andy Miller hasn't returned yet, but he will. Mark my words. He will. And I sure would feel better if he ran into our little obstacle in his attempt."

"I agree. You go break the news to Aurora. I will start pulling some of the men aside that we will need to do the heavy work to get the gate in place."

Aurora was not pleased when Bill informed her of the need to take some of the men and put them to work, but she nodded her agreement. Jack and Bill assembled their crew and went to work. In short order, a team of horses was hitched to the wagon, and a load of material was taken from Bill's workshop down the driveway to the valley entrance.

Work commenced immediately and proceeded for the next several hours, with only short breaks for food and rest. By the time the bell was rung calling the people to the evening meal, the project was completed. Before they went to join the others for supper, Bill and Jack stood on the bridge outside the construction and admired the work that had been accomplished. Two sets of gates stood before them. The first was a livestock gate that was securely fastened across the center of the bridge where the gravel road crossed the small river. When it was chained and locked, it prevented anyone from easily crossing the river on horseback, or by foot. There was no way around it. One would need to clamber over the five-foot-tall gate or to try fording the river.

Jack's work crew had cleared all foliage on the west side of the river up to where the new stockade wall barricaded the narrow entrance to the valley. Blocking the driveway was a metal-clad gate. Bill had taken two large gates that had been scavenged from neighboring farms and attached metal roof sheeting to their faces. The gate and wall were several feet high and prevented anyone from seeing through them or over them. On the valley side of the wall, scaffolding had been constructed that could give the defenders a view of who was beyond the wall. If archers were positioned on the wall, they could see their targets while still being protected. To the side of the gate, the small creek bubbled through a rock and boulder arrangement that would prevent anyone from crawling under the wall.

Bill asked, "What do you think, Jack? Will it suffice?"

"Yes. For now. We have the people to man it, and it gives us time to get more people to it if an alarm is raised. We can rest better with the added security this gives us. How soon do you think it will be before Miller pays us another visit?"

"I'm surprised he hasn't already. He saw we had horses, cattle, and other goods here. We scared him off, but he saw what we had, and knowing him, he wants it."

"I wish there was some way we could help Mayor Peterson deal with him. The wall will give us some protection, but if Miller ends up taking over Oakwood, then we will have a much stronger foe against us."

Bill considered that for a moment before speaking. "Jim will do his best. I've known him for many years. Did you know he taught for a few years at the high school?"

"No. No one told me that."

"Yep. Many years ago he headed the Ag Department. That was before he took a job managing the poultry farms for the Golden Company up north in Princeton. He was actually teaching when Andy Miller went through school. He knows Andy well enough. If anyone can deal with him, Jim can."

They stepped through the bridge gate, looped a sturdy chain through it and locked it with a large padlock. The men entered the valley through the main gate, dropped the crossbar securely into place, and then proceeded up the driveway into the valley. Their guard crew remained at their posts. A relief guard crew would come on duty soon and allow the current guards to join the community for supper.

As Bill and Jack made their way up the driveway, Jack continued to ask questions.

"Just how large is this 'Miller Clan' that folks talk about?"

"That's hard to say. Sometimes it seems like everyone in the Oakwood area is related to everyone else. Even some of the folks here at Spring Hill are related by marriage. For example, Holly married a local boy, Thad Henderson, so Cody, Megan, and Caleb are related to some of the people around here, who are no doubt related in some way to the Millers. So there are numerous relatives. Some of them are good folks, others are bad apples. To top it off, I'm sure some of the 'good' Millers must have disappeared in the rapture event. So, in answer to your question, I'd say that there is no way to tell for sure."

"Thanks so much, Bill. I just love it when you are so specific. Is there any way you could give me a more specific estimate as to the number of 'bad apples' in the Miller clan and those who might be associated with them?"

"Well, I'd say that Andy usually hung around with a half dozen, or so, guys. That would be the gang he had with him the other day. Before the event, Andy probably had a dozen or so in his circle of family and friends that would follow his lead. I don't know how many others he may have dragged into his circle since the event, so I'd say that if he was trying to bring his full 'army' of goons to attack, he could have a couple of dozen at this point. Also, a branch of the Miller clan lives several miles east of here, in the Stone Creek area. If he connects up with them, his number could be more substantial."

"Whew. I sure am glad we have the wall and gates up.

You know, Bill, if he has control over that many, why doesn't he just take control over the rest of Oakwood?" Certainly Jim, and the others wouldn't be able to stop him. From what I observed and from what Jim said, it didn't seem like the town council was very well armed."

"True. But don't make the mistake of thinking Andy is stupid. He's not. Andy isn't the smartest man around, and he may be lazy, but he has a modicum of intelligence. And he can be conniving and dangerous. I suspect he realizes that if he took over control of the town, he would then be responsible for its welfare. At this point, it is easier to let someone else, like the Mayor, handle the initial problems of building and maintaining a functioning community. Food production, sanitation, and the like wouldn't be the types of problems Andy would choose to deal with. But sooner or later, I think he will make a move to take control of Oakwood."

"So how do we help the good folks of Oakwood?"

"That's a good question. I don't have a good answer. Maybe you can come up with something."

"Thanks again, Bill." Jack sighed. "It's something to chew on - that's for certain. And speaking of 'chewing' let's get in line and get something to eat. I'm famished."

Chapter 19 - Night Visitors

The clouds from early in the day had moved out, and the nearly full moon rose brightly in the clear sky shortly after sunset that evening. The continuing display of the aurora added to the stunning moonlight, and the landscape was awash with light, if not with color. The completion of tasks, such as hay gathering, wall construction, and community building gave the people a sense of satisfaction. Almost all of them had feelings of peace and security as they made their ways to their sleeping quarters. Guards were posted at the gate. The community slipped into somnolence.

The peacefulness of the night in the valley changed with the clanging of the alarm bell at the gate. Men, women, and many of the youngsters grabbed weapons and began running down the driveway to the gate. They could hear shouts and cries of pain.

Jack was one of the first to arrive on the scene. He quickly surmised what had happened. The guards had recognized the threat of an attack and had sounded the bell. When the attackers had rushed the wall, the four guards on duty had shot arrows at them, but they couldn't pull and fire fast enough to stop the advance. Already a couple of Intruders with spears and knives had been hoisted over the wall. They had attacked the archers on the wall, and more men were attempting to come over the wall. No doubt the first men over the wall would make an effort to open the main gate. They needed to be stopped.

Jack ordered the defenders with him to shoot at the men who were attempting to slip over the wall, while he drew his sword and rushed the two intruders already on the ground by the gate. He parried their feeble attempts to spear him and cut them down with his sword.

When the attackers beyond the wall realized that whenever someone was hoisted up in an attempt to scale the wall that they were shot by arrows, they ceased their efforts and drew back. Some of the defenders went to give aid to those injured inside the wall, and others repopulated the stockade scaffolding. They carefully peered over the top to observe the attackers.

The attackers had scrambled back over the bridge gate and retreated to the far side of the river, however, they had left their injured lying by the wall. Some of them were crying pain. Others were yelling for help. One was trying to drag himself to the bridge.

When Jack was satisfied that no threat remained within the walls, he stepped up onto the scaffolding and surveyed the scene. The glow from the aurora and the moonlight enabled him to see that there were a dozen or so men on the far side of the bridge. A good bowman should be able to hit a target, even at that distance. He considered the possibilities for a moment and then yelled out.

"You, across the river. You have men hurt over here. Maybe even dead, or dying. Send some unarmed men back over the bridge to get them. We won't attack them."

In short order, a reply was snarled back. "You're just trying to draw us closer so you can shoot more of us."

Jack turned to the crowd of defenders behind him and ordered someone to give him a bow. Mandy handed him his bow, for she had grabbed it before running down the hill. He smiled a grim smile.

Jack yelled again. "Look at that tree several yards to your right."

Then he drew and released an arrow which sunk into the tree with a thud.

"If I wanted to shoot you, I would have. Wave a white flag, and I will let you come and get your men."

The man crawling toward the bridge cried out, "Andy,

don't leave me!"

In the harsh moonlight, Jack could see that the men had moved further away and there was a discussion taking place on the far side of the river, but he couldn't make out what was being said. Then Andy's voice shouted out.

"What about our guys that went over the wall? Open your gates so we can get them."

Jack looked back to where the men were being tended to. He had no doubt that he injured them severely when he slashed them with his sword. One or both of them may even be dead.

"They're injured. We'll do what we can for them in here. We have a doctor. You don't. The gates stay shut."

There was again a pause as the attackers huddled together. Then Andy hurled his reply back. "Go to hell. You can take care of them all. You better stay hiding behind that wall, 'cause I'll be back. You're going to be sorry you messed with me."

Andy's group started walking away. His follower who had cried out as he was crawling to the bridge gate, wailed again, "Andy, don't leave me to die."

But the men ignored him and moved down the road back toward Oakwood. Jack waited a few minutes to make sure they were really gone, then ordered a couple of his best scouts, Cody and Mandy, to carefully scout down the road. They were to go to the crossroads if needed and to make sure the Miller gang was headed back toward Oakwood. He warned them to beware of any sentinels or rear-guard that Miller might have left behind him. He also prepared several of his people to go with him outside the gate and retrieve the wounded attackers.

They swung open only one of the double gates, and that just a couple of feet. Jack was the first one to step out and survey the scene. The one attacker was lying by the bridge-gate and four men lay crumbled at the base of the wall. He motioned for Cody and Mandy to go to the bridge gate. They carefully checked on the man who had cried for help, and seeing no threat from him they slipped over the gate and across the bridge.

Several of the defenders helped Jack bring the wounded attackers inside the gate where they lay them next to the two men who had made it over the wall. There were also two of the defenders, guards who had been posted on the wall at the time of the attack, who were being tended for the spear wounds they had suffered. Immediately, the gates were closed and barred again. Lookouts remained posted, alert for the return of Miller's gang and the scouts.

Doctor Julie Westin had come down the driveway and by the light of lanterns was examining the injured. She did a fast triage of the nine casualties and then went quickly to work giving orders and directions to those helping her.

Two attackers were declared dead at the scene - one from arrow wounds and the other from Jack's sword. The others were given immediate care and then moved up the driveway to the former shed, now converted into a guard shack that had several cots. Wounds were cleaned and bandaged.

The day that had begun with a celebration of the community had ended with a battle defending the life of that community.

After activity had subsided and the scouts had returned with word that all of Miller's gang was headed back to Oakwood, Jack found a solitary place to lie down and rest. It was a long time before he could drift off to sleep. He had killed a man. His tours of duty as a Marine had exposed him to the reality of combat and death. However, the action of taking another's life, even in defense of life and liberty, should never be lightly felt.

Chapter 20 - Oakwood Plans

Maggie met with her council of advisors over breakfast the following morning. The open attack upon their settlement changed the situation. It was one thing for a bully to come into the valley blustering threats. It was all-together a step further for them to openly attack Spring Valley with resulting injuries and death.

They sat around the large table in the clan hall discussing and debating about what actions should be taken. Miller had lost approximately a quarter of the force he had brought to attack Spring Hill. Two of their Spring Hill own had been severely injured, though both would recover. Miller had made threats while retreating. That was not something which could be ignored.

With that in mind, it was Jack's inclination to take the battle to Miller. First of all, Jack doubted that Miller would expect it. Second, it might be best to attack Miller before he could add new recruits to his numbers and while his group's morale was low. Third, it was possible that with news of the damages inflicted on Miller's gang that the town would turn on him.

Julie Westin, who had joined Maggie's advisors partially as a result of her leadership of refugees from Bluffton and partly as a result of her medical expertise, voiced her thoughts. She wondered if it might not be best to stay behind the secure walls of their valley. They could strengthen their defenses. Why provoke more their enemy even more?

Their debate ranged back and forth for a while. Finally, Bill made a suggestion.

"I think that whatever course of action we take, it would be best to do so in coordination with the Mayor and Council leadership of Oakwood. From everything we know, Miller is not really a part of that leadership team. The town leadership may want him removed as a threat as much as we do."

"That would mean delaying any confrontation with him for a couple of days." commented Jack, "That will allow him time to recoup from his losses. Do you think that is wise?"

"You make a good point. My reasoning is that if we confront Miller directly, he may be able to gain the support of those in the town who are undecided. I also have my concerns about what Andy is telling the town already. I wouldn't put it past him to claim that he had come out here to offer us help and that we ambushed his troop."

"Would they believe that? What kind of leader leaves his injured and dying men behind?"

"He was never a Marine, Jack. He doesn't have your sense of honor. He would have no qualms about lying if it served his purpose."

They could see Jack tighten his jaw, then he spoke again.

"Okay, Bill. You've persuaded me. Now how do we go about coordinating this sortie."

Maggie and the others accepted the general principles of Bill's plan and then went on to plan out some of the specific details of their endeavor. As they dispersed from their meeting, Aurora pulled Jack to the side.

"I want to go with you on the sortie to Oakwood."

Jack hesitated and smiled as he answered, "Aurora, I've observed you during our defensive training sessions. You are making progress, but honestly, you are not the warrior type."

"Jack, not everyone who goes needs to be a warrior. I really want to go with you."

"Hmmm, give me a good reason why you should be a part of our Oakwood troop."

She knew why she wanted to go along, but rather than tell him, she calculated what might sway him the most.

"You need someone as an observer, someone who can

watch what is going on and take it all without having the responsibility to attack or defend or take some kind of action. This probably won't be the final time we have to deal with Andy Miller unless you plan on executing him on the spot. Someone needs to watch everything that happens so we can analyze it later. Following up on that, we need a historian. I've started keeping notes for posterity about the founding of the Spring Hill Community. This confrontation will most likely be an important event in our history."

"We need to survive first."

"Do you have any doubts about that?"

"I have a multitude of doubts. Even though the people of our community are a good lot and are working with great diligence, there are many dangers that threaten our existence: military threats, food supplies, harsh weather, winter shelter, diseases, dissension in our ranks; and I shudder to think about the threats from the metro area. Other than our refugees from Bluffton, we have heard nothing of the impact of the event on the larger metropolitan areas. By now starvation and sickness must be rampant. Will huge numbers of refugees make it this far? Will they carry diseases? Might makes right - will men of brute force take over?"

"Is that all?"

Jack exhaled a short snort. "No, but it is a start."

"Well, then, if we succeed against all odds, then it is imperative we document what we do. I promise I won't get in your way. Can I go along? Please!"

Jack sighed. "Alright. You can be a part of the sortie. But you had better stay out of the way. Don't put yourself in any danger. I don't want you getting hurt."

Aurora smiled coyly. "I won't, as long as you care and are in charge."

The comment caught Jack off guard - because he

recognized there was some truth in the comment. He blushed.

"I'll let you know when we plan on leaving. Now, I've got work to do, and I'm sure you do too."

He turned and hurried off. Aurora stood there for several moments, watching him stride away. Then she also left to go about her tasks, but as she did, there was a smile on her face.

Chapter 21 - Confrontation

Jack, Cody, and Mandy made another scouting trip to Oakwood that night. Traveling under cover of darkness, they made their way into the town and met with the Mayor and the town council. They shared their version of Miller's attack at the gate of Spring Hill. To no one's surprise, the story Andy Miller had tried to tell around town was vastly different. However, most of the townspeople knew Andy well enough and seldom believed all that he said. He was given to exaggeration and braggadocio, and in the eyes of many was a self-serving liar. The town leaders feared what he might do to the town and were extremely amenable to the prospect of removing Miller. Plans were made to confront Miller and his henchmen at noon, two days hence. With hope in their hearts, the scouting party quietly slipped out of town and headed back to Spring Hill.

The following day was filled with making preparations for the sortie to Oakwood, as well as conducting the ongoing work of building the settlement. Another party of refugees from the Bluffton area had come north, and the sentries at the crossroads had brought them to the gates. They were initially upset when asked to stay in the quarantine camp down the river road for a couple of days. However, when they saw Dr. Westin, formerly of Bluffton, come to check on them, and when Spring Hill supplied them with food and other necessities, they willingly agreed to the temporary quarantine.

As soon the sky began to brighten on the day of the confrontation, which happened to be the first day of June, the community started to stir, and the troop commenced the process of assembling for departure. There would be thirty "warriors" going on this excursion. They needed to be well-fed and well-armed before they would leave the gates of their safe haven.

Numerous cumulus clouds drifted through the sky giving

them moments of sunshine and moments of shade as the assembled troop proceeded down the driveway and out the open gate. Two pairs of horse-mounted warriors led the procession, and the rest followed on foot. They didn't march in step, but they did walk four-abreast as they trailed their leaders. They were armed with the best equipment the community had to offer: Hempstead crafted swords and spears, bows and arrows salvaged from the hunters in the community, and a scattering of leather and other protective gear that adorned the warriors.

Maggie and Jack were the leaders of the contingent and rode the first pair of horses. Mounted on the second pair of horses were Bill and Mandy. Bill's horsemanship skills were limited, but Maggie insisted that he come along to give his counsel and Jack insisted that he ride as a sign of his role and because it was a long walk for the elderly man. Mandy had demonstrated that she was the best equestrian of the community and Jack wanted her near the leaders. Placing her next to Bill provided him with a sense of reassurance. Mandy carried with her the communities standard on a pole. The flag of the community, designed by Aurora, was a wavy green line on a field of blue. It represented the aurora of the northern lights which heralded the beginning of their new existence. Yesterday, Jack had pointed out to Mandy that the pole of the standard could also be used as a short lance if needed. She had practiced a few runs with it to get the feel of it. Yes, she thought, it could be done.

They walked at a steady but comfortable pace. The objective was to approach Oakwood at noon. The sentries at the crossroads cheered them on as the troop passed their post and headed north up the road. A couple of miles south of town they stopped for a break. Jack reasoned that the Millers might have a lookout posted on the final curve of the road before the town of Oakwood came into sight, so it would be best to take a break before a lookout could spot them.

They resumed their march after their short break, and when they began to approach the final bend in the road to Oakwood, they could see a flurry of activity. Jack raised an arm commanding the column to halt. He pulled binoculars from his pack and scanned the road and treeline ahead. There was activity ahead.

Jack turned and announced to the troop. "They've spotted our approach. Be prepared to stop and spread out into position when I command it. Let's march on to the town." He turned back to face forward, but before they began, he muttered to Maggie, "Bicycles. Their sentries are using bicycles. I should have thought of that. We should be doing that."

As the column moved forward, Jack could hear Bill telling Mandy about the use of bicycles during WWII, including the use of foldable bikes used by paratroopers. Jack thought, "That man is a goldmine of knowledge. I need to mine him better." He pulled his grandfather's hand-wound pocket watch from his pocket. It was noon. At this very moment, Mayor Peterson and the Council members should be assembling north of the high school.

The Spring Hill contingent rounded the final curve, and the town of Oakwood came into view less than a mile away. They could see two figures on bicycles reach Miller's Headquarters, the High School on the southern edge of the town. As they proceeded up the road, they could see many people gathering on the drive in front of the school. They could also see that beyond that group, past the school, a large group of people was assembled. A scattering of people was working in the field between the river and the road that passed in front of the school.

Jack kept his people moving forward until they were only the length of a football field distant from Miller's men. At that point, half the walking members of the troop moved out into the tilled and planted field on the west side of the road. There were football, baseball, and softball fields on the east side of the highway, but no warriors moved onto them. The chain link athletic fences surrounding the ballfields had been closed off, and a dozen cattle grazed there. The Bartels boys, who were in the Spring Hill force, were quick to point out to their comrades that some of those cattle belonged to them.

It was apparent to Jack that Mayor Peterson and the Council had been successful in recruiting a sizable number of residents to back them in the confrontation with Miller. They were gathered beyond the parking lot north of the school. Jack quickly estimated their number to be in the range of forty to fifty.

On the driveway in front of the school, Miller's crew gathered about him. They numbered twenty men with weapons. Several women, children, and old men sat and stood nearby, near the main entrance doors to the school.

Jack motioned his followers to move forward and they slowly stepped forward. When they passed the southern entrance drive to the school and were directly in front of the school, only fifty yards distant from the Millers, Jack held up his arm and the troop on the road stopped. Meanwhile, the warriors walking carefully through the field proceeded several additional yards, and then they turned to face the school. Meanwhile, the town delegation led by Mayor Peterson came down the road and spread out through the northern parking lot of the school property.

Miller's men began to spread out in anticipation of action. They stopped when Jack shouted out. "There's no need to fight. If you want to leave, we'll allow you safe passage out of town."

Miller's men stopped immediately. Their heads swiveled back to look at their leader. Andy Miller stood there, paralyzed in thought.

Jack yelled again. "You aren't wanted here. The town doesn't want you. We don't want you. Look around you. You are out numbered and out armed."

"Who are you to tell me what to do!"

"I'm no friend of yours, but I'm giving you a chance to save your life. If you fight, many of these arrows will be headed in your direction. You will be the first to fall."

Jack gestured to his archers and then to the Oakwood troops to the north. Nearly two dozen of them had bows, at the ready to be drawn and fired. Andy glanced at the Spring Hill warriors and then at the townspeople. Then he gave a quick glance to the south. The driveway to the road and the road itself was clear.

"If we leave, you're just going to take all our stuff!"

Maggie, seated on the horse next to Jack, declared, "Whatever is in the school rightly belongs to the town, not to you. Leave it. You can take what you can carry on your backs. No livestock. No horses. And if any of you don't want to go with Andy, you are free to stay and petition the Town Council to stay on permanently. If you haven't been a problem, they'll be merciful. If you want to take your chances with Andy, then go with him."

Andy spat, "You are so high and mighty, sitting up there on that horse. Who made you queen over us?"

Bill replied, "Well, Andrew, she isn't exactly a queen, but our Spring Hill community did elect her to be our leader. I personally think that she, and the town leadership, are being generous in allowing you to leave unscathed. By the way, and now I'm speaking to the rest of you, why are you still following this guy who deserted his injured comrades? He may not have a sense of honor, but I know some of you must."

"Hempstead, you old piece of crap, you've got no right to butt your nose in here. I'll get even with you someday."

Andy looked over the crowd again and quickly made up his mind.

He spoke to his followers, "Grab as much as you can. We're heading to Stone Creek."

Most of his followers knew what he meant. Stone Creek was a small village several miles to the southeast where another large contingent of the Miller clan lived. Several of the Millers rushed into the school to grab belongings while Andy remained defiantly glaring at the Spring Hill leaders.

The old man of the clan, Zeke, who had been sitting by the school doors slowly ambled with his cane to Andy's side. They whispered furtively back and forth. There was apparently some disagreement among them, but the observers were too far away to hear the words. Their voices started to rise and finally were loud enough for others to hear Zeke respond to Andy.

"I don't care what you say. I'm staying here. I'm too old to be walking all the way to Stone Creek." He turned his attention to Maggie and yelled, "You! Missy! You said we could stay if we wanted to. Well, I want it! Are you going to keep your word, or are you going to chase me out of here?"

"Mr. Miller, that's not up to me. It's up to the Town Council. Let's go talk to them."

She started to walk her horse up the road toward the town contingent. Jack motioned for Mandy and a couple of the foot soldiers to go with her. Andy just glared at Zeke as the old man made his way down the school driveway and over to the parking lot where the townspeople were deployed. Jack kept his focus on Andy.

Sitting on the horse next to Jack, Bill muttered, "I wouldn't be surprised to see that idiot grab a bow from someone and try to skewer his old man."

Jack, keeping his attention on Andy, queried back, "Really? Is there that much bad blood between them?"

"It's a sort of love/hate relationship, near as I can tell. Always has been. The old man was a nightmare parent for coaches back when Andy was in school. He was vocal in his criticism of everyone: coaches, officials, and especially Andy; but let anyone else criticize Andy, and he would be all over that person. Ultimately, it seemed though, that Old Zeke was disappointed in his boy because Andy didn't amount to much."

To their relief, Andy didn't take any rash action, he stood and watched from a distance as his father conferred with the town's leaders. Meanwhile, Andy's followers were bringing personal items out of the school and tying bundles to carry away.

After a couple of minutes, Mandy started walking her horse back from the group of townspeople and Zeke. She brought her horse to a halt next to Jack's mount before announced.

"The Town Council has accepted Zeke's request to stay in Oakwood and repeats their offer to others. They did, however, mention that there are a couple of men, and you know who you are, who have done a few things they don't like. They wouldn't want them to try and stay."

Andy spat. "This town is just a bunch of sheep. I'm glad to be leaving. You guys will be sorry I left." Then he glanced at Jack and then pointed at him. "And that one, I don't know where he comes from, but I bet he'll be running the whole show before long. I seen guys like him before - seems all nice and friendly, but he'll be taking power when he can. You mark my words."

With that said, Andy turned and ordered his followers to load up and move out toward the south. Not all of his followers followed his orders. Two of the women, four of the children, and two of the older men turned the other way and started walking toward where Zeke stood with the Mayor. Andy gave them a surly look and a few curse words and then turned and started walking with his people.

Jack and his troops observed them carefully. The total of nearly three dozen men, women, and small children was loaded down with as much as they could carry. Even if the men of the group chose to fight, it would take them some time to shed their burdens and arm themselves.

They were about a hundred yards south on the road when there was a sudden flurry of activity. Andy had set his gear down and grabbed a bow from one of his men. It was one of those plastic bows that were used by high school physical education classes. The bow was already strung. He took an arrow from a quiver and then quickly shot the arrow at the cattle grazing on the ball fields. It plunged into one of the animals, resulting in the animal bellowing pain and running in fear.

Kyle Bartels, one of the archers that Jack had with him screamed, "That son of a bitch shot one of my cattle."

Kyle grimly lifted an arrow to his hunting bow, determined to shoot Andy Miller where he stood. Several others shifted their weapons as well.

However, before any could take action, Jack shouted, "Stand down!" He lept off his horse and grabbed Kyle by the shoulders. He looked him in the eye, before saying, "Kyle, listen to me. His is the action of a vindictive child. He is just lashing out trying to get under our skin."

"But he hurt the cattle, for no reason!"

"Aye, that he did. He is a mean-spirited, lousy, son of a bitch. But he is leaving town. We got him to do that without anyone having to fight and die, or even get injured. That's what we wanted. Understand?"

"Yeah, I think so. But what now?"

"Now we are going to following him down the road and make sure he doesn't cause problems for our folks back at Spring Hill. But I need you and your brother to stay here with the Oakland folks. As you say, that was one of your cattle he shot. See if you can do anything for it. If not, then help the Oakwood folks butcher it. I'm sure they will appreciate your help."

Kyle nodded his acceptance, and Jack gave orders for a couple of men to stay and assist Kyle. Maggie rejoined them, accompanied by a couple of people from the town riding bikes. One of them was Mandy's friend, Amber.

Maggie grinned and explained that she had made an agreement to secure a couple of bikes from the town and to have a couple people representing the town come on a visit to Spring Hill so that they could bring a report back to Oakwood about their neighbor and ally to the south.

Chapter 22 - Grady Farm

The Miller clan turned to the east at the crossroads. The Spring Hill sentries had pulled back from their post at the crossroads when the Millers came into sight. They were ready to flee back to Spring Hill at a moments notice and give the community a warning if Miller was headed in that direction. But no warning was needed.

Miller halted his crew for a few minutes at the crossroads. A couple of Miller's men began walking to the south but, the rest of his minions turned to the east at the crossroads and continued their journey toward Stone Creek.

A few minutes later the Spring Hill troop arrived at the crossroads, and the sentries returned to their post. The leaders dismounted and had a brief discussion with the sentries. They made the decision that Jack would take the three best riders and follow the men who had gone south. A group of six fighters would temporarily stay with the sentries at the crossroads. The rest of the party would return to Spring Hill.

Jack's squad consisted of himself, Mandy, her brother - Dylan, and Danny - one of the Bluffton men. The road to the south had numerous bends and curves as it progressed through farm fields and woodlands, and Miller's men occasionally slipped from view as they made their way south. Soon they would be to Grady home. Jack could sense the anticipation growing in Mandy as he rode next to her.

When they rounded the final curve, and the Grady house came into view, they were surprised that they couldn't see the men on the road in front of them.

Mandy exclaimed, "They must have gone into our place! Why would they be doing that?"

Jack's brow furrowed as he considered what sort of mischief the men might be about. Then he ordered, "Let's pick up the pace, but be careful. We outnumber them, but we don't want to be ambushed."

They brought their horses to a trot and soon reached the driveway to the Grady homestead, where they stopped and looked over the buildings. The yard was overgrown and it was eerily quiet. The family dog that had greeted Jake when he first came up the road to the Grady home had gone with them to Spring Hill.

Dylan blurted out, "They broke the front window. They must be in the house." He moved to get off his horse.

"Wait!" was the quick command from Jack. "We don't want to rush into a trap." They may have broken it just to draw us there. Certainly, they knew we were following them. We didn't hide that from them. Stay mounted for now and be prepared to move out quickly. Mandy, Danny, circle behind the sheds and barn."

Mandy directed her mount off the primary drive and around the barn on the southern side of the property. Danny went around to the north to circle behind the shed.

Dylan asked, "Shouldn't we yell at them to come out? Like you yelled when you first showed up here? Then they'll know we are here."

"Oh, they know we are here. They knew we were following them. No need to yell. Watch for signs of movement in windows and around the corners of the buildings."

He gently nudged his horse to start moving up the driveway. The slow clomping of its walk echoed off the barn. Halfway up the driveway, he stopped and motioned for Dylan to stop.

He whispered to Dylan, "I don't think they are in the house. But, you wait here and keep your eyes and eyes open. I am going to head towards the barn. If you see any movement, shout out where it is."

Jake started his horse heading to the barn. The day had started out sunny, but a cloud bank had moved in and was thickening as it revealed the threat of an early summer storm. The wind was shifting to come in from the east, which was a sure sign that a storm was brewing.

Jack was past the house and approaching the barn when he heard Mandy's voice from the south around the corner of the barn.

"Hey, there! You stop that!

Jack spurred his horse to a gallop and rounded the corner of the barn. He quickly took in the scene. Smoke was rising from a smoldering pile of leaves pushed against the barn. One man had been knocked to the ground and was struggling to get up. The other man was using his spear to poke at Mandy's rearing horse, while at the same time trying to avoid the beast's flashing hooves. With a swift movement, Jack pulled his sword from its sheath and urged his mount forward into the action.

The man made a strong lunge at Mandy's horse just before Jack's sword slashed across the man's shoulder and neck. The man tumbled in a heap to the ground, but his spear had hit its mark. Mandy's horse screamed in agony, and it bucked her from the saddle. She lay where she fell and didn't move.

Jack turned his attention to the other man. He was staggering to his feet and raised his hands in a sign of surrender. Danny had come into view from the opposite end of the barn and quickly approached them. He jumped off his horse and pushed the man back to the ground as he told him to stay down and grabbed a piece of twine that was lying on the ground to tie the man's hands. Jack slipped from his saddle and knelt by Mandy. She was stirring slightly and moaned when she started to move. Dylan came riding his horse around the corner quickly dismounted. Jack ordered him to extinguish the smoldering leaves that had just burst into open flames. Dylan looked at

Mandy, and briefly hesitated, then did as he was told, stomping on the leaves and smothering the fire.

Jack told Mandy to lay still. She opened her eyes and tried to focus, but she did as she was told. Jack gently felt around her head and neck and looked into her eyes. They appeared slightly glazed over, but the pupils were not severely dilated. He found himself thinking that they were a pretty shade of blue and then pushed that thought aside. He asked her if she felt pain anywhere. She shook her head slightly and then grimaced.

"Oh, my head hurts. And my shoulder a little bit."

Jack nodded. "You probably have a concussion. Just lay here for a while. Everything is under control."

As soon as the flames were snuffed out, Dylan checked on his sister and then went to tend to Mandy's horse. The cut wasn't deep but was obviously causing the horse to suffer.

Dylan started leading the horse away and said, "I'm going to take him to the barn. There is some horse liniment in there, and I'm going to dress this wound."

Jack got up from kneeling by Mandy and went to check on the man he had sliced with his sword. There was nothing that could be done for him. He was dead. The sword stroke had severed arteries in the man's neck.

Jack turned to the man who was sitting on the ground with his hands tied.

"What were you doing?"

"We were only doing what Andy told us to do. He told us to go burn the Grady barn and loot the house. We knew you were behind us, but we figured you'd go past the place, or at least go into the house once you saw the broken window. We would have fired the barn for sure if she hadn't come storming around the corner of the barn and knocked me over with her horse."

"Well, you failed. And your friend is dead."

"That's not my fault. You're the one who cut him up!"

Jack sighed because he felt the weight of contributing to another death.

"Aye. The sword can be a fatal tool. But he bears responsibility for his own death. He was following evil orders. As were you."

The man sort of snarled at him, "So I suppose you're fixing to stab me too."

"As tempting as that may be, no. But I imagine you'll pay for your crimes."

"What crimes? There ain't no law anymore, so there ain't no crimes."

"Now that's an interesting proposition, but I'm not about to debate it with you. You are obviously part of the Miller group, how are the two of you related to Andy?"

"I don't need to tell you."

Jack looked at Danny, who shrugged.

"Don't look to me, Captain. I don't know him. I'm from Bluffton."

Mandy remained lying on the ground, but she spoke up, "I went to school with the one you killed. He was a younger cousin. The one you are talking to is Brady, Andy's younger brother. I always thought he was the smarter of the two, but I'm beginning to doubt that."

Brady spit. "You little bitch. What do you know? I wish we had burned your place to the ground."

Jack exclaimed, "Enough! Get your ass up! Danny, take him around to the front of the house. And wait with him on the porch. And if he gives you any problems, you have my permission to give him a few whacks."

After they had disappeared around the corner of the barn, Jack knelt again by Mandy. He checked her over again and then asked her to try and sit up.

When asked how she felt she bravely tried to smile and

responded, "I'm okay. My head aches and I feel a little woozy, but I'll live."

Jack smiled in return. "Don't hurry it. Just stay sitting here until I return for you. And if you feel too woozy, lie down again. I'm going to go check on Dylan and your horse. Then I will be right back."

Upon checking in the barn with Dylan, it was determined that the horse's wound appeared to be superficial, but to prevent infection, Dylan had cleaned it and treated it. The horse was in its familiar stall in the barn. Jack instructed Dylan to round up the other horses and bring them to the front of the house.

Jack pulled out his pocket watch. The time was 4 o'clock. He looked to the skies. The cloud cover had thickened, and the east wind had picked up a little more. He estimated that within a couple of hours a storm would be upon them. He didn't think that Mandy was up to a gallop, or even a trot, on horseback. Her concussion, while perhaps not critical, was severe enough that she should rest if possible. He made his decision and went to tell the others.

Quickly, Jack went behind the barn to Mandy. He lifted her in his arms and carried her into the barn. There he placed her upon the old sofa that the family had put in the barn. When they converted the barn into a stable for the horses, they had made a corner of it into what the family called - the horse trainer's quarters. In addition to the sofa, they had added a couple of overstuffed chairs, a small wood-burning Franklin stove that vented out the side of the barn, a small refrigerator, and an old television. Obviously, the fridge and television no longer worked, but the Franklin stove was a gem. He told her his plans and told her to wait there while he went and talked to the others.

First, he went to the shed and grabbed an old tarp. As he walked to the front porch, he could see that the other three horses were tethered securely, but saddled and ready to go. He had Dylan go with him to where the slain man lay. They wrapped him in the tarp and carried him to the front of the house.

Then he gave them their instructions. They were to take the three horses and Brady and to ride quickly back to the crossroads. Once there, they were to briefly explain the situation to the sentinels posted there, and then they were to make haste to get to Spring Hill. Hopefully, they would arrive before the storm broke. Jack would remain with Mandy, allowing her to recover from her concussion and her horse to begin to heal. On the morrow, they would make their way back to Spring Hill.

Jack made sure that Brady's hands were securely tied and that he had no weapons on him. Then Jack removed his personal gear from his horse. The men helped Brady mount the horse and then hoisted the dead man over the horse's withers. Danny and Dylan mounted the other horses. Dylan led Brady's horse by the reins, and Danny followed behind. They took off in a walk but soon moved to a fast trot. Hopefully, they would beat the rain.

Chapter 23 - Choose this Day

Jack returned to Maddy in the barn, where she was relaxing on the old sofa. She was no longer sitting but had slid down so that her head was resting on one of the arms and her legs were stretched out onto the sofa.

Jack smiled and asked, "Comfortable?"

"As comfortable as one can be who just got knocked senseless."

Jack nodded in understanding as he sat on the opposite arm of the couch.

"I sent the others on their way. Hopefully, they will make it back to Spring Valley before the storm breaks."

"So it just us and my Dolly. You're sure she's going to be okay?"

"Dylan treated her cut, and he says she will be fine."

"I hope it doesn't storm too hard. Dolly doesn't like thunderstorms."

"It's hard to say how bad it will be. I was going to suggest we go to the house and find a bed for you so you can rest comfortably for the night, but maybe you'd rather that we settle in here for the night - so Dolly isn't so frightened."

"Yes. I'd rather do that. The couch would be fine for me, but there's no reason for you to be uncomfortable."

"I'm not going to leave you out here alone. One of these chairs will work just fine. Either that or I'll just spread a little straw on the floor and curl up on that."

"Why don't you go into the house and pull one of the mattresses out here. They're not doing any good in there anymore."

"That sounds good to me. What about food? Your folks didn't have any extra stashes hidden away, did you? All I have on me are a couple of the venison jerky strips that I slipped in my pocket this morning before we left."

She started to shake her head, but then winced and stopped when she felt the pain. "No, we got it all when we made the trip back here after moving to the valley." She hesitated as in thought, and then went on. "But Mom might have planted some early spring vegetables in the garden before the aurora happened. They wouldn't have been watered or weeded, and the rabbits might have gotten into them, but there might be some radishes, lettuce, and peas in the garden."

Jack grinned and said with mock formality, "Well, thank you, M'lady. You've given me some important tasks. I shall be about them promptly before the weather prevents me."

She gave him directions to the garden behind the shed. He got up, grabbed a bucket, and went off. Several minutes later he returned with a bucket of radishes, lettuce, and peas.

"It was as you said, Mandy. The critters have been at them, but I was able to forage enough to make a feast for us tonight. I see the stock tank has some water in it from the rains this month. It's probably not healthy to drink as is, but I can make a little fire in the Franklin stove and boil some water."

Mandy smiled and replied with mock seriousness, "Why, Sir Jack, that would be most appreciated."

Jack grinned back and then set about gathering some wood and making a fire to boil the water. Once he had those tasks in hand, he made a trip to the house and returned with a single mattress, probably from Dylan's bed from the look of the football sheet that covered it. He leaned it against the wall.

"I'm going back to the house to grab a couple of blankets. Is there anything else you want me to bring?"

Mandy thought for a moment. "Well, if you wouldn't mind. I could use some fresh clothes. My room is the first one on the left at the top of the stairs. I shared it with my sister." She went silent for a moment as she thought of her sister. Then she went on. "My dresser is the white one. Hers was the pink one. Could you grab a few clothes for me? And if you see a brush or comb, grab that too?"

"Your wish is my command, m'lady."

Thunder rumbled in the distance, and Mandy said, "You'd better hurry. It sounds like the storm is coming."

Jack scrambled to the house and soon returned with a couple of blankets in one arm and sheet tied into a bundle in the other.

Mandy giggled when she saw him. "You look like a burglar carrying his bag of loot."

Jack chuckled in return. "I felt a bit like one when I went into your room and started pulling clothes out of the dresser."

Mandy sat up slowly. She felt no pain as she moved, and smiled. "Let's see what you brought me."

"I'm going to get this water boiling and clean these veggies off. I can step outside for a couple of minutes if you want to change clothes."

She was already looking over what he had brought from the house and replied, "I'm no prude. We're living in new times, and we've shed a lot of our modesty since establishing the commune at Spring Hill. It won't bother me. Will it bother you?"

He swallowed and said with mock seriousness, "I think I can handle it."

Almost immediately she found something she liked and started unbuttoning the blouse she was wearing. Within moments it was off and she had also unclasped her bra. She grabbed a sports bra from the pile to replace it. Slyly she looked out of the corner of her to see if Jack was looking and could see that he was trying to act like he wasn't, but that he had, indeed, been observing.

From Jack's perspective, he admired his friend's openness, and he admitted to himself that she was actually a beautiful young woman. He had already experienced her athletic prowess and now was struck by the sensual beauty that she displayed.

"Jack, the clothes are great. Thanks."

"You're welcome."

"Too bad you couldn't rig up a hot shower for me, too. That's one of the pleasures I miss from the before times."

At that moment there was a rumble of thunder. It was noticeably closer than the distant rumbling from before.

"Well, by the sound of it, we should be having a rain shower soon. Maybe you'll have to make do with that."

"Ooo. .. that sounds like fun. You too!"

"What?"

"You could use one, too, Jack. But how about some towels? How do you expect me to get a proper shower if I don't have a towel to dry off with?"

"I can take care of that," he said as he leapt up and was out the barn door on the way to the house.

The wind had lessened and the rain started to patter down upon the farm. A few large droplets, at first, and then more and more. By the time Jack returned with the towels, sprinting across the yard from the house, the rain was steady. He came through the open barn door, and the first sight he saw was Mandy sitting on the couch, without a stitch of clothing on. She had pulled the tie from her ponytail and her hair lay loose about her shoulders. She unashamedly stood up and started walking toward him. She staggered slightly and briefly closed her eyes.

"Are you okay?"

"I'm fine. Just a bit of the dizziness."

"Maybe you should sit back down."

"What? And miss my shower?"

She walked to the door. It was now a heavy downpour. She put a hand on the door frame to steady herself for a moment.

Jack called out, "Wait!"

Then he quickly slipped his shoes and socks off. He looked up at Mandy, gave a slight shrug and then stripped off his shirt and pants. Finally, he pulled off his undergarments and then stepped forward to take Mandy's hand.

"You might need some support in your shower. I wouldn't want you to fall and hit your head again."

She grinned. "So gallant. Such a gentleman."

They stepped out into the rain. Immediately they were drenched, but yet they walked several paces forward and stood in a grassy area. Jack released her hand from his, and she raised her arms upward, as if in prayer. She tilted her face upward, mouth agape, and felt the pleasure of the rain forcefully pummeling her face and body. Jack imitated her posture. For several moments they stood there - drinking in the refreshing power of the rain.

Then Mandy turned to face him. She lowered her hands slightly and placed them on the sides of his face. He was several inches taller than her, so she lifted herself on her tiptoes and pulled him down towards her. He did not resist. He lowered his arms and took her in a full embrace, lifting her off the ground as their lips met. For a moment they lost themselves in each other.

Suddenly there was an explosion of light, and the boom of thunder shook the air. Their eyes flew open. He lowered her to the ground, and they dashed toward the barn. She slipped slightly as they reached the door and he grabbed her again. He pulled her into another embrace. They stood just inside the doorway and kissed again.

Then she smiled and said, "Now, mister, where's my towel?"

He slowly released her from his embrace and stepped to the side to grab the towels. They were huge fluffy bath towels, and the thought flashed through Mandy's mind how serendipitous it was that they had not taken these towels to Spring Hill when they had made a foraging trip to the farm.

They dried themselves, wrapped themselves in their towels, and stood in the open barn door watching the rain. For long moments they were silent as they enjoyed the sight and sound of the storm.

Mandy spoke first. "Jack, do you believe in free will . . . or fate?"

"I'm not sure. What do you mean?"

"How much of our future do we determine, and how much of it is determined by fate?"

"Ahh . . . the age-old question of free will or determinism."

"Yes, that's what I'm talking about. I can still remember discussions about the subject that we had in Mr. Hempstead's high school classes."

"I'm no philosopher."

"None of us are. But don't you wonder if there is a 'why' about what happened?"

"Do you mean about what we just did, or do you mean about the aurora event?"

"Well, both, I guess ... but I was talking about the aurora. Was it fate? Or did God make a choice to rapture some people, and leave the rest? Did you just show up on my doorstep by chance? Or were there personal choices that made it happen that way? I mean - I didn't have to come home from college for the weekend. I choose to."

"Whoa! I can't answer all that. I really don't know. Really ... how can we know?"

She pursed her lips. "That's the problem. I want to know."

"I'm sorry I can't help you. But what I tend to think is that we are responsible."

"So you believe we are responsible for the choices we make."

Jack nodded. "Yep. We were raised a certain way. We were taught certain things. Yet ultimately we have choices. And the choices we make, determine the things that will come and the future choices that we will have before us."

Mandy nodded thoughtfully and paused before she spoke. She shifted her gaze from the pounding rain and looked up into his eyes.

"And, if tonight, I choose you, what then?"

He returned her gaze and replied, "Then that decision is made, and we live with the consequences."

She paused and then asked a similar question.

"And, if tonight, I don't choose you?"

He made a slight thoughtful smile before saying, "Then we live with the consequences."

She shifted the mood by playfully punching him in the arm and saying sarcastically, "You are such a romantic. Now let's get to that food you promised. I'm hungry."

Chapter 24 - Brady's Escape

The east wind was gusting, and droplets of rain were beginning to splash on the road when Dylan and Danny reached the bridge gate at Spring Hill. In anticipation of the storm, a guard had just come and locked the gate for the night, but he quickly swung it back open as he saw them approach. Their faces were grim as they rode past the guards and hurried through the gates. Without pausing, they trotted their horses up the driveway to the buildings. They headed directly to the barns to take care of their horses. They dismounted and a couple of boys took the reins of the horses and led them into the barn to care for them. With resignation, Dylan and Danny started walking to the main hall to report to the Chief.

Even though the residents of the Spring Hill community were scrambling to get everything under cover before the heavy rain started, Dylan and Danny felt that everyone was looking at them and wondering what was happening.

They entered through the main door and found Maggie, Mike, Bill, and Aurora sitting at the large oak table. Aurora had paper and pen in hand and was making notes as they talked. Their faces turned toward the new arrivals and upon seeing the grim expressions and noting the absence of Jack and Mandy their curiosity soared. Nonetheless, Maggie invited them to join them at the table. Holly, who was working in the kitchen, brought the men some food.

It was a painful story for the men to tell, yet they described in detail what had happened at the Grady place. They were obviously distressed to discuss the action that occurred on the road home, but they relayed the events faithfully.

They recalled that as they rode up the road to the crossroads, they could sense the building storm and had been hurrying toward the crossroads. The sentinels had stepped out from their shelter, the old long-empty farmhouse on the northeast corner of the crossroads, and were standing in the center of the junction when the real action started.

Dylan felt the reins from the trailing horse yanked from his hands. This pulled him off-balance, and he struggled to maintain control of his mount. The startled sentinels leapt to the side to avoid the commotion. Meanwhile, Brady had flung the tarp-wrapped body of his friend from his horse and kicked his mount to a gallop, heading down the road to the east - the direction the Miller clan had gone.

Danny was momentarily stunned by the action, but then recovered and took off in pursuit. It soon became apparent to him that his horse was not as fast as the other horse and that he was losing ground on the fleeing man. Regretfully, he gave up the chase. Brady had escaped, and to top it off he was delivering one of the valuable horses to the Miller clan.

The riders dismounted and stood in the center of the crossroads with the sentinels. They decided the best course of action at this point would be to leave the tarp-wrapped body with the sentinels. They would bury it in a hastily dug shallow grave. The riders would ride to Spring Hills and give their report to the leaders.

After sharing their story, Dylan and Danny sat quietly at the table. They knew they had failed in their task and they waited for a rebuke. For several moments no one spoke. Then Bill broke the silence.

"The loss of life is mournful. The loss of the horse is regrettable. But the loss of Brady Miller is perhaps fortunate."

The others turned and looked with surprise at their elder statesman, so he explained.

"Many of us here know Brady. He is a braggart, but he has a certain amount of charisma when he chooses to use it. In many ways, he is more dangerous than his older brother. Had he come into our midst, even as a prisoner, he could have spread his poisonous ideas in our community. He certainly could have observed our community in depth and spotted our weaknesses. No, I think we are better off that he wasn't brought into our settlement."

The others at the tabled nodded their heads in understanding and agreement. There were several moments of silence as they sat in silent reflection and thought. Aurora stopped her note taking and raised the next question.

"Why was Jack the one to stay with Mandy? Why didn't he have one of you stay with her while he brought the prisoner back?"

Dylan and Danny looked at each other and shrugged.

Danny spoke, "I don't rightly know. He didn't explain it. It seemed logical to us, after all, he was the guy in charge. Maybe it was his military training. A leader doesn't leave one of his team behind."

The answer didn't seem to satisfy Aurora completely, but she didn't pursue it any further. Maggie gazed thoughtfully at Aurora but said nothing. By this time the rain had picked up in intensity. Everyone had found a place of shelter in one of the houses, barns, or sheds.

Mike looked out of the large living window that gave a view over the valley and commented, "It appears that all our folks are under shelter and out of the rain, but I think we need to do some more building. Some of our folks have been sleeping in tents, which is fine for summer nights, but come next winter, we need to have some solid winter habitable structures for them. We're over a hundred people in the valley now, with more people showing up almost every day. We need housing."

Bill asked, "Do you have some suggestions?"

"No. I was hoping you would."

"Hmmm. I would think a longhouse type of construction

might be best. It would be most efficient, though it would have less privacy than individual homes."

"I'll think about that. Maybe I can come up with some simple plans. What about housing some of the people in the deserted houses - like the ones on the way to Oakwood? After all, the Millers are gone now."

Bill shook his head. "I don't think so. They may be gone, but they are still a threat. There is also the possibility of threats from people who have fled the cities. Looking ahead, perhaps we can repopulate the countryside, but I think it will be best if all our people winter safely in our valley."

Maggie chimed in, "That's a long way off. Summer has hardly begun. We have a lot to do before them, but I agree - we must plan ahead."

Chapter 25 - Smoke

The storm passed through the area during the night, and when the sun lifted into the skies the clouds were gone. Spirits were high in the Spring Hill community because of the decisive action that had been taken against the Miller's. But optimistic attitudes soon turned pensive when a plume of smoke started billowing up in the eastern sky. It was in the direction of the crossroads sentinel post, and some feared that perhaps it had been set ablaze by lightning during the storm.

The team of replacement sentinels for the crossroads post was just about to leave Spring Hill on the newly acquired bicycles when they were given instructions to check out whatever was causing the smoke in the east and then to report back as soon as possible. Hastily, they took off down the gravel road. As they approached the crossroads, they could see Jack and Mandy walking up the southern highway. The couple was leading Mandy's horse which was carrying a couple of bundles of supplies.

The plume of smoke was not coming from the sentinel house. It was from beyond the hills to the east - the direction the Miller clan had taken. With growing apprehension, Jack estimated it would probably be in the area of the Bartels farm. The sentinels gave a brief report to Jack about Brady's escape the previous evening. Jack was more upset about the loss of the horse than Brady, but he tried not to show his disappointment.

When he learned the newly arrived sentries had been instructed to check out the fire, he decided to accompany them. He asked Mandy to stay with the other sentries at the crossroads and then he borrowed one of the bikes already at the crossroads. He would accompany the two replacement sentries on their bikes, and the three of them would reconnoiter to the east.

What they found was disappointing. Apparently, the

Miller group had camped overnight at the Bartels farm, riding out the storm within the protection of the buildings. When morning had come, they had intentionally torched all of the buildings and then departed eastward toward Stone Creek.

The overnight rains had dampened the exteriors of the structures, but when ignited the house and outlying buildings had burned readily. The middle of the road was strewn with human excrement as if to send a message to anyone who might be following them.

A cursory appraisal of the homestead revealed little reason to linger. The buildings were mostly burned down and still smoldering. Nothing of them could be salvaged at this point. There might be metal and other farm equipment that could be recovered, but there was no need to so at the moment. A salvage crew could be sent at a later date. The Miller strategy of revenge and devastation had been foiled at the Grady place, but here the destruction was substantial. Even with the Millers moving to Stone Creek, Jack knew that Andy and Brady would continue to be a threat to Oakwood and the Spring Hill community. For a few moments he second-guessed his decision to allow them the opportunity to escape, but then he shrugged his shoulders and set about moving on. It was an action of the past that couldn't be changed. They'd have to live with the consequences.

Chapter 26 - Summer Solstice Plans

The next couple of weeks passed quickly. Men, women, and children worked feverishly on tending the crops, building structures, foraging for food, as well as securing other supplies from the deserted homesteads in the vicinity. They also welcomed more people into their community. More people from west of the county forest had come up the gravel river road. After a brief quarantine, they had signed the community charter and had become full members.

Maggie was adamant that some sort of summer solstice celebration would take place. At one of their council meetings, she spoke her mind freely.

"As you folks know, I'm not a believer in any god. I don't rightly know if there is a deity or not, and I won't force my beliefs on anyone. However, I think it is obvious that for the immediate survival of our Spring Hill community, we will be an agricultural community. Our lives and our survival, are intimately tied to the seasons. From our inception we need to observe the coming and going of the seasons - so I declare that we shall have a summer solstice celebration. I'll take suggestions from you as to what we call it, how, to celebrate it, and so on - but I'm telling you - we need to do this. We are old-timers in this area, and we are newcomers. We've been working hard and working out our differences while living together. Now we need to play and celebrate together."

And so it was that they developed plans for a celebration of "Midsummer." Technically speaking, the summer solstice was the astronomical first day of summer, but many countries and cultures had developed "midsummer" celebrations at this time of year when the northern hemisphere had the most daylight hours. Some fruits and crops were already maturing - life was in full abundance. It felt proper to take the time and celebrate life in all its fullness.

Bill, the history teacher, and Aurora, the official historian of the community, did most of the work of researching and presenting ideas and possible activities to Maggie's council. Plans were made to celebrate Midsummer on June 22. The day would begin as an ordinary work day, for much work needed to be done, and the celebration activities would start later in the afternoon. Archery contests, feats of strength, games for the children, a "feast" of available food, dancing about a "green pole," and a huge bonfire at twilight were some of the planned activities.

Word of the planned events spread throughout the community and excitement for the day grew. It was as if the promise of a celebration spurred the residents of Spring Hill to work even harder than in previous days.

Holly suggested that it might be "neighborly" to communicate with the town of Oakwood and invite them to send a delegation to join in the festivities. Maggie and the council sensed the wisdom in that and dispatched a team to walk to Oakwood and extend the invitation. Mandy (now fully recovered from her concussion) and Amber (who had come from Oakwood) left for Oakwood two days before Midsummer with the intention of returning with some Oakwood representatives on the day of the celebration.

Chapter 27 - Princeton Refugees

Mandy and Amber enjoyed their walk to Oakwood. It was a beautiful sunny summer day. They were armed with staffs and daggers and felt confident they could fend for themselves, having practiced their skills under Jack's tutelage.

As they rounded the final bend in the road and Oakwood came into sight, they could see several dozen people working in the fields between the school and the river. Such activity did not surprise them, but what did surprise them was that there were dark-skinned people, including some wearing colorful headscarves, working among them.

People were going in and out of the former school building on the edge of town, so that seemed the logical place to go. By the time they had reached the entrance driveway to the complex, a young man carrying a spear had come walking out to meet them. He was apparently a guard of some sort. Amber and Mandy immediately recognized their former classmate, Nate Howell. Nate had lived with his brother, sister, and parents about a mile north of town, but when the aurora happened, and the parents had disappeared - the young folks had come into Oakwood where Jim Peterson had taken them under his wing.

Amber greeted him first, "Hey, Nate, how's it going."

"Well enough. But you two have to stop and answer a few questions before you can go on?"

"Really? You know who we are!"

"Of course I do. But I have to make sure you aren't carrying any sicknesses in with you. Neither of you has been sick, have you?"

After a brief question and answer period, Nate started walking them to the building entrance. The large sign in front of the building still said "Oakwood High School" but a small sign taped to the door read "Oakwood Guriga."

Nate explained to them that once the Miller clan had vacated the premises, the town council had decided that since the school building was the largest building in the community, it made sense use it. They had cleaned up the mess that the Millers had left - including the freeing of several people who had come as refugees from the south before the Spring Hill sentinels were posted at the crossroads. The Millers had taken them as prisoners and subjected them to harassment and abuse.

Nate walked them past the school and explained that now the building was being used as the home ("guriga" means home in Somali) for the contingent of Somali refugees from the north. As they made their way to the town Community Center to meet with Mayor Peterson, Nate told them of how the Somalis had arrived several days ago and how the Town Council had decided to welcome them into the community.

Before the aurora, the large town to the northeast, Princeton, had a large poultry processing plant. Throughout the last decade, the plant had trouble hiring local workers. Their response was to recruit and hire immigrants, mostly Somalis, to come and work in the plant. Racial tensions had sometimes flared, but since the Somalis provided work and contributed to the local economy, they had been grudgingly accepted into the community. When the aurora happened, a group of Princeton locals - the Kapps, who were much like the Millers of Oakwood - had threatened and persecuted the Somalis so much that they felt they had to leave. They bundled up what they could of their possessions and started trekking south. They ended up in Oakwood.

Having reached the Community Center, Nate escorted the two visitors into the Mayor's office and then left to return to his post.

"Welcome, ladies!" Mayor Peterson greeted them warmly. "What brings the two of you to our neck of the woods?"

They laughed and told him about the Spring Hill invitation to the Midsummer celebration.

"Great minds must think alike," responded the mayor, "we have decided to do a similar thing here. Part of our reasoning is to build a community that includes all of our members - including our new Somali friends. So we want to do some things that are new for all of us."

Mandy nodded thoughtfully. "That makes sense to me. I knew there was a large group of Somalis living in Princeton, but I never really got to know any of them. All their kids went to high school there."

"Yep. The Somalis tried to fit into the Princeton community, but there were some real haters up there. You know, folks who just don't like immigrants."

"Nate was telling us that the Somalis got chased out of Princeton after the aurora happened."

"Blame it on the Kapps. They're of the same ilk as the Millers."

"So why did they head this direction?"

"I don't rightly know. None of the Somalis have really explained it. But there is something strange about what happened to them. I'd like to talk to Bill Hempstead about it sometime."

"Mr. Hempstead? Why?"

"You know how we've speculated that there was some sort of 'rapture' event. All of the real fundamentalist believers disappeared."

A sad expression settled onto Mandy's face. "Yeah. My parents and sister vanished."

"Oh, yes, of course. I'm sorry. I knew that. Well, the Somalis had a similar occurrence happen to them."

"But they aren't Christian."

"No, they're Muslim. But they tell us that their most

fundamentalist and fervent believers also vanished."

"A Muslim rapture?"

"That's what is so strange. It's what I want to discuss with Bill. I don't know if Islam has anything in its theology that is comparable to a 'rapture' event, yet fundamentalist Muslims disappeared in the same way fundamentalist Christians did."

"Then maybe it wasn't a rapture."

"Yet the only commonality across the lives of those who are gone - at least that we have come across - is that they were all fundamentalist believers in their faith - whatever it was. That's what I'd like to talk about with Bill. You know he taught history, but did you also know he studied religions?"

Mandy and Amber looked at each other and gave knowing laughs.

Mandy replied, "Oh we know that. Anyone who was a student in one of Mr. Hempstead's class knew he had a thing about understanding religions."

Amber added, "But I never figured out what religion he actually was. He was just always asking questions. He never really said what he believed."

Mayor Peterson nodded. "Yep, that sounds like Bill. He's always trying to make people think critically. He doesn't like just to tell people what to believe."

Then the mayor changed the direction of the conversation, "I was in the process of getting a couple of people to head north to visit the Rudd place, you know, the bison farm. We heard reports that people are gathering there and the town council wanted to see if they want to be our allies, sort of how you folks at Spring Hill are."

"Who is running the show up there?" asked Mandy, "Is it Jason, or his sister Karla."

"I don't know. Would it make much of a difference?"

"I think so. If it is Jason, well, he is a friend of Andy Miller.

I always thought he was kind of creepy. He tried hitting on me once. I don't know if he would be very receptive to you after you kicked the Millers out of town."

"Ewwhhh," said Amber with disgust. "Why do older guys always think it is okay to chase after younger chicks?"

Mandy replied, "Older guys aren't always bad. It's just the older creepy ones." Then she turned her attention back to Mayor Peterson, "Why tell us about visiting the Rudd farm?"

The Mayor sighed, "Well before I knew your impressions about Jason, I thought that I might ask you to go with the group. The fact that you are from Spring Hill might give added weight to our offer of friendship and cooperation."

Mandy paused a moment before answering. She felt conflicted. She really wanted to return to Spring Hill in time for the Midsummer celebration, but she also felt a compulsion to represent the community she now called home.

With determination, she answered, "I'll go - to represent Spring Hill. I think that's what my leaders would want me to do."

Amber turned and looked at her to protest. "But you'll miss the midsummer celebration at Spring Hill. Are you sure?"

"Yes, I'm sure. Oh, I'd love to get back in time for the celebration, but I think it is my duty to go to the Rudds with the mayor's group."

"Well, then, I'm going with you! Maybe we'll at least get back in time for Oakwood's party."

Mayor Peterson looked at them and smiled. "My plan is that our delegation will travel there today and come back tomorrow. So I think you should be able to be back for the evening bonfire and festivities."

Mandy confidently replied, "Then it is settled, Amber and I are going with. Let's get this group assembled and let's get going."

Chapter 28 - Bison Farm

Within an hour, Mayor Peterson had assembled his group, and they were on their way to the Rudds. Mandy and Amber felt safe enough as they followed behind the two representatives of Oakwood. One of the men carried a hand-fashioned spear, and the other one had a hunting bow. They bantered conversation back and forth with their friends for the first couple of miles, and then the young women dropped several steps behind the others so they could converse privately.

Amber whispered to Mandy, "When you made that comment earlier about 'not all older men being so bad' you were talking about Jack, weren't you? I've seen the way you look at him."

"He's not that much older than me." Mandy protested.

"Really? He might not be as old as Andy Miller, but he is several years older than you."

"Well. . ." she hesitated and then continued, "we're close enough in age, and he is a great guy."

Amber's voice rose in intensity but was still quiet enough so the others wouldn't hear her. "I knew it! You've got the hots for him! Does he feel the same about you?"

Mandy blushed.

"I think so. We enjoy each other's company."

"Tell me more." Amber urged.

Mandy shared with Amber about how she felt that Jack looked at her in a special way but said nothing to her friend about what had happened the night that she and Jack had spent together on the Grady farm. Then their conversation shifted to other matters. It was late afternoon when they crested the last rise in the road and could see into the valley where the Rudd bison farm was located.

The Rudd farmhouse, barn, and sheds stood about a

quarter of a mile away and appeared to be the way the travelers remembered them, but they could see that several tents and temporary shelters had been constructed nearby. A herd of several dozen bison grazed in the fenced pasture behind the buildings. In a separate field, they could see several horses grazing. The Rudd Bison Farm was known in the region both for its bison herd and for the quarter horses it raised. Smoke rose from a cookfire that was burning in the fire ring behind the house. There was also an outdoor wood-fired pizza oven and grill that had smoke rising from it. On the opposite side of the county road from the Rudd farm was another farmstead with a smaller farmhouse and fewer buildings. Fields around that farmstead were tilled and people were hard at work in them. Men, women, and children were moving about, but there was a sudden flurry of activity as the inhabitants spotted their visitors on the road.

Within moments four riders on horseback, armed with spears, were headed their direction. The walkers stopped, and one of the men began waving a white flag of truce. At a distance of several yards, the riders brought their horses to a halt. They recognized the man apparently in charge. It was Jason Rudd. He had no warm words of welcome. He was harsh and brusque.

"What do you folks want here?"

Jimmy Karstens, a middle-aged man who had been a worker at the lumberyard, was the leader of the Oakwood delegation. He responded for the group.

"Hi, Jason. It's good to see you're doing okay. We've come out from Oakwood because we heard rumors that there was a group of people gathering at your place. Just being neighborly. Seeing if we can help."

"Hmmmph. You're carrying weapons. That doesn't look so friendly."

"Well, we are - friendly, that is. The weapons are only to

defend ourselves if needed. Are you in charge here, or is Karla? Who do we talk to?"

Jason snorted again. "Sometimes she thinks she's the boss. She gives people their work orders. But I'm the one really in charge. You can talk to me."

"Okay. Can we come down to the farm and talk with you there?"

They could see Jason's eyes flicker back from them to the farm and then back to them, with his eyes finally settling on Mandy and Amber who stood behind the others. His expression changed to a noticeable leer and then Jason spoke.

"Wait a minute, is that Mandy Grady hiding in the back? And Amber Hill? How nice of you ladies to visit me. Sure, you folks can come on down to the farm."

Without waiting for a response, he wheeled his horse around and spurred it onward back to the farm, without waiting for them to follow. The others looked at each other, and they copied his lead, racing back to the farm and taking their mounts into the horse barn. As the visitors walked their way down the road to the farm, Amber leaned close to Mandy and whispered, "I don't like this. Did you see the look he gave us? Like we were fresh meat on the hoof that he was going to tear into? My stomach is turning."

Mandy returned the whisper. "I saw it. I don't like it either. I can't wait until we get on the road heading out of here."

Dogs were barking at them as they walked up the driveway to the house. Karla Rudd came out of the house and greeted them as they approached. Karla was known to all the locals as an intelligent and caring person, but also one who could be strongly opinionated and stubborn.

"Hey, guys. It's good to see you. I was wondering when we would see someone from Oakwood. How are things going there, Jimmy?"

138

Her friendly greeting relaxed the Oakwood delegation. Jimmy Carstens responded, "It's good to see you too, Karla. Things are going okay, I guess. But we'd like to sit down for a spell and talk things over with you and Jason - if that's okay?"

"Of course, of course. I've got stew for supper cooking over the fire, but my helpers can handle it from here. Pull up some chairs on the porch and let's talk." Then she turned toward the horse barn and yelled to Jason who had just left the barn. "Hey, Jason, get over here. These folks want to talk to us."

Jason yelled back, "Hold your horses! I'm coming."

As he reached the porch and began moving to sit down, he said with a slight tone of arrogance, "You may not have noticed because you were working here in the house, but I already met these folks on the road. They said they wanted to talk about Oakwood helping us out."

Karla ignored what Jason said and asked turned her attention to the Oakwood visitors, "So, Jimmy, what is it that you and your people have to say to us?"

Jimmy took a deep breath and began.

"Well, Mayor Peterson and the Town Council were wondering if you folks would be interested in making some sort of agreement with us. It'd be along the lines of doing what we could to help each other if we could, and also not trying to attack or steal anything from each other."

Karla furrowed an eyebrow. "Are you saying we're stealing from you?"

"No, no," protested Jimmy, "We're not accusing you of anything. We want to be good neighbors. We want to work together if we can."

Jason interrupted. "Or maybe you're trying to get in good with us and get some of our bison herd. I hear you chased Andy Miller out of town. How neighborly is that?"

"How'd you hear about Andy?" asked Jimmy.

"I got my ways," Jason smirked, and then he went on, "from what I heard Andy wasn't doing anything to you folks, but then you chased Andy and his friends out of town and confiscated all the stuff they couldn't carry away on their backs with them. Ain't that true?"

Jimmy stammered and sputtered as he tried to form a response, but before he could answer, Mandy replied.

"There's some truth to what you say, but it's not the whole story."

Karla turned her full attention to Mandy. Jason started to say something, but Karla held up her hand to forestall him and then she spoke.

"You're Bob and Marge Grady's daughter aren't you? From south of town?"

A flash of grief at the mention of her family hit Mandy, but she politely responded.

"Yes, ma'am."

"How are they? Did your folks move into Oakwood?"

"My folks disappeared in the rapture. Dylan and I ended up moving to Spring Hill. There's a bunch of us living there now. I'm here to say that Spring Hill is a good place and that our folks would also want to establish a friendship agreement with your community."

Jason snorted and said, "I heard your Spring Hill group was a part of kicking out the Millers," and then he added a challenge, "say that ain't so!"

"I won't deny that we played a role in removing the Millers from Oakwood. But they attacked us first. They were lucky we let them leave town peacefully and go to Stone Creek."

Jason was about to make another retort when Karla turned on him.

"Jason, keep your mouth shut. I want to hear their story, and I don't want you interrupting. When they are done - then I'll want your comments."

Jason clamped his mouth shut and just stared at the visitors. Karla turned back to the others and bade them tell their tale. Jimmy took the lead and related a brief summary of what had transpired in Oakwood during the days that followed the aurora. As Mandy listened, she appreciated how Jimmy detailed the events and included the apprehension and fear that many of the surviving residents of the town felt about Andy and his actions. She didn't know the extent of the relationship that existed between Karla and Jimmy, but it was apparent that there was some sort of history between them. They were of approximately the same age and had lived most of their lives in the area, so it was likely they had shared some past experiences. Karla seemed to trust what Jimmy was telling her. Then Karla turned her attention to Mandy.

"Tell me about Spring Hill. What is this attack you were telling me about?"

Mandy related some of the details about the daytime visit of Andy Miller, his threats, and then the following nighttime attack. When Mandy was finished, Karla turned back to Jason.

"You didn't tell me about that."

Jason avoided making eye contact with her and muttered an excuse, "I, uh, d-didn't know about it."

Karla cleared her throat and then said, "I'll have to think about this. The Millers were an important part of the Oakwood community. It sounds like some of them, like Andy, might have done a few questionable things, but just chasing all of them away in these tough times. That doesn't seem right."

Jimmy nodded. "I understand, but I assure you Andy was a real threat to us." He paused and glanced toward the western ridge on the far side of the valley, "Seeing how it is getting late, would it be okay for us to stay overnight? We'll head back in the morning."

Jason replied, "I'll find a place for our Oakwood friends to bed down in the barn. Unless, of course, the ladies would like to share my bed."

"Jason!" exclaimed Karla, "No way. My daughters aren't about to see such a thing!"

At the mention of Karla's daughters, Mandy recalled that Karla Rudd was divorced and had a couple of middle school-age daughters.

"Awhh. I was just kidding."

"Sure, you were," retorted Karla, "you can find a place for the men in the barn, but Mandy and Amber will be bunking with me and the girls in my room tonight."

Thereupon, Jason took the men to show them where they could sleep for the night and then the whole bunch gathered at the fire ring behind the house where the simmering stew was served for the evening meal. As they ate and visited, Karla continued to probe the visitors about ways that their respective communities might be of assistance to each other.

At one point Jimmy expressed curiosity about any interactions the Somalis might have had with the Rudd folk. Almost for a certainty, they would have come down this county road from Princeton and would have passed between the two farmsteads. There were other routes they could have taken, but this was the most direct and logical path. They learned that Jason was responsible for their quick passage past the bison farm. As soon as the Somalis had appeared coming into the valley from the north, Jason had rounded up several of the men who had settled in with the Rudds and had led them in confronting the Somali caravan. There was no bloodshed, but Jason made it clear that foreigners were not welcome. Ostensibly, Jason said it was because they wouldn't have food to feed them, but more likely it was because they were different. He had his men immediately escort them down the road toward Oakwood.

Soon dusk began to deepen and people started settling for the night. True to her word, Karla brought Amber and Mandy to her room where she insisted they take the large queen-size bed, while she shared a bed with her daughters.

Neither Mandy or Amber slept well that night, even though the bed was comfortable. While they liked Karla, they couldn't help but feel as though something was amiss on the farm.

Chapter 29 - Morning Surprise

Mandy and Amber rose early the next morning, when Karla did, hoping to get an early start away from the farm. They were surprised to find that the men from Oakwood were gone.

Jason explained to them that the Oakwood men had decided to leave in the middle of the night. Jason said he didn't know why, but they had grabbed their gear and taken off saying they were heading back to Oakwood. Jason surmised that if they had been walking the whole time, then they probably would have already returned to their town.

Mandy and Amber were skeptical. They couldn't think of any logical reason the men would have left without them. They wondered if something had been done to the men, or if the men had been forced to leave. Karla muttered something to herself, but to Mandy, it sounded like "that doesn't sound like Jimmy."

When Mandy and Amber voiced their thoughts that they would grab their gear and leave immediately, Jason objected.

"That wouldn't be a smart thing to do," he said with a certain edge in his voice.

Mandy, Amber, and Karla all turned and stared at him.

Jason went on, "I don't think it would be safe for you - two young women - to go walking alone through the countryside. There are some crazy people out there."

Mandy shifted her gaze to Karla, "Is that true? Is it that dangerous around here?"

Karla shrugged. "I don't know. If Jason says it is, then it probably is. I have more than enough work organizing life and work on the farm for all the new folks we've brought. I don't really have time to worry about life outside our farm. Jason and his crew go out on patrol and make sure we stay safe in our valley."

Mandy looked at Jason and saw a strange gleam in his eyes. She didn't like the thought of staying on the farm any longer than she had to and she knew Amber felt the same way.

"How about if you let us borrow a couple of your horses? That would enable us to escape anyone who might try to stop us. We could send them back later."

Amber leaned close to Mandy's ear and whispered, "I don't know how to ride."

Karla responded, "Hmm. Maybe we could work out a trade. We are running low on some supplies, like flour and sugar. If we could get some supplies from you, we might consider it."

Jason shook his head.

"No way. I'm not giving away any of our stock. Besides, with as many folks as they have in Oakwood, I doubt they have much of those basic supplies on hand. Isn't that right, you two?"

"I don't really know," replied Mandy, as Amber shrugged her shoulders, "I'm from Spring Hill."

Karla sighed, "Perhaps it would be best if you stayed here a couple of days. Maybe some more folks from Oakwood will come this way when you don't show up."

Mandy sized up the situation in her mind. Staying on the farm certainly had its risks - she didn't trust Jason in the least. However, hiking out of the valley and attempting to return to Oakwood had more significant risks. Perhaps there were "crazy folks" out there who would try to harm the two of them. Even with their staffs and knives, a large enough group could overpower them. And then there was Jason; he could easily have his men follow them on horseback and do who knows what to them. The option of riding out had been taken off the table, because even if Jason and Karla had been willing to loan them horses - Amber didn't know how to ride. Their options were limited, and none of them were good. At least if they stayed, they would have Karla to protect them against whatever Jason might have in mind for them.

Mandy pulled Amber to the side and they quietly discussed their situation. After a few minutes, they returned and Mandy announced their decision.

"Karla, we'll accept your gracious offer. We'll stay - but only until we can safely return to Oakwood."

Karla nodded in acceptance, "That seems the sensible thing to do."

Standing to the side, and slightly behind Karla, they could see a sickening grin spread across Jason's face.

Chapter 30 - Midsummer

The Spring Hill Midsummer celebration was in full swing. Daily tasks had been completed, and for the moment any thought of work was placed out of mind. Now it was time for the members of the community to relax, enjoy each other's fellowship, and to celebrate life. Fresh venison and wild turkey were roasting over cook fires, and the eternal stew was simmering with fresh summer vegetables. The laughter and play of children and adults echoed throughout the valley as they played and competed in games for all ages.

So that other members might participate fully in the activities, Jack and a couple of the older men had taken over guard duty at the gate. Bill Hempstead instructed a couple of the food servers to prepare plates for the guards, and he walked them down to Jack and his men. He sat with Jack on the parapet of the wall as they ate.

"Jack, you seem somewhat pensive this evening. Could it be that you are missing someone and worrying about her?"

"Yeah, Bill. I can't seem to hide much from you. Mandy should have been back by now."

"The folks who came out from Oakwood to celebrate with us said she was going to make a trip with their representatives to the Rudd farm. Do you really think she'd be able to be back by now?"

"They said she planned on being back here in time for the festivities. She's pretty strong-willed. I can't see her failing it unless something happened."

"You have a point there," agreed Bill, "when she was one of my students she demonstrated determination and perseverance. She was never one to give up. I seem to remember calling her stubborn to her face once. I think she took that as a badge of honor."

Jack chuckled at that.

"Yeah, she's a tough one, alright." He paused and then said softly, "But she's also tender-hearted."

Bill nodded knowingly. Then he sighed before he went on.

"Jack, I don't want to speak out of place, so stop me if I do, but there's something I feel I should say."

"Go on."

"It is obvious to me, and I think to some others, that you and Mandy have feelings for each other." He paused and waited.

Jack nodded in agreement but said nothing, so Bill went on.

"There is someone else who has strong feelings for you. I'd hate to see her get hurt."

Jack grimaced. "You mean Aurora. Don't you?"

"Yes. The lady has quite a crush on you. I mean, think of it: you are the warrior who has stepped into a threatening situation to save the day; you are, in your own manner, mildly handsome; you are intelligent and compassionate. Need I go on?"

"Those are some nice compliments, even if they aren't totally deserved. I'm no saint."

"Ahhh, but in her eyes, you are close to it."

Jack frowned before speaking, "Bill, I do like her. And I do respect her. She is intelligent, funny, and cute. If it wasn't for Mandy, I might pursue her."

"But there is Mandy. Have you made a commitment to her?"

"Well . . ." Jack hesitated and then acted as if he was going to say something, but stopped.

"That says it all, my boy. You can leave it unspoken for now, but it is obvious there is something there. I think you owe it to Aurora to be open about it with her. She deserves that. I don't think she'll be happy about it." He paused, but when Jack said nothing, he went on, "Actually I know she won't be happy about it, but if your feelings are so strong for Mandy, it is better for Aurora to know now."

Jack sighed a long, deep sigh.

"I reckon you're right, but I don't want to hurt her."

"You'll hurt her more if you let her keep believing there is a chance for the two of you when there isn't."

Jack shook his head slightly. "I never thought that taking my father's ashes to the cabin up north would result in being in a situation like this. I wonder what he would say about this."

Bill chuckled, "Well, with what I remember of your old man, I think he would be having a little laugh at your dilemma. He would probably say, 'What are you complaining about? Two beautiful women are falling in love with you. Everyone should have it so tough."

Jack dryly responded, "Thanks, Bill. I can always count on you to make a joke at my expense."

"Think nothing of it. It seems to be my calling in this situation."

"You better head on back to the festivities, Bill. I'm sure they miss your erudite musings."

Bill gave a hearty laugh as he stood and made his way to go down the parapet ladder.

"I hope you're right about that. In any case, I suspect I've given you enough to think about for a while. And try not to worry too much about Mandy. She's a competent and resourceful young woman. I'm sure she can fend for herself - in any situation."

The older man made his way back up the driveway, and Jackson Stewart sat looking over the wall. His eyes scanned the trees and road on the other side of the river, but all his mind could see were the faces of the two women.

Chapter 31 - Bonfire

When the setting sun touched the top of the trees that lined the western ridge of the Spring Hill valley, the Chief of the Spring Hill Clan, Maggie Nelson, took a torch and held it to an assembled stack of kindling and logs, thereby igniting the Midsummer bonfire. The surrounding crowd hollered and cheered as the fire leapt to life on the. Maggie tossed her torch into the blaze and then threw her hands into the air declaring that it was time to dance.

The sound of a fiddle soared into the air. It was Maggie's husband. While Mike was no professional musician, and this was the largest crowd he had ever played for, he was accustomed to strumming his fiddle at small gatherings of family and friends. Soon, many members of the community were 'kicking up their heels' as they danced around the bonfire to the robust rhythms of Mike's fiddle.

In the back of the crowd, Bill noticed Aurora glancing down the driveway toward the gate. He knew she was thinking of Jack. He began moving toward her, but when he saw Cody step up to her and ask her to dance, he turned to the side and started a conversation with one of the recent additions to the community.

The folks partied into the night, but when the bonfire began to burn down, those with younger children began leaving to put them down for the night. Some of the older members, aware of the work before them on the morrow, also retired for the night.

Bill had spent much of the dancing time mingling through the crowd of non-dancers but now finding one of the Nelsons' original Adirondack campfire chairs empty he pulled it close to the fire to watch the flames surrender to the night and burn down into embers. A few minutes later, Aurora pulled up another of the chairs and sat next to him.

Bill commented, "I saw you dancing with Cody. You looked like you were having a good time."

"It was fun, I enjoy dancing."

"I could tell. It also appeared that Cody was enjoying it. He's developed into quite a resourceful and competent young man. I think he likes you."

"What? Cody?"

"Yep. Cody. What do you think about him?"

"He's nice, Cody has grown up a lot since he was in high school, and he is a good dancer, but I can't get beyond seeing him as a former student."

Bill said nothing, but as he looked beyond the fire, he could see Jack and the other guards who had been replaced walking up the driveway. He noticed Aurora's eyes lift from gazing into the fire and recognize Jack emerging from the shadows. Her eyes lit up and a smile appeared on her face.

Bill stretched his arms and yawned. Pushing himself up from the chair he said, "I think it is time for me to turn in for the night. I've got lots to do tomorrow." He turned himself toward his approaching friend and continued, "Jack, you can have my chair. I'm calling it a night."

A flickering look of resignation crossed Jack's face, but then his expression settled into one of resolution. Thanking Bill, he lowered himself into the chair and said hello to Aurora.

"It was a nice party you planned, Aurora. From the sounds I heard, the people were having a good time."

"It too bad that you couldn't be here for all of it."

"That's okay. Somebody needed to watch the gate. I'm sort of an introvert anyway. Big parties aren't really my thing."

"I understand. I'm sort of that way too, but sometimes I enjoy a good party. And I don't mean to brag, but I think this was a good gathering, and I think it was good for our community."

"Yeah," agreed Jack, "we needed it."

They made small talk conversation for several minutes with each other and with the others who had joined them in sitting around the dying fire.

Then Jack leaned over and whispered to Aurora, "There's something I want to talk with you about. Would you take a walk with me?"

They bid the others a cheerful goodnight and then stepped away from the fire. As they walked away from the fire their eyes adjusted to the partial darkness of the night as the glow of the aurora and the light of the rising moon washed the landscape.

After several moments of silence, Aurora asked, "What is it you wanted to say, Jack?"

Jack gulped a swallow, and then began, "Aurora, I think the world of you. You are talented, intelligent, charming, and pretty."

"Awwh, thanks. You aren't so bad yourself," she joked.

"Wait. Please let me finish. I don't want you to get any wrong ideas."

"About what?"

"Aurora, I'm afraid I might have given you the impression that I wanted to be more than friends."

"And you don't?" She said it as a question, but her tone it more as a matter of fact.

He stammered and then blurted out, "I do want to be friends, but I'm interested in someone else."

He couldn't see it, but her jaw clenched, then she said, "It's Mandy, isn't it."

He meekly replied, "Yes."

"Well, she is quite attractive. I understand why guys would be interested in her."

"I'm sorry. I haven't meant to lead you on."

"Lead me on. Whatever are you talking about? We're just friends. You never suggested more." She paused, then added, "It is getting late. Bill was right. There is much to do tomorrow. I think it is time I should be turning in. Let's head back."

They turned about and walked toward the fire. Neither one spoke. When they reached the bonfire, Aurora said goodnight to the folks that remained and went to her sleeping quarters. Jack stayed at the fire. The chairs were all taken, so he sat on one of the logs that were circled about the fire. For a long time, he sat and gazed at the burning embers as the other people conversed. They were telling each other the stories of what each of them was doing the night of the first aurora. That made him think of Mandy, and he became lost in his thoughts of her.

After a time he heard someone, it was Dr. Julie Westin, saying, "Jack. Jack!"

He shook his head to alertness. "What?"

"Where were you? You look like you were a million miles away in thought. The rest of us were sharing our stories of the first night of the aurora. What was your experience that first night?"

Jack made a small joke about being lost in his thoughts and then launched into his tale about that first night. It was a new story for the more recent members of the community, and since Jack was one of the key leaders of the community, they leaned forward in rapt attention. Several them smiled when Jack described Mandy, in his first meeting with her, as a 'cute, ponytailed college girl.'

One of the crowd asked, "Why isn't she here tonight? Where is she?"

"She went on a mission to Oakwood. We thought she would be back by now, but she didn't make it. Hopefully, she'll return soon."

Conversation resumed as the next person shared their

story, and Jack slipped back into his silent reflections. The sizzling of the embers and the friendly voices around the fire were peaceful and calming, but the stress of his conversation with Aurora and his worries over Mandy left Jack tense and anxious. He sighed. Sleep would come, but it might not be soon - or restful.

Chapter 32 - Maximus

Bill's small dog, Maximus, passed away during the night of Midsummer. Bill insisted he wanted to take him back to Bill's shack in the county forest beyond the western ridge of the Spring Hill valley and bury him there. Several people offered to accompany him, but the only offered he accepted was that of his young friend, Jack.

Bill gently wrapped Maximus in an old towel and carefully put him into his shoulder satchel. Armed with their regular weapons and a small spade, the men headed up the path to the pass in the hills.

For a while, they walked without speaking, but after several minutes Jack broke the silence.

"Bill, I talked with Aurora last night and told her."

"I thought you would. How did she take it?"

"Well enough, I guess. She didn't make a scene or anything. But then she didn't stay and visit with anyone. She went right to bed. I think she'll be okay."

"Silent acceptance doesn't mean she's good with it, my boy. She's hurting. But it was the right thing to do."

"I think so. I do feel better about the situation in general. I'm still worried about Mandy, though. If she doesn't come back today. I'm going to make a trip into Oakwood and see what is going on. I suppose it is possible she just wanted to stay in Oakwood with old friends and celebrate there, but . . ." his voice trailed off.

"It's okay to worry. Just don't let your emotions overrule over your reasoning. Keep them balanced."

They walked the rest of the way in silence, enjoying the peace and calmness of the woods on a summer morning. They reached the end of the game path and stepped near to the edge of the woods and scouted the clearing before approaching the cabin. It appeared that nothing had been disturbed during the several weeks Bill had lived at Spring Hill.

Surmising that nothing was amiss, Bill said to Jack, "I'll take that spade now. I know of a spot near my meditation garden where I'll bury him. Why don't you go scout around for a while? Give me about half an hour, okay?"

"Sure, Bill take what time you need. And say a word over old Maximus for me. I liked that little fella."

While Bill went about his task, Jack hiked down the driveway toward the chained gate. As Bill had told him previously it was nearly a mile away. An examination of the gate and surrounding ground revealed no indication that anyone had tampered with it or gone around it. Apparently, at least to this point, there was no one who had survived the aurora event that knew about, or deemed it worthwhile, to examine Bill's cabin in the woods."

Jack walked back up the driveway and as approached the cabin he could see Bill waiting for him on the front step of the cabin.

"I was beginning to wonder where you were," the older man said, "did you hike all the way to the gate?"

"Yep. It doesn't look like anyone has bothered to come this way. Though I did see a lot of deer tracks."

"There is plenty of deer about, for sure; but as for people, just because they haven't come here, doesn't mean they won't. Folks do know about this place."

"You know, Bill, this county forest is a pretty nice hunting grounds. How would you feel about having a detachment of our community living here at your cabin? It could be our hunting headquarters to help supply us with fresh game. It'd also be a good defensive post to help guard the pass over the hills into the Spring Hill valley."

"I'd have no problem with that. I guess I don't really

consider it mine since I joined Spring Hill. What's mine is ours, so to speak."

"What about water? Is there a spring around here?"

"Not that I know of. But there is an old well. It used to have one of those long handled pumps on it, but the folks before me put an electric pump on it. The old pump was sitting with a pile of other old stuff in the shed. After we lost electricity, I reattached it and got it working again. It takes a little elbow grease to use. But it is functional."

Jack smiled, "Is there anything you can't do?"

"Your faith in my abilities is duly noted and appreciated. Who do you have in mind to post over here? You aren't trying to find a place for you to hide away are you?"

"Ha! There are days where I would welcome it, but no, I know my place is over there. I have a few people in mind. Foremost of the bunch is Cody. He's a natural in the woods."

"He'd be a good choice. He's a solid thinker with a good heart and a steady disposition. And he has always been crazy about hunting."

"Help me run the idea by the Chief when we get back. Okay?"

"Sure, but I don't think there will be a problem with it."

"Great. Are you ready to head back, Bill? Or do you have anything more you need to do for Maximus?"

"Naw. I'm ready. I may put up some sort of marker later. Max was a gentle soul, and he bears remembering, but I'm not going to do that today. Say, what about your father's ashes? I doubt you'll get up to the family cabin any time soon. You could consider scattering them in these woods. It's a peaceful place."

"That's a good idea. I'll think about."

The men made their way back into the woods and trekked the path over the pass into the Spring Hill valley. They emerged from the shaded woodlands and stopped to survey the activity that lay spread out before them in the valley. Men, women, and children were going about their tasks in fields and farm. There was also a building crew that was hard at work on the construction of a longhouse. They had worked to level and smooth the land for it, and now they were digging holes to set the main structural posts into place.

They stood still for a few minutes under the eaves of the forest, then Jack mused, "I wonder if we could make a mechanical, water-powered lumber saw."

"I reckon we could, but it would have to be on the river. Our little spring doesn't provide enough water power for that. Even though we have built a little holding pond near the spring, it only provides our community with enough for our basic needs. Maybe in the future. For now, we are better off using salvaged lumber and material from nearby structures."

"You're probably right. I know nothing electrical seems to work yet? Do you think it ever will?"

"I'd love having my computer back online," mused Bill, "but I don't see that happening. It is as though, somehow, and don't ask me how, the laws of science have changed since the aurora came."

"Hmmm. What about steam power? Could we make a steam engine?"

"I don't think I could do that from scratch. But that's a good idea. I wish Geoff were here."

"Who is Geoff?"

"He was our tech ed teacher in the high school. I know he worked on some steam engines in the area. He might even know the location of some working ones that they used for the 'old times farm days' festivals."

"Did he live close by? Do you think he disappeared in the rapture?"

"He lived several miles east of town, over in the Stone

Creek area. I know he was Christian and went to church, but I don't really know if he a was a fundamentalist."

"I'd say we should search for him, but I don't know that this would be a wise time to go prowling about Miller territory. I doubt we get a friendly welcome."

"You're probably right about that. But sooner or later we are going to have to make contacts with our neighbors to the east."

Jack nodded in agreement then the two men stepped forward and went to join their comrades in the work of the day.

Chapter 33 - Bison Bluff

Throughout the day Mandy and Amber went about the tasks that Karla set aside for them. Neither of them was averse to hard work, and they readily went about doing chores around the farm that would benefit the struggling community. It was a way to keep themselves occupied as they considered what to do about their situation.

As they worked at cultivating in the large garden across the road from the main farmhouse, they made their plans. As night fell, they would identify the locations of the nighttime sentinels. Then they would plan how to sneak past those posts. Late into the night they would make their escape from the farm. They reckoned that they should be able to make it to Oakwood before the light of the sun started to brighten the skies - even on one of the shortest nights of the year.

Throughout that day, they noticed Jason watching them. It was unnerving. Many of the times they observed him, he was not looking directly at them, but on several occasions they caught him staring at them from a distance.

After the umpteenth time, Amber said, "He's creepy, the way he looks at us. Why doesn't he just leave us alone.?"

"'Cause he's a creep, that's why. Don't ever let yourself get caught alone with him."

"I don't intend to!"

Other than the near-constant visual surveillance by Jason, the two young women experienced nothing overtly unusual about the community of the Rudd Bison Farm. The people gathered at the farm were merely struggling to survive in a world that had changed. Similar to the folks of Oakwood and Spring Hill, they hoped to make a go of it through hard work and cooperative effort. Without a doubt, there must be lone survivors and families scattered throughout the hills and valleys of this region, but this growing community was developing into a center point for survival. By the time the evening meal rolled around, Amber and Mandy had developed a feeling of dogged appreciation for Karla and her people. They still didn't care for Jason and the men who followed him closely, but they could see potential in having the Rudd farm as allies in the days to come.

It was a warm summer evening and the soft breeze of the afternoon fell away to a still evening and a sultry sunset. Giving the warm evening as a rationale, Mandy and Amber ask Karla for permission to sleep on the front porch of the farmhouse, rather than in the bedroom of the previous night. Karla gave them a look of thoughtful consideration but made no objection.

From their sleeping pallets on the porch, they watched the night sentries go to their places. The gloaming light after sunset was fading into twilight and soon would descend into full darkness. They would wait a couple of hours before the crescent moon rose to give more light to the unfamiliar landscape. Attempting their escape before the moonrise would give them more cover, but it would also provide a more significant opportunity for them to stumble and reveal themselves. They lay still on their pallets until the moon broke over the eastern horizon. Carefully making sure their daggers were securely in place, they picked up their walking staffs and quietly stepped off the porch.

Slowly they slipped away from the house and made their way to a large oak tree that was in front of the house, near the driveway. They waited there for a moment before crossing the driveway. They planned to make their way south along the roadway ditch. With great caution, they stepped softly and quietly as they crossed the gravel driveway. But it was not enough. They noticed a slight movement in the shadows along the wooden barnyard fence, and a voice came out of the darkness before them. It was Jason.

"And where do you think you ladies are going?"

They stopped dead in their tracks.

Mandy was going to reply but never got a chance. They heard the clanging of an alarm from the behind the barns, followed by shouts and screams of pain.

Jason spat out, "Damn! The bastards are attacking us!" He started to move toward the alarm, but then stopped and gave a warning, "Don't run off you two. I'll track you down!" Then he turned and ran toward the commotion.

Amber grabbed Mandy's arm. "What do we do? Should we run?"

Mandy thought briefly before replying, "No. We can't. Not when they are under attack."

"But it is our chance to escape."

"These are Karla's folks as much as Jason's. We need to help them. We'll go back to the house to protect Karla and the girls."

They ran back to the house and up the porch steps. As they reached the door to open it, Karla burst out of the door with a baseball bat in her hand.

"What's going on?" she demanded.

Mandy replied, "I don't know. Jason blurted out something about being under attack and then ran towards the barn."

"Ugh!" grunted Karla. "Amber, you stay here with the girls. Mandy, come with me."

She ran from the porch with Mandy on her heels. They went to the cookfire. It was kept burning throughout the night by a guard, but that guard was now gone - perhaps running towards the attack. Stacked next to a nearby tree were some unlit torches. Karla handed one to Mandy and grabbed one for herself. Thrust into the fire, the torches quickly ignited.

With torches in one hand and weapons in the other, for

Karla still carried her bat and Mandy had her staff, they hurried across the yard, went between the barns, and headed toward the bison and horse pens.

They could see the movement of men on horseback by the dim glow of the rising crescent moon, the pulsating light of the aurora, and the light cast by their torches. The sounds of clashing weapons and wild shouts of men in combat punctuated the night. Defenders of the farm were rushing from where they slept in barns and tents. There was general confusion as they milled about. Some of them lept the high wooden fences of the bison and horse pens and rushed into the melee.

Soon the sounds of combat died out as the attacking men on horseback galloped away into the darkness. Additional torches were brought forth and added light to the scene. It would take a full accounting in the bright light of day to determine their losses, but it was apparent that some of their prize horses had been stolen, and that a hole had been created in the bison fence allowing a portion of the bison herd to escape. A couple of defenders were lying on the ground. Karla screamed when she saw one of them. It was Jason, and he wasn't moving. She ran and knelt beside him. His right leg was twisted in an obscene manner which should have him crying out in pain if he was conscious, but he was not. He was breathing, but shallowly. If Jason had been awake, the pain of his contorted leg would have sent his body into shock. In the light of the flickering torches, they rigged a stretcher, and four men carried him to the farmhouse. They brought him into his bedroom and transferred him onto the kingsize bed that filled most of the space in the small first-floor bedroom that before the aurora had been used as a den. Karla chased the men out of the room ordering them to go tend to the critters and anyone else who was injured in the attack.

Karla's daughters and Amber had been peeking out of Karla's bedroom when Jason was brought in. Karla ordered them back into the bedroom and told them to close the door. A couple of the farm's women had come to the house to help Karla when Jason was brought in, and she started to give them and Mandy orders.

"This isn't going to be pleasant, but his leg is obviously broken. It may be a blessing that he is unconscious because we are going to have to manipulate that leg and set it. Let's get those boots pulled off, and his pants cut away from that leg and see what we can do before it swells."

Mandy asked, "Do you know what to do? I mean, have you set a bone before?"

"I'm no nurse, but I watched the doc set Jason's arm when he broke it in middle school. I'll do the best I can. I know we can't leave it like this. Now, give me those scissors."

One of the ladies went to the foot of the bed to remove Jason's boots and the other handed scissors to Karla. Once the boot was removed and the pants cut away, it was apparent that either one or both of the bones below the knee were broken. Tibia and fibula - Mandy thought to herself, as she recalled her anatomy class.

Karla spoke. "I'm pretty sure both bones are broken. I can't be sure without an x-ray - but there won't be any of those. I'll just try to line them up the best I can and then I'll use splints to stabilize the leg. He won't be able to put any weight on it for a long time."

Karla worked methodically setting the bones as best she could and then arranging and tieing wooden splints along the leg to hold the bones in place. It wasn't until after she had completed her work that Jason began to moan and eyes fluttered as he struggled to open them.

One of the ladies said, "He's going to be in a lot of pain. What can we do for him?"

Karla responded, "There's not much we can do. We do

have a few of the drugs we use for horses, but I don't want to risk giving him any of that. We have a few ibuprofen tablets left. As soon as he is awake enough to swallow them, we give him some. I'll sit with him for a while. You ladies can leave. Mandy, would you check on the girls. Let them know that their Uncle Jason has a broken leg, but that he will be okay."

After Mandy relayed that information to the girls and tucked them back into their beds, she stepped outside with Amber.

Amber whispered, "What are we going to do? There is still much of the night left. Should we take off?"

"No. I don't think we can. Let's wait until morning. Jason won't be bothering us now."

"I almost feel sorry for him. He looked in bad shape when they brought him in."

"Don't feel too sorry for him. He may be hurt, but that doesn't change who he is."

"Did anyone say who the attackers were?"

"No. But they were on horseback. It appears to be an organized attack. It must be someone from the north. I don't think it would be anyone from Oakwood."

Amber agreed. "Yeah, I think we'd know about it if they were."

They continued to talk as they settled back into their places on the porch, finally managing to fall asleep deep into the night.

The light of a new day gave the residents of the farm an opportunity to survey the damage and evaluate the effects of the night raid. It was determined that the raiders had, in addition to the injuries to Jason, given minor injuries to three of the guards, made off with six of the farm's quarter horses, and allowed a portion of the farm's bison herd to escape. The bison could be seen grazing on a distant hilltop to the north. More terrifying to many of the residents was the realization that even though they had banded together in an effort to survive the difficulties of this new era, they knew now that others could attack and harm them.

Chapter 34 - Rescue Plans

After talking to Bill about Geoff, Jack persuaded Maggie and her advisors that with the skill set and personality Geoff had, he would be the type of person that would fit into and benefit the Spring Hill Clan. Someone should be sent to the Stone Creek area to search for him. The problem was that the Millers of that area, and the Millers from Oakwood that had joined them, would be suspicious of anyone from Oakwood or Spring Hill that came searching for him. They briefly considered Danny from Bluffton, since he was demonstrating skills as one of their best warriors, but then Jackson reminded them that Andy Miller's brother, Brady, who had escaped from them after the incident at the Grady farm, would likely easily identify the man.

Ultimately, Maggie and her counselors decided to send a husband/wife team that had joined the Spring Hill Clan after making their way from Bluffton. They were in their mid-twenties, with no children, and had been married recently. Nick had driven a truck for a Bluffton trucking company, and Michelle had been a medical secretary at the Bluffton hospital. Both were avid hunters, and it had been their love of the outdoors that brought them together.

Before departing for the Stone Creek area, Bill and Jack met with the couple to give them background information, discuss their cover story, and to go over a map of the area. There was no guarantee they would find Geoff, or any of his family because they might have disappeared in the rapture. The plan was to avoid the village of Stone Creek and go to Geoff's home. If he weren't to be found, they would circle around and approach the village from the south, which would give credence to their cover story of fleeing the troubles of Bluffton. They should avoid speaking of any sickness, or problems from there, using as their purpose for leaving a fear of the man who was taking control of the city, Professor John Neizner.

Bill and Jack stood at the open gate of the valley and watched the couple depart.

"Bill, I hope you are right about Geoff. And I hope they are able to bring them safely here."

"Me too."

"You realize that we are sending them into real danger, don't you? If Andy should figure out that they are coming from us - I fear what might happen to them."

"They know the risk. I explained it to them. We are all taking risks for our community now. They are a part of us, and they are willing to do it."

Jack nodded and replied, "Duty, honor, country."

"Yep," Bill agreed, "though perhaps we should replace country with clan - for we've seen no evidence in these last couple of months that country still exists."

"I think you are right. In the back of my mind, I still hoped the "lights would come back on" but now I doubt they ever will. Somehow we must rebuild our society."

"Perhaps we can make it better than before."

"I don't know, Bill. There are still plenty of bad folks out there."

Bill nodded thoughtfully and agreed. "True. The rapture event may well have removed an element from our population, but it didn't take the bad apples. Well, it may have taken some of them, but certainly not all of them. I wish I could figure out exactly why certain folks were taken and not others."

"When you figure it out, tell me."

"You'll be the first to know. Now, what are you going to do?"

"What am I going to do about what?"

"What are you going to do about a certain young lady that left a couple of days ago and hasn't returned?"

Jack took a deep breath before responding.

"She left on a mission for our clan. We have a responsibility to her. It's not like her not to return or not send word with others. If something has happened to her, we need to help her."

Bill gave a wry smile and said, "Maybe the young lady just wanted to get away from you for a couple of days. You can be a little intense at times."

"What?" Jack looked at him incredulously.

"I'm just joking with you. What are friends for, if they can't tease each other a bit!"

"Thanks a lot, Bill." He paused and then added sarcastically, "You're always there for me."

"Think nothing of it, my boy. But, seriously, what are you going to do?"

"I don't like the thought of taking workers away from productive tasks here at Spring Hill, but come morning, I'm going to take a couple of warriors and head toward Oakwood. You understand how it is. We leave no one behind."

Chapter 35 - Search for Geoff

Geoff was sitting on a high stool tinkering at his newly set-up workbench in the old semi-truck repair garage in Stone Creek when he heard someone clear their throat behind him. Holding a wrench in his hand, he slowly turned to see his visitor. It was a man he didn't recognize. Having lived in the area most of his life, and now having been in Stone Creek for several weeks following the event, he was startled to see this unfamiliar man. The visitor was a sandy-haired, husky man who appeared to be in his mid-twenties.

Geoff sat still and looked at him, but said nothing, waiting for the man to speak first. Finally, the man cleared his throat again and spoke.

"Are you Geoff? I was told to see if you could use some help."

"I'm Geoff. Who told you? And what type of help did you have in mind?"

"My name's Nick. I guess it was the fella in charge here who told me what to do. I think he said his name was Andy Miller. My wife and I are out of Bluffton and looking for a place that's safe. Wherever we end up, we're willing to help."

"Well, come on in. Pull up a chair and tell me more about yourself so I can decide how you might be of help."

There was another stool near the workbench, so Nick pulled it close and leaned in to talk to Geoff. Before speaking, he glanced toward the door.

"Are we alone in here?"

Geoff snorted. "I don't see anyone else in here, do you?"

Nick accepted the sarcastic comment without reaction. Instead, he smiled and said, "I bring you a message from your faculty friends: Bill, Maggie, Holly, and Aurora. They want you and your family to come and join them at Spring Hill. That's the

Nelsons' valley."

"I know where Spring Hill is. If you're from Bluffton, how do you know about them?"

Nick glanced furtively towards the door. "My wife and I settled there. They sent us to see if we could find you. They wanted you to know you're welcome there. You'd be among friends. They seemed to think that you might not want to be in the midst of the Miller clan."

"Does Andy know you came from them?"

NIck's eyes widened slightly. "No. And please don't tell any of Andy's men. I don't think they'd treat me, or Michelle, very nice if they knew."

"That's probably true. Why did you bring your wife with you? Didn't you realize it might be dangerous?"

"We did. But traveling together was a good cover for our searching you out. Will you, and your family, come back with us to Spring Hill?"

"I have no family."

"What? The Spring Hill folks said you did."

"I did. But everyone close to me disappeared when the aurora first happened. I have some shirttail relatives here at Stone Creek, but no one close."

"I'm sorry. So, will you come with us?"

Geoff glanced toward the open door of the garage. He nodded before he replied.

"There have been guards posted outside of town ever since Andy and his gang showed up. I'm sure you saw some on the bridge when you came in."

Nick smiled. "We saw some, but not on the bridge. They were on the road south of town. We thought that if we came over the bridge, we might be suspected as coming from Spring Hill, so after we couldn't find you at your place, we headed south, forded the Pine River, and then came up the road from the south. That way it'd look like we had made our way from Bluffton."

"Smart. We'll have to do something similar when we leave. If we let 'em see us crossing the bridge, they'll track us down before we can get very far. For now, let's play it quiet. We'll tell them you can be of help to me in the shop. Maybe we'll see if we can make an unsupervised trip back to my place to get some more of my tools. Then we could take off from there."

Nick nodded. Soon enough they would find their way to Spring Hill.

That evening, after the evening meal, Geoff took his new assistant and his wife on a walk around town, ostensibly to show them the community and to help them get settled in, but primarily it was so they would have a chance to talk privately. The more they talked, the more convinced Geoff was that he wanted to leave Stone Creek and join his old friends at Spring Hill. As long as Nick and Michelle's cover story held, they would be safe. It would be wise to take the time to plan an escape.

Chapter 36 - Jack's Search

When Jack left for Oakwood in the morning, he took three of his trainees with him - Megan Henderson (Cody's sister), Tony Bartels, and Thomas (a young man from the Bluffton area). He left behind the two people he considered his most capable warriors (Cody and Dan) with instructions to draw up a plan for the establishment of an outpost at Bill's cabin.

They arrived in Oakwood at mid-morning and were quickly taken to meet with the Mayor at the town hall. Mayor Peterson was noticeably worried.

"We sent a delegation to the Rudd bison farm to propose some cooperation between our groups. The envoys should have returned by now. Mandy and Amber went with them to represent Spring Hill. I was sure they would be back here for our midsummer celebration, but they never showed up. I was just debating with my council about what we should do."

"How far away is the farm?"

"It is about five miles north of here."

"Hmmm. Even if they didn't leave until this morning, they should have returned by now."

"Yes. But there is no word of them."

"If you don't have any objection, my team will accompany whoever you send to check up on them."

"I'd appreciate that. We hate to pull any of our folks away from their work tasks, but if you go along, that will help. You should be able to march there, check things out, and still return by this evening. Will you do that?"

"That sounds like a good timeline. How many men will you be sending?"

"We sent two with Amber and Mandy. I think we had better send more, even though we could use their work here. How about five?"

"Your five and our four. That's nine. We'll have our guard up, so unless there is a major force out there, it should be enough. In any case, we'll try to avoid being spotted by going off the main road before we get there. We'll be cautious. It might be dark before we come back, but we will plan on coming back tonight."

The crew was assembled quickly and soon departed on the road out of town to the north. As Jack had indicated, when they reached the point where a sentry (if posted on the rise of the road to the south of the farm) would be able to spot them, they left the main road and walked through the adjoining fields and woods. They came to the top of the ridge southeast of the farm. Lying flat on the ground, they scanned the farm for activity. They could see that people were hard at work in the gardens and that there was a group gathered about the bison fence on the far side of the valley.

One of the Oakwood men commented, "I'm sure that's fewer horses and less bison than they used to have on the farm. I wondered what happened."

After surveying the scene for several minutes, Jack made his decision. Given that there was no evidence of a large military force that might threaten them, Jack decided his team would make their way back to the main road and then down the hill to the farm.

Just as happened to the first team of envoys, they were spotted on the road as soon as they crested the ridge south of the farm. Almost immediately a couple of men on horseback came riding out to meet them. Megan and Tony recognized them as former classmates.

Brief introductions were made, and the new visitors were invited to come down to the farm. One of them stayed with Jack's group, while the other one went galloping to alert his leaders. He dismounted and hurried into the house. Within moments, Karla, Mandy, and Amber came onto the porch.

As the visitors approached, Karla recognized Megan, Tony, and the men from Oakwood; however the man who obviously led them was unfamiliar to her. She turned to Mandy and asked who the man was.

"That's Jack. He was stranded on the road by our place the night of the aurora. He's a good guy and is a part of our Spring Hill community. You can trust him."

The tone of pleasure and admiration in Mandy's voice when she spoke of Jack was obvious to Karla. She gave Mandy a studious glance.

Jack acknowledged that he was gratified to see Mandy and Amber, but neither of them gave any verbal indication that they were more than comrades in arms. Then Jack asked about the two men from Oakwood.

Karla gave a puzzled look. "You mean they never returned to Oakwood?"

Jack shook his head.

Karla went on, "Yesterday morning, we were told that they left in the middle of the night to return to Oakwood. Something must have happened to them. Maybe they encountered the raiders from Princeton that attacked us last night. Maybe they were even in on it with the raiders."

Jack pondered that for a bit before asking, "Did you see them leave? Who was it who told you their plans?"

Mandy replied, "Amber and I were in the house with Karla and her girls. The men were staying in the barn. It was Jason who told us in the morning that the Oakwood men had left."

"Jason?"

Karla said, "My brother, Jason."

"I'd like to talk to him if I could."

"That won't be possible. He broke his leg and also

suffered a severe concussion during the Princeton raid. He's delirious at the moment."

Jack nodded in understanding. "Maybe some other time. Would you mind if we looked around a little bit? And maybe ask a few of your people if they have more information?"

Karla replied, "I'm not sure I want you poking around here, checking on our defenses. How can I be sure that you aren't planning on attack us? Maybe you are all in it together."

At this point, Megan Henderson spoke out, "Karla, you know me. My mom was one of your teachers in high school. We aren't your enemies."

Karla lingered a long gaze on Megan. Then she looked at Mandy and Amber. Her eyes finally settled on Jack before she spoke.

"How can I be sure about you?"

Jack turned his arm so she could see the Semper Fidelis tattoo. "Trust me, or don't trust me. This is the best I can offer. The choice is yours."

Karla only took a moment to make her decision.

"Go ahead and look around. And if you see anything that might help us against any more raids from Princeton - let me know."

"Thank you. We'll make it short. We want to get back to Oakwood before the sun sets."

They did spend some time visiting with the residents of the farm and asking questions about the missing men and the raid of the previous night, but they turned up no leads concerning the missing Oakwood men. Jack did give Karla a couple of suggestions for increased security, but whether or not she would implement them would be up to her. As they bade farewell to Karla and her people, Mandy made one more offer of help.

"Karla, I don't know what happened here, and I don't

know how Jason will heal, but I want to offer again - on behalf of both Oakwood and Spring Hill - that we want to be your friends and allies. Call on us if you need help!"

"I'll consider it."

During the walk back to Oakwood, Jack questioned Mandy and Amber as thoroughly as possible, but the fate of the two men remained a puzzle. Perhaps, the men had taken a long circuitous route home, or maybe the mayor could clarify the situation when they returned.

Mayor Peterson was troubled when the team returned to Oakwood and informed him about his missing men. He recoiled sharply against Karla's suggestion that Jimmy and the other man might have been agents of Princeton. He insisted there was no possibility of that for either man. They were both long-time residents of Oakwood, and there could be no doubt of their loyalty.

The Spring Hill contingent was hosted by the Somali refugees overnight in the old high school. As they left the high school in the morning, Mandy commented to Jack, "These Somalis are really nice people, if the Rudds had accepted them into their community, I wonder if the Princeton folk would have dared to mount their raid."

"You might have a point. But by the looks of it, they really aren't Somalis anymore. They are Oakwood folks now. Wherever people build a home, that's who they are. Oakwood will be stronger because of them."

Chapter 37 - Bill's Outpost

Upon Jack's return to Spring Hill, and after his team had been debriefed by Maggie's leadership council, Cody and Danny presented Jack with their plans for the outpost at Bill's cabin. They had more extensive plans than Jack had envisioned. They wanted it to be a way station on the expansion of the Spring Hill community. They envisioned the outpost intentionally going down the county forest driveway, and into the surrounding farmland. They thought this might be a necessity, since during the days since Jack was gone additional refugees had come to the valley gate and asked to join the clan. Spring Hill continued to grow. They would need more farmland.

Jack promised to broach the idea with Maggie but told them that at the present time Bill's cabin was to be a defensive outpost and a hunting center to procure game for the community. In Jack's mind was the previously expressed wish by Maggie's husband, Mike, that the Spring Hill would expand their farming to the east and the south.

When Cody handed Jack the list of people they were asking to be assigned to the outpost, he was surprised to see Aurora's name on the list.

Jack asked, "Why is Aurora's name on the list? She's not much of a hunter."

Cody and Dan looked at each other.

Cody was the one to answer. "No, she's not really much of a hunter, but the outpost needs more than hunters. Aurora is smart, she's a great organizer, and she asked to join our team. Do you have some objection to adding her to our list?"

Jack stammered, "No. No, I don't. It just caught me by surprise, that's all. If that's what she wants, okay. I will have to clear it with the Chief, since Aurora is a real help at the Chief's house, but if you want her at the cabin, then I'll have her assigned there."

The next morning, Bill led the newly formed outpost team over the pass to his cabin. For the next few days, Bill would stay with the team, as the team repurposed the dwelling and sheds to make it into their defensive outpost and hunting center. Bill had previously opened up the wall between the kitchen and the living room. A small wood-burning Franklin stove in the living room was the source of heat for the house. Bill insisted that Aurora take his small bedroom and make it hers, but she refused. She declared that the room would be the "office" for the outpost. The common room would be converted into a bunk room, and she insisted she would sleep in the bunk room with everyone else.

Years ago, when Bill had purchased and moved into the cabin, he converted the garage into a shop, and he had installed a wood-burning barrel stove to keep it warm when he was not using the forge. It was decided that since the garage could be heated, they would use it as the common room for the outpost. They also dug a new hole for the the old outhouse that stood to the side of the house.

Out of one of his cabinets, Bill pulled out some old topographic maps of the county forest and surrounding area. Even though some of the hunters were long-time local residents of the area, the maps would prove to be valuable tools in planning their hunts and establishing defensive plans.

A couple of hours into the work, and while the men and women of the outpost were busy at their tasks, Bill slipped away from the others went to his meditation garden. He sat on the bench and looked at the spot where he had buried his old friend, Maximus. He spoke softly, as though his old friend would hear him.

"Sorry about all the noise and commotion, old buddy. I know it has been nice and peaceful around here, and now that's all changing."

He went on for several minutes - talking to his old friend. Aurora watched him from the kitchen window that looked out into the back yard. After several minutes, she exited through the back door of the cabin and went to him. Bill noticed her approaching and motioned for her to join him on the bench.

"I'm not interrupting you, am I, Bill?"

"No. I was just talking with my old friend, Maximus. I - we - appreciate your joining us."

"In the little time I knew him at Spring Hill, I grew to love him. Such a tiny dog, with such a big personality."

Bill chuckled. "So true. I do miss him. Even with all that is happening. I still miss him."

"Yeah. Maximus is someone that can't be replaced. Only missed."

"But the memory lingers. As long as I live, he lives on in me."

Aurora nodded in agreement but stayed silent. Bill said nothing for a few moments. Then he asked her a question.

"Aurora, tell me if I'm speaking out of turn, but appeared to me as though you were becoming enamored with our new friend. Is everything alright with you?"

She sighed and attempted a weak smile. "I won't deny there was some infatuation on my part, but . . ." She stopped and did not go on.

Bill lifted an arm and patted her on the knee. "It's okay. You don't need to say anything more. He does care for you, you know."

"But as a friend, that's all."

"Do you think there is a chance that could turn into more over time?"

"I don't think so. He's interested in someone else."

"That could change. One never knows."

She covered the hand that Bill had placed on her knee with her own, and smiled. "Thanks, Bill. I know you're trying to be a good friend and cheer me up. I appreciate that. But really, I'll move on. It appears to me that his future is with someone else."

"Okay. But you know, anytime you need a friend to talk to, I'm here."

"I know that. Ever since I started teaching at Oakwood, you've been a mentor and a friend."

"Aurora, if only I were a couple of decades younger . . ." His voice trailed off.

Aurora seemed not to notice what Bill was implying, and asked, "Bill have you ever wondered - why not us? Why are we still here? We are good people. Why weren't we raptured?"

"Yes, I've wondered. From what I've observed, it doesn't seem to be a question of whether or not someone was good. Good people were taken, and good people remain. Likewise, there were people who we might call 'bad' who were taken and some who remain."

"Then why? Why are we here?"

"Perhaps there is yet something for us to learn."

"Us? Do you mean individually, or as a group?"

"Perhaps both."

"And what might that be?"

Bill chuckled, "As the old saying goes - that is far beyond my pay grade. But maybe it has to do with learning to live and love each other. Maybe it has to do with living with, or without, a purpose in life. The "fundies" sure seemed to have lived with a purpose - a very restricted purpose. I know I'm throwing out a lot of "maybes" here, but what if the higher power - if there is one - took them all away, not as a reward, but as a punishment?"

"What?"

Bill became more animated as he spoke, "What if those who were taken away, were taken because they were too close-minded? They had their minds made up, already. Maybe we are left because we are open-minded and because the "higher power" wants us to use our open-mindedness to achieve something?"

"Like what?"

"Maybe acceptance of each other, a peaceful society, or something I haven't thought of."

"That's a lot of maybes and what-ifs."

Bill nodded. "True. And quite likely it is all wrong. But it is worth considering. I don't know that we'll ever know the deep philosophical answer behind the rapture event. But as of now, we live in a new world. What we make of it is up to us."

PART 2 - A NEW ERA IN BLUFFTON

Chapter 38 - Darkness fell upon the land . . .

Lord Neizner of Bluffton was ready to proclaim judgment on the man who stood before him. Neizner sat on his throne, an ornate wooden chair, which had been placed on the steps in front of the chalet-looking museum that he had taken over as his headquarters.

When the fundamentalist believers were raptured during the aurora event and the world changed, the small city of Bluffton changed along with it. Bluffton was one of the original logging towns of the north woods which then later developed into a center of agriculture, industry, and education for the area. A large portion of the city consisted of the sleepy campus of Bluffton State College. In the days following the event, the campus was taken over by the followers of Professor John Neizner, who now ruled it as his personal fiefdom.

Professor Neizner had been a professor of history at the college, as well as its athletic director. He was a stocky and well-muscled man in his early forties who maintained excellent physical condition through his practicing the martial art discipline of Taekwondo. Professor Neizner had stepped into the void and taken charge when people suddenly vanished and the lights went out plunging the world back to medieval technology. He gathered his remaining athletes and took control of the campus. His control soon expanded throughout the small city. That brought him into conflict with several authority figures of the pre-event era that remained. One of those was the man who now stood before him - County Sheriff Dan Lester.

Standing on the walkway, several yards in front of the seated Lord Neizner, was Sheriff Lester. He wore his now tattered and dirty uniform, and his hands were securely bound with zip-ties behind his back. On each side of him stood a guard holding an arm. Lester glared defiantly and disdainfully at Neizner, and at the two women who stood close beside his throne - one on each side of the lord. Neizner noticed that Lester had glanced at the women, so he reached out with his right hand and patted the woman to his right on her derriere. She neither smiled nor flinched.

She was a local girl from north of town. Her name was Krystal Miller. She was finishing her junior year at the college and was a member of the women's volleyball team. Typical of Lord Neizner's student-athletes, at his command she was wearing athletic clothing - a tank top and running shorts. Neizner expected his action to irritate Sheriff Lester because Lester's daughter had been a part of the college volleyball team before she vanished in the rapture. Lester would certainly know Krystal and would be bothered by seeing her touched in such a manner.

Neizner wasn't disappointed. He laughed inwardly as he could see Lester's face twist in disgust.

"So, Mister Lester. You have been brought before me because you were interfering with the work of my foraging crews. Do you have anything to say in your defense?"

"Bullshit!" The word was spat out of the sheriff's mouth. "They weren't foraging. They were stealing. And you know it. You've got no right to do what you are doing,"

Neizner smiled. "And in today's world, who are you to claim authority over me. I seem to have the power here, not you."

"Might does not make right," protested Sheriff Lester, "what you are doing is wrong. You have no authority here."

Neizner slowly rose to a standing position. He took one step forward, to the front of the top level, and then slowly drew his sword from its scabbard. It was a beautifully balanced katana sword that had been gifted to him by a fellow martial arts master when Neizner had completed his Taekwondo weapons training. He looked at it with an admiring eye and then shifted his gaze to Sheriff Lester.

"This katana is a sign of my authority. Perhaps you would like to make a personal acquaintance with it."

Lester sneered in defiance. "You wouldn't dare. You know I'm the Sheriff. If you commit murder of a police officer - you go to jail."

Lord Neizner laughed loudly. "What world are you living in? Our world is not the world you remember. I am the law here. I am judge, jury, and executioner. Do you doubt that?"

"You're the man with the sword. But that doesn't make it right. It never will."

Lord Neizner made his way down the steps. He stopped a couple of paces in front of the prisoner.

"Former Sheriff Dan Lester. You are a relic of a time gone by. And you are a fool. Your sentence is death." Lord Neizner took a deep breath and then went on. "Stand still and this will be quick and relatively painless; move, and you may inflict needless pain in your demise. Men, release his arms and stand back."

His men did as they were ordered. They let go of the sheriff's arms and quickly stepped back. A startled look crossed Lester's face and then changed into a grimace of determination. With his hands still bound behind him, he lowered his head and charged at Lord Neizner. Neizner deftly stepped aside and slashed downward with his sword. It sliced deeply into the neck of the sheriff, who tumbled to the ground. The crowd watched in silence as the blood flowed out of him and his movements ceased.

Lord Neizner looked at the body for a few moments, then he muttered to himself, "Never ask someone to do what you're not willing to do yourself." Speaking in a louder voice, he added, "Someone, get rid of this trash. Get the blood washed off the pavement, and get me a cloth to clean this blood off my blade!"

Lord Neizner walked back up the steps to his throne and said to the gathered crowd, "The time for foolishly holding on to old times is finished. Go get back to your work." Then he turned to walk into his headquarters. To the two women by his throne, he simply ordered, "You two come with me."

They meekly followed him.

Chapter 39 - A New City

Lord Neizner sat in the library of his Northwoods styled chalet and looked out over the lake. For centuries there at been a lake at this place where the waters of the Pine River backed up before plunging down a narrow ravine. Bluffton Lake of the present had been expanded when, after the early logging days of the community, a dam had been built across the gorge. On the lake, Neizner could see several fishing boats plying its waters. They provided fresh fish for the struggling community and would provide sun-dried fish for the months to come.

The days were quickly moving through summer, and Lord Neizner was proud of what he was accomplishing. Many people had vanished in the rapture. Civilization had been set-back with the loss of everything electrical. Trade and transport of goods across the countryside had ended. Chaos had ensued. In the face of such adversity, he felt as though he was the man who had saved this community. He had asserted control and brought order to the town. He had organized means to secure and begin producing food for his people. He had insulated his people from some of the ravages of illness and disease by quickly banishing anyone who showed signs of sickness. His analytical mind had soon realized that the Bluffton area carrying capacity of available resources in the near future was less than the number of residents. In response, he had forced some of the weak and less able workers to leave. Unfortunately, some of the people with desired skills sets had escaped when he tried to keep them, but that couldn't be helped. They would have been malcontents in his orderly society. He could do without them. He was better off to be rid of them.

He pulled his gaze from the lake and swiveled his head to look at the young woman standing near the door. Some people might have considered that by having people constantly at his side he was keeping them from doing some productive task to help the community's survival, but he knew it magnified his stature to have people see his followers waiting at his beck and call. In addition, having someone available to jump at his smallest command, running an errand, or communicating an order, was productive. Besides all that, she was rather attractive to look at. He made sure of that. All of his personal assistants, and there were several of them, were young women who had been members of the college's athletic teams. They were all fit, and the ones he had chosen for his assistants were also very attractive.

He chuckled to himself about how some people in the previous era - only a few short months ago - would consider him a male chauvinist pig. Let them think what they want. He was in charge now, and he'd do whatever he damn well pleased. And it pleased him to have attractive young women at his beck and call.

Lord Neizner lifted his hand and beckoned his assistant to come to him. She quickly came and stood before him. For a moment he admired her figure. She had never been fat, but she had slimmed down slightly since the beginning of the aurora. He enjoyed the way she looked in her tank top and shorts. She was brunette, slender, petite, and displayed well-toned muscles. He was proud of himself as he looked at her, for he thought that undoubtedly her fine physique was a result of the Taekwondo instruction that he gave to all his personal staff.

"Lacy, you've been doing well in your Taekwondo instruction. Do you enjoy it?"

"Yes, my Lord Neizner. Very much."

"I thought as much. You have an intensity about you."

"Thank you, my lord."

"As you know, I've been teaching sword fighting classes for some of my armed groups. Some of them have become quite adept in the use of the katana." She nodded as he spoke and he continued. "I've decided that it would be a beneficial skill for my personal assistants, as well. Would you like that?"

A grin spread across her face. "Very much, my lord."

"Lacy, you are one of my favorite assistants. You've been a big help to me, but there is one thing that concerns me."

A worried look settled onto Lacy's face. "What would that be, my lord? I don't want to disappoint you."

"Oh, you don't disappoint me, Lacy. you have done everything I have asked of you." He hesitated, and a smug smirk appeared on his face. "You have pleased me greatly. However, I wonder about your relationship with one of my other assistants - Krystal Miller. I thought that the two of you were friends and teammates, but there seems to be some sort of tension between the two of you. What is it between you?"

Lacy hesitated, but then took a deep breath and explained that the two had gone to high school together in Sandstone and had played together on numerous sports teams, but that during those years they had suffered through some tough times in their relationship. With a little prompting, she explained.

"I don't want to say anything bad about her, but I considered her a "mean girl" - if you know what I mean."

Lord Neizner grinned at the use of the colloquial phrase. "I think I understand. Tell me more."

"She was like the golden girl. Blonde. Cute. Smart. She came from a large and influential family in the area. We were best friends in elementary school. She could do anything she wanted and get away with it. In some ways, she was a natural leader, but if you ever crossed her - well then the "mean girl" came out. She could make life miserable for you."

"And you didn't care for that."

"No, sir."

"Is she acting like the "mean girl" now? To you, or to the

other assistants, I mean?"

"Well, no. But I know it is still in her."

Neizner thought about the situation for a few moments and then grinned slyly and said, "Don't worry your pretty head about Krystal. I'm in charge, and if there is any problem, I will take care of it. But I am counting on you keeping me informed. I am putting Krystal in charge of all my female assistants, including you. She is talented and capable. Be a good teammate, and you will be rewarded. Understand?"

Lacy's eyes went wide as she tried to understand all the implications of what he said. Slowly she nodded. He dismissed her with orders go fetch his weapons chief. There would be a need for several new katanas to be crafted for his bevy of female assistants. He would want the weapons slightly lighter in size and weight, yet also durable.

He smiled as he watched Lacy Millbanks walk away. She did have a rather delightful sway to her walk. Then his smile broadened as he thought of Krystal Miller.

Chapter 40 - Sword Lesson

The sweat trailed from Krystal's forehead into her eyes as she went through the individual practice forms of gumdo (a Korean sword training regime) using a mokgum (a wooden practice sword the size of a katana). It was late morning and the summer day was hot. The sky was free of clouds and, though it was scarcely noon, the day was sultry and stifling with only an occasional breeze.

Twelve of Lord Neizner's female attendants were following his instructions as they practiced their martial arts under his watchful eye. Lord Neizner was wearing his black dobak with a black belt, but his disciples were wearing their typical attire of tank-tops and shorts. While it was an idyllic-looking scene, as in unison they went through their practice forms on the plaza between the Lord's chalet and the lake, it was also an intensely physical and mentally demanding exercise.

After working through the prescribed forms, Lord Neizner ordered them into pairs and they practiced making moves of attack and defense. Krystal was paired with Lacy Millbanks and they were sparring furiously. Krystal's attention was focused on her task as they repeatedly advanced, parried, and retreated.

Suddenly, an unanticipated gust of wind fluttered a couple of flags on the edge of the plaza. Krystal was distracted as the fluttering colors made her think that in the 'old' world this would be the Fourth of July - a day of gatherings and celebration. She paid the price for her distraction. A wooden sword came smashing into her shoulder. Lacy had taken the moment of Krystal's loss of focus to twirl and strike. The pain surged through Krystal's body. She dropped her mokgum and hurtled herself forward, smashing into Lacy and tumbling the both of them to the ground.

Before either could cause severe damage to the other, Lord Neizner ordered the others to intervene and they were pulled apart. As the others held them apart, Krystal was rubbing her shoulder and glaring at Lacy, while Lacy was sputtering out apologies.

Neizner declared, "That will be all for today, ladies. Take the equipment back to the armory and get something to eat. Dismissed!"

Then he added, "Krystal. You stay here!"

Krystal stood there, rubbing her shoulder in pain and fuming. After the others had moved away, Lord Neizner beckoned her to come to him and began walking along the path that followed the edge of the bluff.

"You lost your composure, Krystal."

"Yes, sir. But she didn't have to hit me so hard."

"Why was she even able to land such a blow?"

Krystal hung her head in shame. "Because I lost my concentration. I started thinking about something else."

"Let this be a lesson for you. You must maintain your focus at all times. If this had been combat with real katanas - you would be dead."

"Yes, sir. I understand."

He stopped and looked her directly in the eye.

"Do you? I would sorely miss you. Not only are you the Captain of my Attendants, but you are someone who gives me great pleasure. Would you deprive me of your service by making such a mistake?"

"No sire. I understand. I will do better. You can depend on me."

With a glint in his eye and steel in his voice, "You will serve me well, Krystal."

With a slight glint of her own that and with a slight blush on her face, she nodded her agreement.

Lord Neizner turned and began walking the path again. He motioned for her to continue walking with him.

"Now, Krystal, tell me more about your background, your family, your hometown, and what you saw for your future in the old world, and what you see for your future now."

She opened up her past to him, describing her early years north of Bluffton in Sandstone and the nearby Stone Creek area, her success in school and sports, and then of her success in college. She expressed that she had considered pursuing a career in veterinary medicine, but had lately been rethinking it in favor of sports medicine.

He had to prompt her again to speak of what she saw for her future in this changed world.

She looked at him coyly and replied, "I'm not exactly sure. I want to serve you. You are a natural leader, and we wouldn't be here without you. I want to be by your side as we build a new world."

"By my side, Krystal?" Would you really like that? A young thing like you."

She was embarrassed and tried to recover, but she stammered in reply.

"Well ...I mean ... you know ... help you ..."

He chuckled, "I know what you meant. I like you by my side. You keep doing what I tell you, and you will stay by my side. Understand?"

"Yes, my Lord."

She couldn't fully see his face, for they were facing forward as they walked. But had she been able to see it, she might have been startled to see it turn from a benign smile to an almost feral grin.

Chapter 41 - His Mark

August was coming to a close, and the thoughts of many residents of Bluffton had turned to school. In years past, students and teachers of all ages would be starting their new school year. But not this year. These were changed times and the old patterns of life were gone.

The college campus that had become the center of Lord Neizner's realm bustled with daily activity. Traditional medieval crafts were being relearned, and summer harvests were being preserved and stored for the coming winter. A new society of obligations and responsibilities was being forged.

Lord Neizner's iron-handed rule was apparent in the manner in which his subjects followed his every command - and the commands of others to whom he had delegated authority. The residents of Bluffton knew that it was "Neizner's way - or the highway!" Early on, when Lord Neizner was just beginning to assert his authority, there were some (for example, Sheriff Lester) who had disputed his rule. Those people were either dead or banished. Others had fled when they were able to find such an opportunity. Those who remained accepted former history professor John Neizner as their Lord, and as such, they had pledged their loyalty to him. Professor Neizner had used his knowledge of medieval history and life to mold the Bluffton community into his personal fiefdom. For the most part, the people were grateful, for Lord Neizner gave them a sense of belonging and security as they dealt with a changed world. Rather than despairing of what the future might bring them, now they had hope for survival.

This late August day still felt like summer, although people could sense there was a change in the air. On the plaza outside the building that had been the college sports complex, blue and white banners fluttered in the breeze. Blue and white had been the colors for the now-defunct Bluffton State College Blue Demons. When Neizner took over control of the college and city, he had merely co-opted the colors and mascot of the college to become the signatory heralds of his fief. He even had a few moments of mirth as he considered how the seemingly religious event of the rapture had left him (a Blue Demon) in charge. Why, his ex-wife (now living as far away from him as possible on the west coast), had even declared on several occasions that "he didn't have a religious bone in his body!"

The east facing front lobby of the sports complex was awash in the morning light of a sunny day. Several training/massage tables had been brought out from the training rooms and were lined up near the windows to take advantage of the bright light. Stationed at the open front doors and throughout the lobby were several of Neizner's warriors. They still wore their summer gear of t-shirts and athletic shorts. About their waists, they wore symbols of their position - belted scabbards with katanas that had been crafted from leaf springs of abandoned cars. They also wore blue baseball caps with the Blue Demon logo emblazoned on them. The former college store and the supplies of the athletic department were good sources of clothing and gear that identified Neizner's men and women. Several dozen important members of the Bluffton community were assembled in the lobby as they waited for the beginning of today's important event.

Lord Neizner was seated on a raised dais in the lobby. He wore royal blue nylon running pants and a grey compression shirt with the Blue Demon logo emblazoned on the breast. A thick gold chain adorned his neck, and his omnipresent katana was sheathed in its scabbard at his waist. His thinning black hair was close-cropped and his beard was neatly trimmed. He was a picture of strength and power. Standing slightly to his side and behind his throne stood two of his chief counselors. Both of them had been on the staff of the college before the aurora event. The tall and lean man with a brooding look about him was Woody Larson, who had been the men's basketball coach and who was now the Marshall of Neizner's military forces. The bespeckled man with a scraggly beard and sandy blonde hair was Larry Smuder, the former head of the Engineering Department who was now Neisner's designated Chief Scientist.

At Lord Neizner's command, there was a drum roll, and one of the interior doors opened into the lobby. Captain Krystal Miller and several of Neizner's attendants filed in. They came and stood at attention before their lord. Lord Neizner looked them over admiringly and then spoke.

"My faithful attendants. You have chosen to follow me and serve me. You have been rewarded with my protection and my favor. During the last several months you have demonstrated your loyalty and commitment to me. Today, as a mark of your fealty and as a promise of my continuing favor, you will receive a branding. It is a great honor. Prior to this date, only your captain has worn a mark of Lord Neizner's favor."

Captain Miller turned and faced the assembly. She reached her right hand up to the left strap of her tank top and pulled it low, off the shoulder. Above her left breast, for all to see, was a stylized tattoo of the letter "N."

Neizner went on, "Both branding and tattooing are temporarily painful. Both are permanent. Your Captain's tattoo is dark as a sign of her deep loyalty to me. In time, each of you may earn the right to have such a tattoo. Today, as you pledge your loyalty and receive this first mark, know that I accept your allegiance. Take your places on the tables by the windows that you might be prepared to receive your marks."

Dutifully the women went to the tables. They stood beside the tables and then servants did as they had previously been instructed. They assisted the women in stripping to the waist and getting positioned, face up, on the tables. Each of the women to be branded was given a rolled up cloth that they might clench between their teeth when the moment for pain would come.

Through the outer doors, two men carried in a brazier full of hot coals and a fire red branding iron.

Krystal went to stand by the first woman to be branded - Lacy Millbanks. The servants attending her had placed the cloth in her mouth and were firmly holding her hands to her side. Lord Neizner had risen from his seat. He went to the brazier and pulled the glowing brand from the fire. Krystal looked down at Lacy and said the words that she and Neizner had chosen for the ceremony.

"With the fire of this brand, we affirm the fire of your fealty to Lord Neizner. Wear his mark proudly." Then she moved close as she moved to hold Lacy's shoulders steady against the table. She leaned right next to Lacy's head and whispered softly so only Lacy could hear, "Feel this pain, bitch. You ever touch me with a sword again, and I'll brand your ass."

Lacy's eyes went wide in surprise. She thought the sword strike during practice was a forgotten incident. She could say nothing in response, for the attending servant had already shoved the rolled up cloth into her mouth. Almost immediately Lord Neizner was before her. He touched the searing brand against the flesh of her upper breast. The skin sizzled briefly as the pain flashed through her body and tears welled in her eyes. The smell of burning flesh wafted through the lobby. But then the sharp pain was gone because the nerve endings in her skin were destroyed.

Lord Neizner stepped away from Lacy and plunged the branding iron back into the red hot coals. Still holding Lacy's shoulders, Krystal leaned forward to whisper again into Lacy's ear, "Good girl." As Krystal lifted her head away from Lacy, she brushed her lips against Lacy's cheek and gave her a light kiss.

Krystal moved away and went to the next table. The same procedure, minus the whispered personal words would be repeated with each of Neizner's female attendants. After they moved away from Lacy's table, a sports trainer stepped up to her and washed the mark with cool water. He then liberally applied some healing salve to it.

Lacy watched the other women receive their branding from Krystal and Lord Neizner. Instead of her mind dwelling on the residual pain from the hot iron, the thoughts that filled her mind were that her Captain was a very confusing, and a very dangerous, woman.

Chapter 42 - Summer's End

It was the end of October. The growing and harvesting seasons of the new era drew to a close. With the cooler temperatures and the lessening hours of daylight, the Bluffton community began transitioning toward winter life. People knew that winter was coming, but since none of them had ever experienced living through it without "modern conveniences," they viewed the approaching season with some trepidation.

It had been six months since the aurora began and life changed. The aurora still flared every night, though perhaps not quite as brightly as the very first night at the beginning of May. Despite the intense efforts of Chief Scientist Larry Smuder to understand what had happened to basic scientific principles concerning electrical current and certain combustible elements, no progress had been made in restoring the basic rudiments of modern technology. The world had morphed back into a mechanical world powered by humans, animals, wind, water, and steam.

Human society of the Bluffton area had also changed from a representative democracy to an authoritarian realm ruled by John Neizner. Recently, Marshal Larson suggested to Lord Neizner that they should begin calling the area that Neizner ruled "a kingdom." The area that was controlled included the city itself, the college campus, and spread a couple of miles out into the surrounding countryside. At Marshal Larson's urging, the nearest block of houses ringing the college campus (which was the center of the current community), had been salvaged of any possible resources, and then razed. At present, this provided an open space as a defensive perimeter that any enemy would have to cross to reach the main buildings. In the future, this would provide ample space to construct a defensive wall and fortifications.

During the last couple of months, Bluffton had experienced some bedraggled groups fleeing death, disease, and the complete breakdown of human society in the large metropolitan area fifty miles to the west. According to the survivors, they had come to a bridge on the major river and bribed their way across it. The group that held control over the span brutalized them and then forced them to march down the old interstate to the east.

This type of news alerted Lord Neizner to the fact that there were future dangers for Bluffton. Such people could bring disease to the realm. And the fact that there were powerful organized groups to the west meant that they could be future military threats to Bluffton. There was no doubt that the military forces that Neizner had put in place were sufficient to control the population and to intimidate those in nearby rural areas, but it would take more than his personal attendants and guards to defend the realm against significant threats. They would need to build up their defensive and offensive military forces. There was work to be done, and winter would be an excellent time to begin training a more massive army.

A celebration marking the end of harvest and the transition to winter was planned for October 31. Taking relics of old Halloween, Lord Neizner declared that Bluffton would observe a festival to be called "Summer's End." People could individually adapt whatever Halloween traditions they desired, but as a community, Bluffton would celebrate with a bonfire and ceremony on the open plaza in front of the former College Student Center.

Lord Neizner met at his chalet with his major advisors for several hours the day before the Summer's End celebration. They ate together and then after dismissing all of them except Krystal Miller, he asked her to join him in front of the blazing fire that was burning in the central fireplace of the hall. Once the two of them were seated, he asked all the other attendants and servants to leave. The final one pulled the door shut behind her as she went.

He said her name and then hesitated, "Krystal."

"Yes, my lord."

"You've spent a great deal of time by my side these last few months."

"Yes." She didn't know what more to say.

He went on, "Both day and night."

She smiled slightly.

"Yes, my lord. It has been my pleasure."

He chuckled lightly as he added, "I hope so. You do seem to have enjoyed yourself greatly at times."

She blushed slightly but said nothing.

He went on, "I've been thinking I should make that permanent."

"What? What exactly do you mean?"

"Tomorrow, at the Summer's End ceremony, I am going to make an announcement. I will be naming you as my Consort."

She smiled a broad smile, but then she shifted to a quizzical look as she considered whether that meant she would wield more, or less, power.

"Will I still be the Captain of your attendants?"

"Yes. At least, for now, you will be. Until I change your duties."

"Will the people understand what you mean by consort?"

He laughed. "Good point. The masses can be quite ignorant. I will tell them it means you are my partner. I am their Lord. You will be their Lady." Then, with a note of sarcasm, he added, "They should be able to understand that."

She asked yet another question, "Don't we need some sort of ceremony?"

He laughed a full-throated laugh. "I rule here. I have said

it is so. No ceremony is needed for I have declared it."

She smiled. "John Neizner, you are my king. I shall be your queen."

He chuckled. "So I shall be King John, and you shall be Queen Krystal."

As she snuggled her head into his shoulder, she thought, "And they WILL call me Queen! I wonder what my family in Sandstone and Stone Creek would think of me now."

PART 3 - WINTER AT SPRING HILL

Chapter 43 - The Longest NIght

Without the modern conveniences of electrical power and heat, even mild northern winters are challenging. They often seem to start early and go on forever. The residents of the Spring Hill community, which now numbered close to two hundred souls, found the cold and snowy days of the first post-rapture December to be days filled with hardship, yet also days of warmth and fellowship.

In the eyes of some, the long dark nights of December were nights of dazzling light shows. The aurora continued unabated and every clear night was spectacular. The pulsating skies reflected off the snow-covered landscape, washing it with gleaming luminescence.

Many cultures throughout history had some form of observance of the Winter Solstice. In recent centuries, American culture had developed and observed many "Christmas" traditions at the time of the solstice. Some were religious, but many were secular. It was a foregone conclusion that the citizens of Spring Hill would have some sort of solstice observance - the big question was as to what kind of observance it would be. Clan Chief Maggie and her husband, Mike, claimed to be agnostic, but many of the clan were spiritual folk of varying stripes. Some had traditional Christian beliefs; however, the fundamentalist "Keep Christ in Christmas" believers were gone.

Since its inception, the Spring Hill community had operated on the premise that no religion would be forced onto any of its members, but that each member was allowed to practice their own faith as they saw fit - unless it harmed someone else. So it was easy to encourage each member of this community to observe the season in their own way, including their Christian religious observances as well as their secular practices. Yet Clan Chief Maggie saw the wisdom in having some common community observances. In the later weeks of November, Maggie summoned her advisors to come together and offer suggestions as to what the formal community celebration would include.

One difficulty they discussed was that given the number of people now living in their community, there was no structure which could accommodate all the people at one time. Seasonal celebrations when all could gather around a bonfire were enjoyable in the warmer months, but in the unpredictability of the frigid winter season, such a gathering could be uncomfortable, to say the least. Currently people were being housed in several locations: the Nelson's house (now called the Clan Hall), the old farmhouse, Bill's cabin in the county forest (now called the Cabin), the crossroad's farmhouse, and the two longhouses (called North and South) that were constructed during the summer and fall months.

Several ideas were bandied about, but then Bill made a comment that "with all the personal traditions people have, it might be best to let them choose what they wished to observe, perhaps Spring Hill should observe only one specific unifying activity." From then on, the discussion focused on what that activity would be.

Aurora made a suggestion that they built upon. On the night of the winter solstice, there would be a Yule Log lighting ceremony in the Clan Hall. Each place of lodging would send representatives to this ceremony and would then carry flames from Hall's fire to light their own Yule logs. In their separate shelters, they would repeat the ceremony that had been celebrated in the Clan Hall. The fact that the Cabin was beyond the pass and into the county forest, and that there was snow on the ground, did complicate matters. But it was decided that if the weather permitted torchlit processions would carry flames through the darkness to the crossroads house and to the Cabin.

When the longest night came, and after the Yule log was lit in the Clan Hall, it was Cody and Aurora that left the Hall carrying the flame for the Cabin. The skies were clear, and the northern lights splashed their colors across the star-spangled canvas. Both Cody and Aurora carried torches that had been brought to life in the flames of the of the Clan Hall yule log. Cody led the way as they followed the path through the wooded path to the cabin. The sound of crunching snow beneath their snowshoes drifted into the night, and the flickering flames of their torches rebounded off the bare hardwood trees of the forest. At places, tall pines towered above them briefly blocking out the dazzling night sky.

They made their way through the narrow high pass in the hills and started to descend into the western county forest. Leading the way, Cody stepped into a small glen where the trees parted to reveal more of the sky. He took a couple of steps into the open space and stopped, listening and looking. Aurora came up close behind him and whispered.

"What is it? Why did you stop?"

He turned to face her.

"The world is so beautiful and awesome, tonight." He hesitated, looked deep into her eyes, and went on, "Aurora, you are beautiful."

For a moment she didn't know what to say. She knew that when Cody was in high school, he had a slight crush on her. She had always attributed that to just an immature high school boy being infatuated with a slightly older and more accomplished woman. But in the last couple of months, as they had lived and worked together at the cabin, Aurora had grown to see him as a man with tremendous abilities and energy who was also a deep thinker. She respected him. In this moment, when she looked up into his eyes and saw the glow of the northern lights sparkling in them, she knew that she was developing deeper feelings for him.

With one hand holding her torch, she reached up her other hand to the back of his neck. Standing as high as she could on her tiptoes, she pulled him down towards her and gently kissed his lips.

Cody was startled, for although he had hinted several times of his affection for her, she had never responded in kind. However, it didn't take him long to react. He eagerly returned her kiss and reached his arm around her to pull her close. They clumsily struggled to remain standing. The moment of romance quickly dissolved into a moment of humor for it is hard to be graceful when bundled against the cold, carrying torches, and wearing snowshoes.

Aurora said, with a slight smirk, "Cody, I think you are beautiful too. But don't you think we should be on our way? We have a fire to deliver."

Cody stammered, "Why, yes, of course. I'm sorry..."

She stopped him and startled him by saying, "You had better not be - sorry, that is. You better have meant every bit of it. We can continue this at a later date."

"I'm all for that!" He replied as he turned back to the path.

The mirth in their voices was as obvious as the smiles on their faces.

Chapter 44 - Yule in the Longhouse

Late into the darkness of the longest night, long after the Yule fire had been ushered into the North longhouse and the ceremony repeated there, most of the residents had retired to their family units. Only Bill, Geoff, and Doctor Julie Westin remained near the central fire. Julie looked across the fire at the two men with no small sense of admiration. Both men were talented and compassionate human beings. Julie took a deep breath and made her decision. She rose and walked around the fire to sit between them. She thought of the first days and weeks after she had arrived in Spring Hill, and of how she had come to know the two men.

To her left sat Bill. Bill had been an integral part of the community before Julie had arrived with the refugees from Bluffton, but he had quickly befriended her. On her right sat Geoff.

Geoff had comfortably settled into the Spring Hill community after his escape from Stone Creek. The flight to Spring Hill had been a little hairy at times. When Geoff had broached the idea with Andy Miller of making a trip back to his home and shop to get some of Geoff's equipment, Andy was reluctant to allow him to go. Miller was suspicious of anything that had to do with any of his former teachers, and Geoff had been one of his teachers when he was in high school. Geoff had always done his best to be congenial to all people in the community, after all, he was a local boy who had come back to teach in the local high school. He was a shirttail relative of the Miller clan, having married a distant relative of the Millers. His naturally friendly nature served him well, and he had been generally respected throughout the Oakwood and Stone Creek areas.

After several conversations over a couple of weeks, Geoff

finally had persuaded Andy to permit him to make a "salvaging" trip to Geoff's home. Geoff suggested that his new helper, Nick, and Nick's wife, Michelle accompany him. They could take a team of horses and a wagon, load it up with material at Geoff's home, and then return to Stone Creek. Geoff suggested that they could probably do it in one day, but if needed they could stay overnight at the house. Though finally agreeing to it, Andy added a significant complication. Andy refused to allow Michelle to accompany them, instead delegating one of his cousins to go along. Geoff agreed to the arrangement but made additional plans.

On the morning that Geoff and his crew departed on their errand, Michelle had gone about her work with one of the field crews. However, after lunch, through a little subterfuge and deception, Michelle had managed to slip away unnoticed after telling her supervisor that she had been ordered to help at another task. She used all of her hunting skills to move through the woods and fallow lands as she made her way west toward Spring Hill.

After arriving at Geoff's former home, the crew worked hard loading up the wagon with useful tools and equipment. When it came time to leave, Geoff and Nick surprised and overpowered their "keeper." They bound him and placed him on the wagon. They urged the horses onward down some back roads that would eventually bring them to the crossroad house near Spring Hill. Darkness was falling when they neared the crossroads. They stopped and freed the bound man and gave him a choice: He could continue with them on to Spring Hill, or he could hoof it back to Stone Creek. He decided to trek back. Michelle caught up with them at the crossroads house, and the three of them finished their journey, arriving at the bridge gate of Spring HIll well after dark.

Geoff was now considered as much an integral part of the

Spring Hill Clan as were his companions at the fire, Bill Hempstead and Julie Westin. Bill and Geoff had been colleagues at the Oakwood High School for many years, but Julie was a relatively new figure in the area. As a doctor in Bluffton, some of the people in the Oakwood area had met her, but only in her professional capacity as a physician. After the aurora, she had been one of the early refugees from Bluffton. She had fled from Bluffton in the earliest weeks of Lord Neizner's seizing of power. The three of them had taken varied paths to get to Spring Hill, but now here they sat - at the central hearth fire of North Longhouse - discussing what the future might bring. They discussed several aspects of the community as they looked to the future. Defense, shelter, food production, community identity, health issues, technology, and leadership. But then the conversation took a sudden turn toward the personal.

With her gaze focused on the flickering flames of the burning Yule log fire, Julie threw the proverbial "rock into the pond" as if she wanted to see what the ripples would be.

"Have you noticed how much I like you?"

The two men looked at each other with startled expressions, but neither spoke - as if each was waiting for the other to say something.

Finally, Bill responded, "Which 'you' are you making reference to?"

Julie went on, "I mean, guys, I am really interested in you - and I mean BOTH of you."

"Both of us?" asked Bill. "I'm not sure I . . . we . . . understand what you are talking about."

Julie sighed. Then in a soft voice, almost as an aside to herself she said, "Men! Sometimes you need to spell things out for them." Then, louder, she went on, "Look, guys, I'll lay it out for you. I married my husband when I was far too young. We weren't good for each other and it didn't last. Fortunately, we didn't have any children together. I kept myself busy with my work. Then this world changed. Now, I'm here, in Spring Hill, and we are trying to build a new world. I love caring for our Spring Hill family, even with limited medical supplies, but I want more. I want my own family. I want a child of my own. I'm in my mid-thirties and not getting any younger, and I like you and respect you. Both of you! Both of you would be good father material. Let's make a family. Do I make myself clear?"

Bill took the lead in answering. "You do, and you don't. I mean, thanks for the compliment, but have you noticed this grey hair?"

Geoff added, "And neither of us have fathered children; mine were step-children. My wife had three children by her first marriage."

"I am aware of all that - I have written down your medical history, after all. I'm a Korean adoptee myself. I understand that family is more than blood. We've been friends for several months, now. I know a few things about you. Besides, Maggie and Holly told me all about you guys and how you might react."

"What?" Bill blurted out. "You talked to Maggie and Holly about this?"

Julie grinned, "Sure. It seemed to be the wise thing to do. I reasoned that If anyone here knew a lot about you - it would be them."

"And they thought this would be a good idea?"

Julie gave a light laugh and gently placed a hand on the nearest knee of each man. "Well, Holly did seem to think that both of you might feel a little prudish about the idea, though they thought you'd be open to it."

Geoff gave a snort and defensively replied, "Prudish. I'm nothing of the sort. And neither is Bill. Why you should have heard some of our conversations in the teacher's lounge."

Bill protested, "Geoff, we weren't that bad." But then he said to Julie, "Julie, speaking for myself, I'll admit I am attracted to you. I'd say we could work out some arrangement. What about you, Geoff? Any objections, religious or otherwise?"

Geoff answered, "What if those who disappeared, suddenly reappear? I love my wife, but is she gone for good? Is there a chance she could return? Just like she magically disappeared - could she magically reappear?"

Bill sighed and answered, "I don't know the answer to that. None of us do. We can't explain for sure what happened and there is no way we can know if what you suggest could happen. All we can do is live in the present and deal with what we have."

Julie looked thoughtful. "Geoff, I don't want to infringe on the feelings you have for your wife. I'll honor and respect whatever you decide. And if a 'return' would happen, you would be free to follow your heart. But as Bill said, we live in the present. Will you join our family?"

Geoff was silent and thoughtful for a moment, and then they could see that he made a decision. "No objections. I think you are a special woman. I'm up for it. The past is past and now is now. I'm not sure exactly how you want to work out all the details, but we're all adults here." He paused briefly and then added, "Do you think we should call ourselves 'brother husbands'?"

Bill groaned in feigned pain, for this obviously was an oblique reference to the conversations the two men sometimes carried on about the foolishness of a former television show called "Sister Wives."

Julie took charge, "That's funny. But seriously, I think this is something that would be good for all three of us. I want both of you to know that if I do get pregnant and we have a child, that I will consider BOTH of you to be the father."

"No objection here," said Geoff, "I always thought of my

step-children as my own. This wouldn't be any different."

"Same here," agreed Bill, "I never had my own kids, though I did consider my students as 'mine' in some ways, if we have a child - then all of us are the parents. Now, how are we going to organize all this?"

Julie said, "Leave it to me. We'll obviously have to rearrange some of the sleeping arrangements and to let the community know. For tonight we go our separate ways, but in the morning I'll take care of announcing it and making arrangements."

Julie's eyes teared up and sparkled in the light of the fire as each of the men put an arm around her. They stayed in that posture for several moments before Julie turned to each man and gave him a gentle kiss. Then she stood up, smiled at them, and walked away to her bunk.

The men sat in silence as they watched her go. Then after several moments of looking back into the glowing fire, Geoff asked, "Do you think we really know what we have gotten ourselves into?"

Bill replied, "I'm not at all sure . . . but in any case, it should be interesting."

Chapter 45 - Yule at the Crossroads

The Northern Lights blazed through the winter night of Yule as Jack and Mandy trudged on snowshoes through the snow, carrying the Yule fire to the Crossroads Guardhouse. There were several inches of snow on the ground, but the path from Spring Hill to the crossroads was well beaten due to the frequent travel, and they made good time.

About half-way through their journey, they paused for a moment to rest. The aurora's shimmering green and blue lights reflected off the snow of the open fields on both sides of the road, giving the night a magical quality.

Mandy exclaimed, "Isn't it glorious!"

Jack looked up at the heavens and then looked at her. He smiled as he said, "The view takes my breath away."

She blushed for she knew him well enough by now to know he was referring to her as well as to the scene of nature that surrounded them. During the past several months, their mutual attraction had become evident to others around them. They had attempted to conceal it at first, but they had long ago allowed themselves to display it openly.

"Aw, Jack, you can't even see me - all bundled up like this. And don't get all excited. We've got this yule fire to get to the crossroads, and then the ceremony to share."

He grinned, "True, but it is the longest night and much of it is left. Let's get moving."

They proceeded on down the path and before long they could see the lights of the Crossroads coming into view. Their arrival was anticipated, and soon they were greeted by the current contingent of the Crossroads guards.

The old farmstead at the crossroads, now referred to as the Crossroads house, was an important defensive position for both the Spring Hill Clan and for the town of Oakwood. It allowed both communities to get advance warnings of any refugees from the south (the direction of Bluffton), or the east (the direction of Stone Creek and Sandstone); as well to defend against any future raids or attacks from those directions. Currently, there were nine guards (of various ages and sexes) from Spring Hill stationed at the Crossroad, as well as the men from Oakwood. The current contingent from Oakwood consisted of three Somali men. Since their arrival in Oakwood from Princeton, the Somali group had been diligent about integrating themselves into the local community. They had developed a reputation of being loyal and working hard at whatever tasks lay before them. They were accepted at all levels of the community, including participation in the defense forces.

Jack and Mandy led the group through a reenactment of the Yule ceremony at the Clan Hall and then joined the guards in a time of fellowship. After a while, Jack made a comment about how on a cold winter night it would be nice just to have a nice hole to hibernate in. Immediately, Mandy noticed there was some sort of humorous conspiratorial glances being shared among the guards.

She asked, "Okay, folks, what is all the winking about?"

Jack quickly replied, "Oh, not much really. I'm sure they were all thinking about the thermal a-frame I taught them to build the last time I was here."

"The what?"

"A thermal a-frame. It's one of those things we were taught in our cold weather military training. If you are ever caught outside in harsh winter weather, you need to be able to build a shelter that will help you survive."

"Really," she said with false indignation, "and why haven't you ever taught me this?"

His face broke into a broad smile. "You are absolutely right! I should have!" He turned to one of his men and winked so

Mandy could not see, "Is the a-frame still out back? You didn't dismantle it did you?"

"Why, Captain, of course, it is still there," came the reply. "We figured everyone who was posted here should take a look at it and know how to do it. I'd say it is in such good shape that you could even use it tonight if you wished."

Jack turned to Mandy, "I think we should go take a look at it. How about it, Mandy?"

"Right now?" she responded incredulously. "In the dark?"

"We'll take one of the lanterns. I'm sure our friends wouldn't mind."

The now openly grinning leader of the guards replied, "Not at all. Why you can keep it all night, for all we care."

Mandy came to a sudden realization as to what was happening.

"Ahhh. I must say the Crossroads House is most generous. Captain Jack, would you please give me the deluxe tour of the thermal a-frame."

They quickly bundled themselves into their winter gear and grabbed their packs. As they exited the house, Mandy turned to the assembled guards, winked to them, and said, "Don't wait up for us."

Even though it was Jack's plan, he still blushed at the raucous laughter that escorted them out the door. They made their way behind farm buildings and to the edge of a nearby woods. Mandy could see a small sloped mound rising out of the field of snow. One end of the mound was about six feet high and six feet wide, and from there it sloped for about fifteen feet to where it was level with the surrounding snow. Jack lifted the heavy tarp they had used for a door flap, and they entered the shelter, pulling the flap down behind them and propping their packs against it to give additional insulation. The structure of the A-frame was easy to see from the inside. Saplings had been leaned against the central beam and then smaller branches interwoven with them. They were then covered with pine branches, then a layer of leaves, and then covered with several inches of snow.

"I'm impressed," said Mandy, "Nicely constructed! And I might add - the soft bed of pine needles on the ground covered by a blanket is a sweet touch. Why one would almost think you had planned all this to seduce me."

"You found me out. I've been hoping for some time to get you alone in a special place."

"We've been alone before. Our friends give us private time when we need it."

"That is true enough. But I wanted something different. Something special. I thought spending the longest night of the year alone in a small shelter might be the ticket."

"Oh, really! And why is that?"

"Because . . ."

Jack reached into his pants pocket and pulled up a small cloth bag. Slowly he opened it and pulled out a gold band with a diamond on it.

"Mandy, this is for you. It was my mother's. I found it in my father's stuff after he died. He must have kept it when mom died and was cremated. I'd like to give you this ring as a promise to you. Mandy, will you marry me?"

"Yes. Yes. Of, course, yes!"

He slipped the ring onto her finger and took her into his arms.

It was a long night - the longest night.

Chapter 46 - New Arrivals and News

It was one of those misleading warm days that occasionally occur in mid-February that makes one think Spring is beginning. Bill and Geoff were tinkering in the shop and discussing their plans to get their hands on one of the vintage steam tractors that were in the area. Geoff had been a frequent visitor to antique tractor shows, and he knew there were a couple of machines in the area that were owned by collectors. If they could get their hands on a working steam engine that used only mechanical power (no electricity), they could find numerous ways to help their community. The only question would be if they could locate a steam tractor - or even a stationary steam engine - and acquire it before others did.

They were buried in their discussion and dreams when a young boy burst into their shop.

"Come quick. Visitors are at the gate. Refugees from Bluffton."

Bill and Geoff looked at each other and Geoff said, "At this time of year? They must be desperate to be traveling in February - even on a warm day."

"That's for sure," agreed Bill. Then to the boy, he added, "If you haven't already done so, find Dr. Westin and tell her. She's from Bluffton. She might know these folks."

The boy ran off and the two men left the shop. The driveway was muddy with the melting snow, and the men stepped their way carefully down the hill to the gate.

They could see that the gate was open and a group of 20-30 people waited outside of it. Before the group, stood Captain Jack Stewart and a couple of his men. They did not have weapons drawn. But where quietly conversing with leaders of the refugees. Bill and Geoff passed through the gate and went to join them. Within short order, they were joined by Clan Chief Maggie and Doctor Julie Westin.

It was apparent that some of the members of the group recognized Julie when they shouted out greetings to "Doctor Westin." Maggie and her advisors listened carefully and respectfully to the refugees as they told their story.

All of the refugees had been expelled from Bluffton by order of King John (formerly Professor John Neizner of Bluffton State College). They had one common characteristic. The refugees were all noticeably of minority ethnic heritage. Many of them had been students at the college and had contributed their efforts to the stability and survival of Bluffton in this new era. In spite of their talents and contributions, they were ordered expelled from the kingdom. The king had made a declaration that those who were of obviously impure heritage were no longer welcome in his realm. Even those students who had been on the athletic teams of Bluffton College and had been a part of Neizner's defense force were declared persona non grata. A couple of the students had known Dr. Westin, and when she fled Bluffton, she had shared with them her intention to head north to Oakwood. When people of "non-white" ethnicity were expelled from Bluffton, this group had decided to follow Doctor Westin's example. They would head north toward Oakwood and hope to find her. When they reached the Crossroads house, the sentries directed them to take the path down the snow-covered gravel road to the gates of Spring Hill.

Chief Maggie felt immediate empathy for the refugees and her first inclination was to welcome them into the community. Adding so many people to the community might well put a strain on the food resources of Spring Hill, but other than sending them on to Oakwood, Maggie could see no other option. Her conversation with Doctor Westin left her believing that there were no observable cases of infectious diseases among the new arrivals, but both Jack and Bill urged caution. The refugee camp along the river was currently deserted, for few refugees were traveling in the depth of winter, and it could house these new refugees for a night or two. Camping there during these unseasonably warm days of February, might not be the most pleasant of experiences, but it was doable. So it was decided that the new refugees would be accepted into the community, but would have to stay briefly at the refugee camp in order to determine that they were clear of sickness. It was the procedure they had established during the summer and continued throughout the fall. There had been no refugees during the coldest weeks of winter, but it was deemed wise to continue the previous procedures.

The refugees accepted the news of their temporary quarantine with grace - in no small part to the reassurance of the doctor that some of them knew from Bluffton. Jack's crew of guards helped them get settled and fires started, while Julie gave each of them a cursory examination. Before re-entering the gates of Spring Hill, Maggie had promised that food would be provided for them, and in short order, steaming pots of stew were carried into the camp.

By all accounts that the refugees shared with the leaders of their new home, the situation at Bluffton was one they were glad to have behind them. King John's decrees and actions were openly racist and were seemingly supported - or minimally tolerated - by the general population of Bluffton.

Later that evening, Clan Chief Maggie convened her council of advisors. They met around the large table in the Clan Hall to share the stories they had heard and to discuss how to manage this large influx of additional people into their community during the harsh winter months.

After making plans to accommodate and integrate the new arrivals, their conversation turned to a discussion of the revealing information that the refugees shared about the situation in Bluffton. The reality that Bluffton could become a dangerous adversary in the future was apparent. Within the span of a few months, Professor Neizner had seized power and established his authoritarian rule. By all accounts, it was a selfish and heartless rule.

Bill commented, "Over my last several years of teaching, I recall encountering Professor Neizner at a couple of conferences I attended, but I didn't really get to know him. However, I do understand the rise of totalitarianism. This man has the power, and it belongs to him alone by now. When we deal with Bluffton, we won't be dealing with its people - we will be dealing with him."

Maggie asked, "But what about Krystal Miller, who they referred to as Queen Krystal? She's the girl from Sandstone, right?"

Geoff replied, "It sure sounds like the same person. If so, she's one of the Miller clan."

Jack mused, "Which might have some serious implications for our dealings with the Millers of Stone Creek."

Maggie asked, "How much influence do you think Krystal has?"

At his point, Mandy Grady-Stewart (who because she was not one of the primary advisors - was sitting on a sofa in the adjoining living room area of the great room) spoke up, "Probably more than people think."

An expression of puzzlement and concern came over Maggie's face as she invited Mandy to join them at the table and explain what she meant. Jack quickly stood up and pulled another chair over to the table for Mandy.

Once seated she began, "I know Krystal. We didn't go to high school together, and we were never what I would consider close friends, but I know her. We were often competitors on opposing sports teams. She is intense, and she doesn't like to lose. From what I remember about her, she was always the one in charge. She was always the captain of whatever team she was on and was always bossing the others around. She was a strong and positive force for her team, but if things went badly, she could be mean and vindictive. If she's in charge - and if they call her 'queen' then she is in charge - then she won't be happy about the way we treated her relatives in Oakwood."

Geoff added, "That matches what I've seen of her. As you know, I'm a shirttail relative of the Millers, and I was in Stone Creek for a couple of months after the event. The Millers are running the show there. When I was there, none of them mentioned anything about Krystal being the queen of Bluffton. They had a few refugees from the Bluffton area - but to my knowledge, none of them spoke of Krystal. Apparently, her rise to power wasn't complete yet at that time."

When Geoff stopped, there was a moment of silence before Bill took a deep breath and spoke. "It sounds like we don't have an imminent threat before us, but I do think we have a genuine long term threat in our future. Sure, we are building a good relationship with Oakwood, and the danger from Stone Creek seems to be one we could counter - but if Bluffton, with its larger resources, is an ally of Stone Creek - we could be in real danger. I recommend we start making some contingency plans."

Chapter 47 - Spring - New Life

The sun was shining and the temperature was above freezing, but the wind was blustery on this late March day in the Spring Hill Valley. Much of the snow had melted during a warm spell in mid-March, but Winter had not yet fully transitioned into Spring.

Word had come from Oakwood that after another raid from Princeton, Karla Rudd decided to firmly ally her family and farm community with the town of Oakwood. A contingency of troops and supplies had been sent to the Rudd Farm, and plans were being made to begin construction of a hilltop fort on one of the Rudd hills as soon as the weather broke.

There had been no word from Stone Creek. Apparently, the Millers were either keeping to themselves or establishing connections in other directions. Those connections could be with Bluffton to the south, Sandstone to the east, Princeton to the north, or some combination of them. As this point, it appeared that each of those alternatives had the potential of providing allies to Sand Creek which would be in opposition to the Spring Hill/Oakwood/Rudd alliance.

Bill and Geoff persuaded Maggie to approve Geoff taking a troop under Jack's command and travel several miles to the west where Geoff was sure a "steam engine aficionado" had lived. He was certain there must several working steam engines on the man's property. Hopefully, the troop would be returning soon.

A few more refugees from Bluffton had arrived within the days following the arrival of the first group of outcasts. They were welcomed in the same manner as the earlier ones and had already integrated themselves into the "clan."

On this late March afternoon, several women gathered around the large table in the common room of the Clan Hall.

They were talking about pregnancy. The long winter months in this first year of the Northern Lights Era had provided ample opportunities for old relationships and new liaisons to result in numerous pregnancies. It was evident that the Spring Hill clan would be growing - not just by receiving new refugees, but by childbirth.

Among the pregnant women were Julie Westin, Mandy Grady-Stewart, and the Clan Chief herself. At the moment the women were lamenting the fact that they couldn't use the sauna that Mike Nelson had built into the house when he constructed it several years ago. It wasn't that the sauna wasn't available, in fact, it was being used extensively by the community. However, for health reasons the pregnant women were discouraged from taking advantage of it.

The front door opened and a gust of wind blew into the house. Aurora hustled in and quickly closed the door.

"Whew," she exclaimed, "that's a harsh wind that is blowing today!" She scarcely paused for a second before she went on, "The hunters shot a couple of deer early this morning, and we thought you might appreciate some fresh venison. I figured I might as well help them get it over here, give you our monthly cabin report, and run a few errands at the same time. Sorry to interrupt you. It looks like you might be having an important meeting here." Finally, she paused as she carefully looked around the table and took in the scene and it registered in her mind that all the women around the table were pregnant. "Ah, I see. It's a gathering of the mothers-to-be."

Maggie spoke up, "It is. But you're still welcome here. Come sit with us."

As Aurora unbundled and removed her coat, she declared, "I think I will." She glanced at Dr. Westin, "I was going to hunt down the Doc and talk to her about this, but I might as well share it with all of you. I'm late, and I've been sick in the morning. I'm wondering if I might be pregnant."

Maggie grinned and asked, "Cody?"

Aurora grinned back, "The one and only."

Julie said to her, "We'll talk after our meeting, but on the basis of what you said, it sounds possible."

Meanwhile, several miles to the west of Spring Hill, near a community that had been called Sunset Lake, Jack and his men were searching the premises of a deserted farmstead that had a large barn and several pole sheds. According to Geoff, this was the home of Willie Armet, the steam engine aficionado who was thought to own several steam engines. As was proper, they had first approached the house to introduce themselves and to seek permission to search the grounds. When they found the house deserted, and apparently previously ransacked for food, they then moved out to check the other buildings. Given the religious crosses and pictures hanging in the house, Geoff thought it likely that Old Willie and his wife, Lillian, had been some of the raptured folk.

They carefully spread out to search the barn and sheds. It didn't take them long to figure out that they were not the first to search the premises. Doors that had been locked had been jimmied open and closed areas broken into. However, this had not been a "working" farm. It had been a farm where an old man had enjoyed a hobby of collecting and rebuilding old farm equipment. Previous scavengers had found little of value to take for their immediate survival, but to Geoff, this was a treasure trove.

They had brought a team of horses and a wagon with them to carry scavenged equipment back, but when Geoff saw what equipment was in the sheds, he suggested to Jack that they camp for the night and in the morning they could fire up one of the steam tractors and haul even more back.

Jack thought about it and peppered him with questions,

"How long would it take to get one of these machines going? How long would it take us to get it to Spring Hill? Do we have the materials to keep it running for the entire trip? I've heard these things make a huge racket - how much noise would it make?"

Geoff began to answer, "The fastest that of these tractors could travel is 2-3 miles per hour. It would take us at least a couple of hours to prep it and build up a head of steam. And yep, they make a mighty loud racket . . . " he stopped, and Jack could see the realization of what that meant swipe the excitement from Geoff's face and replace it with concern. Then Geoff went on, "Yeah if we did that, anyone in the vicinity will come to see what we are doing. Maybe someone is spying on us now for that matter. I guess we'd be better off just loading up a couple of these smaller stationary steam engines and getting out of here as quick as we can."

Jack nodded his head in agreement. "This really isn't too far away for us to make this trip again. Maybe we can make more detailed plans now that we know what is here, perhaps send some scouts into the area to see how safe the situation is, and then send back a larger force to procure some of the bigger machines."

"Okay. I'll get the men to work loading up the best one I can find."

"Good, and while you do that, I'll scout around. How far away is Sunset Lake?"

Geoff pointed to the northwest. "About two miles that way."

"Then, I'm going to head that way and see what I can find. How long will it take you to get the load ready?"

"I'd say we could be ready in an hour."

"That doesn't give me much time, but I'll scout as far as I am able. If you have the wagon loaded and are ready to leave, but we're not back yet, go ahead and pull out. We'll catch up to you."

Jack set up a couple of men as sentries to protect the others as they worked loading the wagon and then took one of his best scouts with him as he set out to the northwest.

An hour later, the wagon was loaded with one of the smaller steam engines and various other implements. With a worried look, Geoff gazed out to the northwestern horizon. He could see no sign of Jack or the other scout, but following orders, he gave the command and the troop moved out.

Hours later as darkness was descending, Geoff stopped the troop to set up camp for the night. They were near the edge of the county forest and the old Henderson place. They had a couple of hours left in their journey home and had yet to traverse the river road that skirted the southern ridge of the Spring Hill valley. Geoff deemed it a safe enough to camp overnight at one of the deserted farmsteads. It would be a cold night (most nights in March were below freezing), but with a couple of good campfires, they would be alright. He dispatched a scout to head up the dirt road that led into the county forest to the cabin outpost that had been Bill's place and inform the outpost of their presence. An hour later, when his scout returned with Cody Henderson and a couple of his hunters, they had camp set, sentries posted, and a couple of fires burning. Cody and his hunters brought with them a couple of packs of victuals, including fresh venison. The venison was quickly set to roasting over the fire.

The minutes ticked by and still there was no return of Captain Jack Stewart and his companion. The meal was warmed and the meat was roasted. As members of the troop sat down to eat, one of the sentries whistled an alarm. Soon, Jack, the other scout, and another man emerged into the light.

Cody looked up from his meal and exclaimed, "Sammy? Sammy Antonelli, is that you?"

The newcomer looked carefully at Cody for a moment

before the look of recognition came over his face. "Cody Henderson! Good to see you, buddy!"

Cody stood up and strode forward to greet the man in a brotherly shoulder hug.

Jack smiled and said, "Well, it looks like we made the right call in bringing you back with us. If you are a friend of Cody, then you must be alright!"

Sammy looked around the circle. When his eyes lighted on Geoff, he said in acknowledgment, "Mr. Brown."

Geoff chuckled and said, "That was what my students called me. Today, for my friends and companions, it is simply, Geoff. Just call me Geoff."

"Yes, sir. I mean, okay, Geoff."

The newcomers settled into places around the fire, and they were given food and drink. As they sat and ate, Jack updated the troop on what had transpired after he left the steam machine farm.

The scouts had left the farm heading toward the little community of Sunset Lake. They made their way carefully through the untended and overgrown fields. Most of the winter snow had melted in the open and exposed areas, but large patches still existed on the northern slopes of inclines and in the more wooded areas. Apparently, all of the farms had been deserted and scavenged. The farm fields had lain fallow the entire summer following the advent of the aurora and been covered by a blanket of snow over the winter. Now, as the melting snow watered the earth, the land was eager to spring to life. Wildlife abounded, but human life appeared absent.

The small water tower of the town grew in size as they approached. Several times they stopped, and Jack examined the tower through the small binoculars he carried with him. He surmised that if there were any organized occupation of the village, there would likely be a lookout posted somewhere on the tower. There was none.

As they stealthily approached the first houses on the edge of the village, they startled a flock of birds into the air. Jack knew that if anyone were observant, they would notice the alarm. They continued to make their way deeper into the village, which appeared to be uninhabited. They tried to remain close to cover as they carefully they made their way through the town,

Suddenly, as they were crossing an open space between houses, a voice shouted out, "You can stop right there. We see you."

Knowing that a fired arrow or a thrown spear-like projectile has a lesser chance of hitting a moving target than a stationary one, Jack and his partner sprinted away from the voice to gain cover.

They crouched behind a deserted car, and Jack shouted out, "Who are you and what do you want?"

The voice responded, "This is our territory. We're asking the questions here! Tell us who you are an what you are doing here."

Jack bit his lip as he considered what to do. If they were outnumbered, it would be foolish to start a fight, and it might make an escape attempt from the town dicey. Since the others had called out to them rather than attack them, it was likely that they also would prefer talking rather than conflict.

Jack responded, "I'm going to slowly stand so you can see me. If you want to talk - then show yourself as well."

As he stood, he saw a man step out the open door of a house across the street. As the man slowly walked forward a couple of steps, Jack stepped from behind the car and walked a couple of steps toward him. They began a cautious conversation, and it soon became apparent to both parties that neither of them wanted a fight.

The upshot of the conversation was that just as Jack and

his man were on a scouting foray, so also were the other men (for it was a team of three) on a surveillance foray. They were from the town of Eagle Grove, which lay several miles to the north. In the summer and fall months of the previous year, the population of Sunset Lake village had determined that survivability was not viable for them in their town. They decided to move their population north to the larger community of Eagle Grove and contribute their efforts to establishing a new society there. This scouting trip was intended to check on what had happened to their deserted town over the course of the winter.

Jack had studied Bill's stash of maps of the area, and it was apparent to him that the situation in Eagle Grove would be of importance to the people of Spring Hill and Oakwood. The river valley and forested western bluffs and hills of the Strange River ran nearly all the way up to Eagle Grove. The town of Eagle Grove lay several miles to the northwest of the Rudd farm while Princeton lay several miles to the northeast of the farm. If there was a viable and robust community of people at Eagle Grove and if they were friendly to the Oakwood/Spring Hill alliance, this would be important news.

One of the men offered to return with Jack to establish communication between the communities and Jack accepted. Jack asked the other Eagle Grove scouts to communicate the good intentions of his people to the Eagle Grove leaders and then scouting parties separated on good terms.

What came as a pleasant surprise to Jack were the warm greetings between Cody Henderson and Sammy Antonelli. The strength of an old friendship from the past was a blessing in the present.

Chapter 48 - Falling Apart

A few weeks later, at the time of the Spring Equinox, a new problem started to show itself. For several days, residents of Spring Hill had been noticing that their clothing was literally falling apart. Any and all clothing made with synthetic fibers seemed to rip and tear at the slightest stress. Soon they noticed that anything plastic that was made in the previous era with petrochemicals was breaking down. Natural fibers such as wool, cotton, and hemp were not affected. Neither were items made of wood, metal, glass, or ceramics. It was only the plastics.

Geoff and Bill sat in the workshop analyzing and projecting the causes and implications of this situation.

It was Geoff that said it succinctly. "We still haven't figured out what caused the loss of electrical circuitry or the chemical changes with gunpowder. Perhaps this is just another change that doesn't make sense."

"Maybe," Bill replied with a skeptical sigh. "It just seems so strange: electricity, gunpowder, and now plastics. It is as though someone, or something, changed the world to put us back into the technology of the Middle Ages."

"I'm just a simple mechanic and teacher. I'm no great scientific whiz, but it sure seems to me that the laws of science have changed."

"So, maybe whatever god there is did rapture all those folks and then to punish us, or reward us, decided to remove the 'modern scientific advancements' that have changed human life so much the last century."

Geoff chuckled slightly, "Well then, in your humble opinion, which is it? Is it a blessing or a curse?"

"Time will tell. I concede - I'm not very excited about the prospect of the disintegration of every synthetic product derived from a petrochemical base. However, when I consider the

231

positive nature of the human relationships here in the new world of Spring Hill, I have to admit I am pleased."

Geoff grinned. "I know what you mean. When the lights when on that night and all my family disappeared, I was devastated. But I've reconciled myself to that. I see these fine people in this valley, I see old friends like us become even closer, and I see our Julie pregnant, well, I agree with you. I'm pleased, too."

The mention of Julie's pregnancy brought a smile to Bill's face.

"She is quite a woman. We may not have fully known what we were getting ourselves into when we accepted her proposal, but it seems to be working well. Don't you think?"

"Sure does. The world has changed in many ways. Folks here seem to accept our family relationship. I don't think that would have been the case before the aurora."

Bill smiled a wry smile. "No. Lots of those folks would have objected to our living arrangement. But since you mention the aurora - and thinking of our former teaching colleague, Aurora - she seems to be happier now than she ever was before."

"She does. I think it is because she hooked up with a good guy. Cody was always a good kid, and he has grown into a good and honest man.

PART 4 - SPRING IN BLUFFTON

Chapter 49 - Church of the One Faith

King John, dressed in his finest regalia and wearing his ever-present katana as a symbol of his authority, sat in the anteroom of his cathedral. His slightly balding, but now shaven head was covered by an impressive crown taken from the props room of the college art department, and his dark black beard was neatly trimmed. This cathedral formerly had been the Roman Catholic Basilica of St. Peter in Bluffton, but had become the property of King John when he asserted his authority over the environs of Bluffton. Across the table from him sat his queen, Krystal, who was also dressed in her finest. Her appearance was a display of privilege, power, and loyalty. Her long blonde hair was pulled up and tucked behind a tiara (confiscated from a former jewelry store in the city) and then finely coiffed to cascade in waves down her back. She didn't usually wear make-up; however today her face was made-up, and she was wearing a vibrant shade of red lipstick. Her red tight-fitting prom style dress was cut low and exposed the Neizner tattoo on her upper right breast.

Their discussion had drifted into silence as he had retreated into his private thoughts. Unbeknownst to him, his face settled into a wry smile as he considered the twisted humor of the day.

The day was April 1 using the traditional calendar - April Fool's Day - and here he was, using all the trappings of history and human nature to play a huge farce on his people. He chuckled to himself as he thought, "A farce it may be, but it is a farce that only makes my power greater."

As a student of history, Professor John Neizner knew of the power of religion in the lives of people and nations. His personal experience was that he had grown up in a family that claimed to be Christian, yet were not practicing Christians. His non-rapture came as no surprise to himself, he was no believer. However, his study of medieval times made him aware that religion exerted tremendous power over the daily lives and loyalty of people. He planned to use the religious yearnings of human nature to cement his power in Bluffton. He found it to be an interesting challenge, for all of the fundamentalist believers were gone - raptured to their heaven, if one was to believe such a thing. Yet some people remained who had some beliefs in a god and some people had "found" religion after the rapture. His challenge was to take and mold the old human institutions that remained, with basic human yearnings for belonging and purpose, into a new form that would reinforce his grip on power. He had no benevolent desire to tend to the spiritual needs of his people. He desired to use their needs to increase his grasp on power.

To do this, Neizner enlisted the aid of an old faculty friend in the religious studies department of Bluffton State College. Professor Colin Duffy had headed the religious studies department, but he had no faith in any religion. Publically, he presented himself as a searcher for truth in the worship of the deity, but in his heart, he was a skeptic of the highest magnitude. In spite of his spiritual skepticism, Duffy fully realized the power of religion over the lives of people and human society. For several months Neizner and Duffy had discussions about how they could formulate a church that would be a positive agent in strengthening their grip on power.

Neizner knew that throughout the Middle Ages of Europe the church was a source of authority that competed with the power of the secular authorities, indeed, often times the secular authority had become subservient to religious leaders. He would make sure nothing like that would happen to him. There would be no freedom of religion in Bluffton. The newly organized

Church of the One Faith would be the only acceptable religion in Bluffton, and it would be entirely and strictly under the control of the sovereign of the realm of Bluffton. The organizational structure of the church was a simplified version of the Catholic Church's hierarchy of medieval times. However, there was no Pope as the head of the church. The head of the church was the sovereign of the realm - King John. It was the king's responsibility to appoint the Bishop of the Church, just as it was his responsibility to select his military leaders and other personnel. King John's authority was absolute. All other people and entities would be his vassals.

Today the community gathered in the Cathedral of the One Faith for the installation of the first Bishop of the Church, Colin Duffy. King John would preside over the ceremony that would place his loyal friend and confidant as the administrative and "spiritual" leader of his people. The doctrines of the Church of the One Faith would stress loyalty and service to the sovereign; and the promise of an afterlife, or new rapture, would be tied to that work.

King John was shaken out of his reverie by a light knock on the door.

Krystal gave him an enigmatic smile. "That means it is time, John. Are you ready to go make yourself the center of this grand spectacle?"

Her smile and comment made him wonder to what degree she was aware of this farce of a religion he was foisting on his people, but he decided to leave that for a conversation at a later time. She was a pretty thing and had a certain charisma that drew people to her, but he had also found her to be quite intelligent - and even conniving at times. He admired and appreciated that about her. She had been an excellent choice to be his consort, not to mention the sexual satisfaction that was a part of their relationship. It wasn't the defining element between them, but it was a nice side benefit.

He chuckled, "Oh, I'm ready. Are you? I bet there will be more eyes on you during this spectacle than on me!"

"John," she protested, "you wanted me to wear this dress."

"Indeed I do! Let the people see your beauty. Let them desire you. It will make them all the more eager to serve us."

Coyly, she smiled and reached out her hand to him as he approached. "Then, let's not disappoint them. Let's go give them what they want." As he took her hand and led her to the door, she lifted her head near his ear and whispered, "Then later, I'll give you what you want."

He chortled back, "I will, indeed, have whatever I want."

Chapter 50 - Stone Creek

Andy Miller sat in the common room of what used to be the Black Dragon micro-brewery in the town of Stone Creek. Across the table from him sat a man in military camo gear. Three of the man's associates sat at the table near the door, and another three of the men from Bluffton were posted outside the door.

The leader of the Bluffton men had just finished briefing Andy about the situation in Bluffton.

Andy let out a loud exclamation, "Whew! Do you mean to tell me that little Krysy is now the queen of Bluffton? She is in charge there?"

The man cleared his throat. "Krystal Miller is indeed the Queen Consort of King John, the ruler of our land."

Andy chuckled. "Well, I'll be. She always was quite the little vixen, that one."

The warrior was slightly taken aback by the irreverent way that Andy spoke of Queen Krystal, but he held his tongue.

Andy went on, "Well you let Krysy know that her Uncle Andy is in charge here. We've got control of Stone Creek and Sandstone. Things got a little tough around here last winter, and some of the old and weak folks didn't make it, but now with the coming warm weather, we'll get folks working the fields again. But we won't turn away any help you folks can give us."

The warrior from Bluffton again cleared his throat before speaking, "King John has a great concern for the well-being of the homeland of his queen. I have the authority to tentatively offer the people of Sandstone and Stone Creek the opportunity to be a part of the Kingdom of Bluffton. You would, of course as the leader here, remain in charge here and be the chief vassal in this area. I anticipate that King John may even bestow a title, such as Duke or Baron, upon you."

"I'm already the boss here. I don't need his giving me a title to make it so."

"Are you rejecting his offer?"

"No, no. Not at all. I just want him to know that I took charge here on my own."

The man nodded as though he understood. Then he went on, "I have to admit, Mr. Miller, that I'm a little puzzled to find you here. When I was briefed on my mission here to offer vassalage to Stone Creek, Sandstone, and Oakwood. I was told that Andy Miller would probably be found in Oakwood. . . "

Before he could go on, Andy interrupted, "You can forget about that shithole town of Oakwood. I left there shortly after the lights lit up the night sky. Folks there are ignorant and jerks. They have some bad apples there, and they have their defenses up against us. You head that direction, and they will attack you."

"Hmm. That's interesting and something King John will want to know."

"You tell him there's a nasty bunch living at Spring Hill, too. That's a valley south of Oakwood. They got some kind of grudge against us Millers. If you're friends with us - then you're enemies with them. That's the way of it."

The man again nodded in understanding. "Since you are accepting the King's offer of vassalage, I will be leaving a couple of his men posted here to support you, and who can be used as messengers. You should also make plans to make a visit to Bluffton shortly to personally pledge your loyalty to the King as his vassal and to receive his pledge as your lord."

Andy grimaced slightly, as if he didn't like the taste of something in his mouth, but nodded and replied, "I'll do that. The weather is getting good enough to travel. Maybe in a few weeks, I can make the trip. O, and you tell the King that I want my title to be Duke. Duke Miller. I like the sound of that!"

The King's loyal emissary gave Andy an acknowledging

and perfunctory reply, but as he turned away, he couldn't help himself as his eyes did an epic eye-roll.

After the emissary left, Andy gathered his top men together. The group included Andy's brother, Brady, and Andy's uncle, Jeb. Andy explained the arrangement he was making with King John and they made plans for his trip to Bluffton. Brady was eager to travel with Andy to Bluffton. He wanted to experience first-hand this new king's court. Jeb was appointed to remain in Stone Creek and keep things under control. That was fine with Jeb. He was a couple of years younger than his brother, Zeke - Andy's father who had remained in Oakwood, but he had no desire to travel anywhere. The idea of walking that far, or even riding horseback, was decidedly unappealing to him. He promised to keep things well in hand while Andy was gone.

One week later, near the end of April, Andy, Brady, and two of their men rode out of Sand Creek on horseback toward the bustling city of Bluffton. They were still several miles away from Bluffton when they were stopped by some of the King's soldiers. After discerning who they were, the soldiers permitted them to proceed to the city but insisted that some of them accompany them as escorts.

As the troop made its way through the fields and farm dwellings that spotted the countryside, Andy took note of how the King had populated the landscape and put people to work in the fields, getting the land tilled in preparation for the spring planting.

It was the situation that most of the fields that had been mechanically tilled in previous years still lay fallow. However, the King had purposely scattered actual farm work to be done throughout his realm. It could only mean King John was in control of those lands and not afraid of his people being attacked by bandits. This reassured Andy that he was doing the right thing by joining forces with King John. If this powerful man wanted him as an ally, what was there to fear?

Eventually, they came to the outskirts of the city. It was apparent that most of the structures north of the dam and river bridge had been destroyed by fire, or dismantled, to provide a wide open area directly outside the city. The population and structures of the city lay south of the lake and river. Andy wasn't sure what the purpose of such destruction had been, but he was sure there must have been a reason for it.

The travelers were halted by guards when they came to the bridge over the river. It was formerly a four-lane state highway. Since King John came to power, fortified gates had been built across the bridge. They were swung open now, to allow for the daily economic activity of the community, but they could be closed at a moments notice.

As they passed through the fortifications on the bridge, Brady leaned toward Andy and muttered, "Now this is a gate. Spring Hill's measly gate is nothing compared to this. We're on the right side, brother!"

"Sshh!" replied Andy, "Don't go gawking like a country bumpkin. Remember, they came begging us to join them. It wasn't the other way around." But in his heart, Andy was awed as well. He had been to Bluffton many times prior to the aurora event and had regarded it as a just a big town with a small college in it. What he saw now impressed him. He knew firsthand the difficulties of life and maintaining society in the face of a changed world. He saw the organization and efficacy in building a new world that King John was directing in Bluffton, and he knew it must have taken a strong hand to make it happen. Obviously, King John was one to be respected.

Horses clomping down the paved road, they were led to the King's Castle - the former logger magnate's lodge, turned museum, turned into the Neizner headquarters. Above them, unnoticed to their eyes, stood King John and Queen Krystal watching them from a window. The men dismounted and were escorted to the entrance door. The doors were opened by the guards, and then four men from Stone Creek were ushered into the foyer of the building and instructed to wait. There were a man and a woman standing guard at the large doors leading into the man hall. They stood stoically and refused to engage in conversation with the Miller contingent. The only comment they made was to instruct the visitors to stop and kneel before King John at the red line on the floor several paces before him. Andy muttered to Brady that he had no intention to bow before any man. Brady whispered back that if he intended to be Duke Miller, then he had better kneel.

After minutes of waiting, the doors swung open to reveal the throne room of the king. It was a large granite tiled ballroom with several windows and doors opening onto a large patio that overlooked the lake. A couple of windows were open to let in the fresh Spring air. The gauze curtains gently swayed in the breeze. To one side of the hall there was a large fireplace. On the opposite side, there were a couple of large elaborately carved wooden chairs. The chairs were placed against the backdrop of a hanging curtain that was set a couple of feet away from the wall. Behind the curtain, unseen to anyone who stood before the throne, was a doorway. In that open doorway stood Krystal Miller.

A middle-aged man lounged comfortably in one of the chairs. The other chair was empty. The man did not rise to greet them, but they noticed he observed them carefully with his steel grey eyes as they walked toward him. And they couldn't help but notice the scabbard and katana which lay across his lap.

As directed, the Stone Creek men walked toward the throne. Andy and Brady led the way, and the other two men followed them. Upon reaching the red line on the floor, the Millers stopped and knelt.

Immediately, King John said, "Rise, my friends from Stone Creek. I was informed that you had arrived. I trust you have had a safe journey. My servants have informed me that you desire for me you be your liege lord."

The men stood, and Andy stammered, "Huh, liege lord?"

Brady realized that his elder brother didn't know what that meant. Andy had never been one for learning history. Such terminology was foreign to him. Brady covered for Andy by adding, "Your majesty, we have indeed made safe travel through your realm. The honorable Andy Miller, Duke of Stone Creek, and I - his brother - are pleased to place ourselves in your service."

King John grinned wryly. "You have a velvet tongue, brother of the soon-to-be Duke Miller. What is your name?"

"Thank you, my King. My name is Brady."

King John jovially chuckled as he corrected Brady, "The term of address for a Duke is properly 'His Grace,' and perhaps he will soon be entitled to it as a peer of my realm. However, the promise of loyalty must come first."

Brady virtually groveled, "Of course, your Majesty. We meant no offense."

Any observer could see that Andy was getting slightly annoyed with Brady speaking for him and he jumped back into the conversation.

"Begging your pardon, King John. As you say, my brother has a smooth tongue. He can talk himself into, or out of, almost anything - but I'll speak for myself."

King John's face crinkled in humor as he affirmed, "As you should. Will you pledge your loyalty?"

"If'n that means our lands will be a part of your kingdom and that I'm in charge of the Stone Creek/Sandstone area. Then, yeah, I'll be your Duke."

"You do understand that there are specific responsibilities that you will have as my vassal, including providing tax revenue and soldiers as I need, but it also means I'll give my protection to you and your lands, and that I will regard your people as my own."

"Yeah, I get that." He paused and then added, "Sir."

Brady added, "He means 'Yes, your Majesty.' Will there be a formal pact written up and signed?"

King John couldn't help himself from smiling at the interplay between the brothers. It was knowledge that could be useful in the future if he needed to play one off against the other.

"Yes, there will be a formal declaration drawn up and signed. Duke Miller, and you, his faithful brother, Lord Miller, will also have a formal public ceremony pledging your loyalty to me."

There was a rustle behind the Stone Creek delegation as Queen Krystal entered through the main entrance. After listening to the opening exchange from behind the curtain, she had exited the back room and gone around to listen to the conversation from behind the delegation.

As she walked forward, she added, "As well, as pledging your loyalty to your queen, dear uncles."

She walked up to them with confidence. She didn't look like a queen, dressed in sweats and running shoes, but she carried herself as one. She walked past the first two Stone Creek men and gave hugs to her two uncles. Then she walked to King John, kissed him on the cheek, and sat down in the chair next to him.

King John spoke, "As you can see, your niece is alive and prospering in Bluffton. It was she that persuaded me that the Duchy of her homeland could be safely placed in your hands. Her insight will give me additional oversight over the Duchy of Sandstone."

"Begging your pardon, your majesty," said Brady, "don't you mean the Duchy of Stone Creek?"

"No. We like the sound of Sandstone for the name of the duchy. Oh, it will include all the lands of Stone Creek and Sandstone. I would suggest you appoint one of your Sandstone relatives as chief fief holder in the town of Sandstone, or perhaps even Lord Brady would like to control that fief, but the whole territory will be called Sandstone in honor of Queen Krystal of Sandstone."

Krystal could see Andy gulp and shallow. She recognized that look. He wasn't entirely pleased about the situation, but he knew power when he saw it. In this case, he lacked the ability to object. If King John and Krystal wanted it this way, then that is the way it would be.

King John then gave orders for his guests to be provided with lodging and food. He then dismissed them with the promise to have a public pledging ceremony the next day, after which they could depart for Stone Creek.

After the men left the throne room, Krystal turned to John.

"I told you I had interesting relatives. Did you notice how Brady tried to take charge?"

"Oh, yes. I'd say Brady is the sharper of the two. And ambitious. Why does he defer to Andy?"

"I'm not sure. He's the younger brother. Maybe that's it."

"Perhaps." King John mused, and then his thoughts moved a different direction. "You noticed that they rode in on four horses. That's quite a display of power and wealth."

"They probably didn't realize it."

"I think you're wrong there. I think they knew, at least Brady probably did."

"Perhaps. I know sometimes my relatives come across as country bumpkins, but behind that facade, they are sometimes smarter than they appear."

"Why, dear, you sound a little proud of them."

"I am in some ways. They are loyal to family, I know that."

"You don't think I could use that brotherly rivalry against them?"

Krystal chuckled, "Oh, I'm sure you could. You are a genius manipulator. I just want you to know that I think my family is super loyal to the family when an outsider attacks them."

"Thank you for the compliment - I think. Now back to those horses. We could use more horses around here. They are a valuable commodity, and we need to build up our stock. I think I will take two of them as a 'gift' from them to their liege lord."

"They won't like that. But if you tell my uncles that their niece needs them, they'll take it a lot better."

King John laughed and replied, "Oh, I do appreciate your devious ways. You are a most worthy queen."

Krystal put her arms around him and hugged him tightly. "Just doing my best to serve you. And speaking of serving you - what can be done about our clothing. All the uniforms are falling apart. All our leggings and sports attire rip. We are left wearing cotton and wool - nothing that is at all tight, or stretchy."

He shook his head. "I know you like to show off your figure with the tight material, but I don't know what is going on. I've asked my Chief Scientist to look into it and report back to me this afternoon. Maybe we'll get some answers then."

Chapter 51 - The Council Meeting

Later that day, King John gathered with his chief advisors around the large conference table in the library of the lodge. Chief Scientist Larry Smuder explained the situation. He had observed the same degradation of plastics and synthetic fibers as the folks of Spring Hills had experienced.

"I don't have any explanation for it," Smuder declared, "but I think we better plan that it's going to continue. I'd say we raise more sheep for their wool, and try planting and harvesting hemp for its fibers. We're too far north to think of growing cotton, so I think we have to go with hemp and flax. We should be able to harvest the fiber from flax to make linen. We'll have to consider that everything we are using that is made out of plastic will start breaking down - from plastic bottles, to polyester and nylon clothing, and even things like plastic piping that has been used in construction. If the current situation of this breakdown continues, then plastics and polymers will soon be a thing of the past."

King John paused thoughtfully. "That means we had better start researching and re-developing certain crafts too. Pottery making, weaving, metal-working, and so on."

"All those and more."

Marshal Larson spoke added thoughtfully, "That means I had better start an analysis and inventory about the type of material we use in all of our military equipment. We don't want any of that breaking down." The Marshal paused and then added, "What about material such as leather, or natural products such as rubber? We use a lot of bicycles around town."

Smuder replied, "Leather seems fine, but now that you mention it, we had better start a tanning factory to process more of it. As far as rubber goes, it is a natural product, but we are too far north to have rubber trees, we'll have to make wise use of the rubber supplies we have."

"So when we send out scavenging teams," mused Larson, "we should focus on the longer lasting materials - no plastics."

Neizner nodded his agreement.

"Shoes!" blurted out Marshal Larson. "What about shoes? All of our athletic shoes are made from synthetic material. How soon will they break down?"

Smuder replied, "I imagine it has already begun. Leather shoes will be valuable. We better include that in our scavenging."

"What about a cobbler?" asked Neizner. "Didn't there used to be a shoe repair shop down on River Street?"

Larson nodded. "There was, and we have his tools, but the man disappeared when the aurora started."

Neizner grimaced. "Larry, you had better start getting someone working on learning the cobbler business."

They went on and on, identifying potential problems and possible ways to address them. Before the meeting ended Krystal brought up a matter of concern she had. She shared how her relatives from Sandstone told her of the conflicts that had transpired between Oakwood, Spring Hill, and the Miller clan. It was her strong opinion that King John would be well served to have spies infiltrate the Oakwood and Spring Hill communities.

"Did you have something specific in mind?" queried Neizner.

Krystal didn't hesitate to make her proposal. "I think I would send Lacy Millbanks and Lisa Peele, one of my trainee girls."

"Wouldn't they suspect these two obviously healthy and somewhat Sandstone connected women?"

"Lacy isn't a Miller, but she is from Sandstone. Lisa is from downstate, but she sort of looks Asian, although I don't think she is. She could pass as half-Asian. Their cover story could be that they were kicked out of Bluffton. If any previously exiled folks from Bluffton, who know of them, found their way to Spring Hill or Oakwood, I believe both my girls could convince the others that they were also exiled. They are both capable of charming their way into being accepted there."

King John nodded, and said, "Go ahead and send your spies."

After the meeting had concluded and Krystal had left to go check on the "Neizner Attendants" as their captain, Marshall Larson pulled His lord to the side for a private conversation.

"Do you think it wise to allow Krystal to send those untrained spies? What if they are found out?"

King John chuckled, "And what of it. If they are found out, they are found out. It won't hurt us. Besides, they know nothing of our other efforts in the area. Correct?"

Larson smiled in return. "Correct, my Lord."

"Then I'll allow them to go. Maybe they will help. If not, well, I doubt they will cause us any real harm."

Chapter 52 - Lacy's Orders

Lacy Millbanks and Lisa Peele sat with Queen Krystal in the headquarters of the Neizner Attendants. It was one of the sorority campus houses that had been taken over and converted for use by this select group of female assistants and fighters that Neizner trained and used for his personal purposes. Krystal Miller had risen to be their Captain before she had been chosen to be the King's consort. She continued to be their Captain and ruled the house with a velvet fist.

Both Lacy and Lisa were dressed in what was the current uniform of the Attendants. They wore white cotton t-shirts with a Blue Demon emblem on them and blue cotton workout shorts, also emblazoned with the Blue Demon logo. The spring evening was cool, and they also wore the grey Blue Demon cotton zipper-front sweatshirts. Both young women wore white cotton socks, but they were in their home, and neither wore shoes. The Attendants had been some of the first to notice the disintegration of the synthetic fibers in their clothing and had completely made the switch to all natural-fiber fabrics.

Lisa was similar in size to the petite Lacy, but her long straight hair was a darker shade of brown - almost black. It was easy to see why she would be a recruit to the Neizner Attendants because she met the physical characteristics he demanded: athletic, pleasing to his eyes, and intelligent.

Lacy sat with her mouth agape, unable to respond. Krystal had just revealed her plan of infiltration and espionage to the two women.

Lisa was the first to respond. "Do you really think we can pull this off? I mean we haven't really been trained as spies?"

"I wouldn't ask you do to it if I didn't believe in you," Krystal reassured her, "Besides, what woman doesn't know how to fabricate a story, and even to deceive someone when needed?"

Lacy finally found her voice, "But the folks from Oakwood might recognize me! They might suspect that I am a Miller spy from Sandstone!"

Krystal leaned forward and patted Lacy on the knee and then lifted her hand gently touching Lacy's cheek. She left her hand to linger there.

"Then you'll have to convince them otherwise. Besides, they won't think you'll be coming from Sandstone because you'll be coming straight from Bluffton."

"What? That will make them suspicious for sure!"

Krystal laughed, "Of course they will be suspicious. And you will use that suspicion to ingratiate yourself."

"What? How will I do that?"

"I'm counting on the fact that some of them might know you and might raise questions about you. If you play this right, you can make them trust you even more."

Lacy looked incredulous. "Why would they do that?"

"You will present yourself as a disillusioned and disgraced exile from Bluffton. Tell them what you need to about us. You don't possess any state secrets. But convince them that you are finished with us and even angry with us."

"How?"

"I expect you will use your feminine wiles."

Lacy lapsed back into speechlessness.

Krystal went on. "Look at Lisa. She's white, but she looks like she might be partially Asian. Doesn't she?"

Lacy turned and looked at Lacy, who lowered her eyes as if embarrassed.

"Your cover story will be that King John found out that Lisa is an Asian half-breed. That makes her an undesirable who would be exiled. As her lover, you pleaded with me to convince King John to allow her to her stay, but I would not. You couldn't stand the thought of parting with her, and you hate us for this to you. So you fled into exile with Lisa."

Lacy stammered, "But, but, she's not . . . we're not . . ."

Krystal held up her hand to forestall Lacy and spoke to Lisa, "What do you have to say about this?"

Lisa lifted her eyes and said softly, "I'll do what you command, my Lady."

Lacy turned to look deeply at Lisa. Her mind raced. She thought - there is something Lisa isn't saying. Perhaps she has real feelings for me. Perhaps she really is Asian. Perhaps she wants to get out of Bluffton. Perhaps she has some sort of arrangement with Krystal. Can she be trusted? For that matter, how much can Krystal be trusted? Finally, she realized - she had no alternative. If she declined the assignment, she would suffer the wrath of Krystal. The searing pain of the branding still burned brightly in her memory. That was a future to avoid at all costs.

"Okay," she sighed. "I'm in. How soon do you want us to go?"

"As soon as possible. Tomorrow, if you can. Spend what time you need to set your affairs in order. Get your gear ready. Let me know when you are ready so I can see you off."

"Yes, my Captain," declared Lacy.

252

Chapter 53 - Departures

The highest room of the King's abode was a room at the top of a small turret. It was a room designed to be used as a place for reading and reflection. It had windows on all sides to give a view of the lake and the surrounding area and had a large couch with a couple of matching overstuffed chairs. It was late morning when King John and Krystal stood at a window in the turret tower of the old lodge to watch the departure of Duke Miller and his men from Bluffton. They watched a wagon, pulled by Miller's remaining two horses pass through the bridge fortification and head toward Sandstone. The King had taken two of the Miller horses, but he had also bestowed on his new Duke a wagon load of assorted supplies that would be useful and appreciated by his vassals in Sandstone.

Dozens of paces behind the Duke's entourage, but not a part of it, walked Lacy and Lisa. They wore jeans, sweatshirts, and athletic shoes while carrying full packs on their shoulders, including sleeping rolls. Krystal chuckled to herself as she thought of the shoes the girls wore.

John noticed her chuckling and asked, "What's so funny?"

"Their shoes. I bet with the extra weight and stress from those heavy packs, my girls will shred those synthetic athletic shoes before they get too far. They'll be walking into Spring Hill barefoot." She laughed again, this time out loud.

King John feigned surprise. "Why didn't you have them outfitted with leather shoes?"

"What, and have them waste such a valuable resource?"

"True, but it would be more comfortable for them. Why would you do that to your loyal servants?"

She grinned at him, "You know as well as I do that it will make them seem all the more like pretty damsels in distress. Exiled. Tired and in pain. Poor girls. Who wouldn't want to help them?"

He grinned back. "I do like your devious mind."

They turned their gaze back to the bridge. Once the bridge was crossed the Millers would take a road that veered northeast, while the two women would take the route the headed north.

King John was wearing his black dobak in anticipation of heading out to lead some of his troops in a martial arts training session, and Krystal was wearing her Attendant attire of t-shirt, sweatshirt, and shorts. As they stood together, looking out the window, John reached out to place his hand on the small of her back in a display of affection. He rubbed her back gently then chuckled.

With feigned surprise, he asked, "What? No undergarments today, my queen?"

"John, you know full well that almost all my underwear was made with synthetic fabrics. They have just fallen apart."

Again, with feigned surprise, he said, "Ahh, and here I thought you were just trying to seduce me this morning with your feminine charms."

Krystal knew when to play along with him. She slipped the unzipped sweatshirt from her shoulders and let it fall to the ground. She reached up to put her hands on his shoulders, pushing herself up against him.

"My king can have his way with me whenever he desires."

John grinned and then kissed her as he put his hands on her hips and slowly raised them to pull her shirt up to her shoulders.

Krystal broke the kiss and teased, "Are you certain you have time for this, my king? Aren't your men waiting for you?"

He continued lifting her shirt over her head, and pulling her to the couch, he replied, "They'll wait."

In their distraction, they missed the final gestures of Lacy and Lisa, who momentarily stopped to wave toward their benefactors in the tower. They also missed, moments later, seeing a solitary man approach the gates and without being challenged gain admittance to the city. There was nothing unusual about the man, but he would change the course of events in the kingdom - for he was a carrier. He had no visible signs of disease, but nonetheless, what he carried would impact the kingdom.

Lacy and Lisa walked side by side down the road, each silent in her own thoughts at first, but then they engaged in casual conversation with each other. Their packs were heavy, for they were filled with all the personal belongings they were able to carry. They needed to give the impression that they were leaving, never to return.

They had only walked for a couple of miles before they encountered their first problems. The tough ripstop fabric on their backpacks began tearing. As they examined their packs it became apparent that the disintegration that had affected the lighter synthetic fabrics was now happening to the tougher material of their packs. They debated what to do. They tried shifting their packs to their front side and using their arms to help carry them. But the stress and pain from it on their bodies was too much for an extended period of time. After only a short period, they dropped their packs to the ground in exhaustion and frustration.

They didn't know what to do. They couldn't just leave all their gear by the roadside. Yet, they had no way to carry all of it. The fabric was just too weak. Suddenly, Lisa came up with the idea of doing what the early Native Americans did. She suggested making a travois from some saplings on the side of the road and arranging their gear in a sling between them. They could drag their gear. It wouldn't be pretty, and it wouldn't be fun, but it was doable.

They went to work getting the saplings and using their sweatshirts as the material for the sling. Soon they were on the road again. At first, they encountered several travelers on the road taking their goods to Bluffton, but as the women moved further away from the city, there was less traffic on the road. The law of Bluffton extended several miles beyond the city, but they were near, or perhaps had already passed, its limit of authority. Both of them had long knives secured in their belts. Lacy would have dearly loved to be carrying a katana. However, Krystal had forbidden it, since it would draw attention to Lacy's martial prowess when they reached Spring Hill.

By the time the sun was nearing the horizon, they had reached the east-west highway that Jackson Stewart had traveled the night of the aurora. They crossed the state highway at the point he had turned north to take the county roads through Oakwood. They soon found themselves surrounded by trees on both sides of the road. Exhausted, they felt as if they could go no further. So when they encountered a small stream that passed under the road through a culvert, they pulled their travois several dozen yards into the woods. It was far enough so that they would not be easily spotted from the road, and there they set up camp for the night. They unbundled their gear from the travois, and Lisa pulled the two-person backpacking tent from its bag.

Lisa exclaimed, "Well, I hope we can get at least one night from this tent. It is nylon, after all, and that means it won't last much longer."

"Let's try to put it up without putting much tension on it," replied Lacy.

They worked carefully, but at a couple of points of stress, the fabric began to give way.

Lacy sighed. "It doesn't look good. I think we will get

some protection from it tonight. At least the rainfly hasn't ripped yet. But if we get a strong wind tonight, this tent will be shredded."

"Then," asserted Lisa, "let's hope we have a peaceful night."

The sun was setting, and shadows were deepening in the woods. They knew they should build a fire and boil some water for drinking, but they were too tired. They sipped what water remained in their canteens as they nibbled on some venison jerky and hard biscuits that they had brought with them. Then they crawled into the tent and into their sleeping bags.
In the semi-darkness, Lacy heard Lisa whisper to her.

"According to Krystal's instructions, we are supposed to pretend to be lovers, right?"

"That's the cover story."

"Will she know if we don't follow it?"

"I doubt it. But that's what others will use as our cover story if it comes up. I think we'd better stick with it."

Lisa hesitated and then said, "Maybe we should kiss then." She paused for a reply, but then quickly added, "For practice. I mean, won't it be obvious to others if we don't display some affection for each other."

All sorts of thoughts came racing into Lacy's mind. Chief among those thoughts was wondering if Lisa really was a lesbian. But did it matter? Lisa was a sweet enough girl and if this was to be their cover story, well then, she had better make it a good cover story!

"Alright. Let's do it."

Tepidly and with tenderness they touched lips and briefly kissed.

"That was okay," said Lisa, "how about for you."

"It was nice." agreed Lacy.

"Let's do it again," urged Lisa, "but with more passion.

Like we really had to convince people we are a couple."

Lacy agreed, and they kissed again. This time with increased intensity, yet still with a gentleness. With they finished, Lacy spoke first.

"I think we'll be able to convince them. Don't you?"

"Yes. That was pleasant. I enjoyed it. You do have soft lips, you know."

Lacy giggled slightly and then hesitated before asking, "Lisa, can I ask you a personal question?"

Lacy could sense the tension as Lisa replied, "Sure."

"Krystal said that our cover story is that we are gay. Are you?"

Lisa didn't reply right away, but when she did, she did so softly, "No, I don't think so." She stopped but then hastened to add, "Don't get me wrong. I really did enjoy our kisses, and I like you, and I will enjoy doing it again, but I know I like guys." She stopped again then added quickly, "Are you gay?"

Lacy answer, "I guess I'm like you. I don't think so, but you're kind of sweet yourself. I like being your friend."

They lay there in silence for several moments.

Lisa broke the silence, "Can I tell you something? As a friend? Will you promise not to ever, ever, tell this to Krystal?"

Lacy thought about that for a moment. That was a dangerous promise to make, but she agreed to it.

Lisa took a deep breath and then whispered as if she was afraid someone might overhear her.

"I really am Asian. Or at least partly. My mother was a Vietnamese-American. That makes me only a quarter Asian. But in the King's and Queen's eyes that would be enough to make me a mixed breed. Promise you won't let them know."

Lacy reassured her, "It is a part of our cover story. That's what it will remain. I'll keep it at that." Lacy reached her arm out of her sleeping bag and patted her friend on the shoulder. "Don't worry about it."

Darkness had fallen, and Lacy was surprised when she felt Lisa shift slightly in return and then she felt Lisa's lips against hers. Lisa whispered, "Thanks," and then kissed her deeply.

To Lacy's surprise, she returned her new friend's kiss with equal passion.

PART 5 - THE SECOND YEAR

Chapter 54 - Transition

It was the day before the anniversary of the advent of the aurora and plans were underway in Spring Hill to hold an observance of the event. Aurora Cortez-Smith, who had organized her school's "Festival of Nations" event the previous years, was in charge of the planning for Spring Hill's celebration. When she had first proposed the idea that they hold an anniversary observance that celebrated the diversity of their community in the context of this "new era" she was pleasantly surprised by the overwhelming acceptance and encouragement by the community's leaders.

Maggie had declared, "It is the perfect way to observe the anniversary. A year ago we started living in this changed world. It is a new era, and our people have forged a community that is loving, open, and supportive of its members."

Aurora was sitting at the hall's kitchen table with Maggie and a couple of her other advisors having a morning cup of spruce tea. Sadly, all the coffee had been depleted during the course of the year, and since it was a commodity that could not be grown in this climate, they had resorted to drinking locally produced concoctions. This particular mixture of spruce and dried herbs was a recipe that Holly had found in one of the traditional Native American cookbooks she had brought from her home. They were reviewing the agenda for the coming day to make sure all the details were taken care of. Activities would actually start late in the evening, after sunset, to observe the moment when the lights of the aurora first flared to light.

Suddenly, the dogs in the compound started barking. It was their way of announcing visitors. The "kitchen council" as they called themselves, quickly stood up from the table and went outside to see who was causing the commotion. Maggie immediately recognized the two bicycle riders that made their way up the driveway. They were former Oakwood students of hers. Their faces were grim. She could tell they were official messengers for they wore the gold oak leaf armband of Oakwood that symbolized their official capacity.

Almost before they brought their bikes to a stop, one of them announced, "Chief Maggie, we have bad news."

Everyone within earshot stopped what they were doing to listen. The dogs, however, continued to bark until their owners commanded them to stop.

Maggie asked, "What's happened?"

The youngster, still out of breath, blurted out, "Mayor Peterson is dead."

Several comments were voiced by those in the immediate area, "What?" "The Mayor?" "How?" "Oh, no."

Maggie asked the messenger to go on.

The second messenger went on to explain, "We think it was a heart attack. He hadn't been feeling well the last couple of days. We thought it might be that he was just thinking about his wife, Carol. You know she died shortly after the first aurora. But then, during the night he got up out of bed and just keeled over. We tried CPR, but it didn't help. He's dead."

Maggie replied with genuine care and compassion, for Jim had been a colleague and friend. She teared up as she said, "We are so sorry for your loss. He was a good man, and he was a dear friend."

The first messenger said, "Thank you, Clan Chief. The Town Council sent us to share this news with you - and they sent us with a request as well."

"Really? What is it you need? We will help in any way we are able."

The young messenger looked surprised. "But you don't even know what we are asking."

Chief Maggie smiled. "We are friends. Friends help friends. So as we are able, we will help."

The second messenger spoke up, "When Mayor Peterson died, the Town Council met. They didn't want to choose a new mayor."

Maggie tipped her head and prompted him to continue.

He continued, "The Council wants to be a part of Spring Hill."

Maggie blinked her eyes. "Can you give me a bit more detail?"

"Well, they said to tell you that they'd be willing to work out the details with you, but that they hoped that we'd all be part of one community."

Maggie was surprised enough by this development that she was momentarily left without words. She was about to respond when she overheard Bill remarking to Geoff, "Consolidation of small political units into larger entities. It's a reenactment of the early Middle Ages if you ask me."

Maggie turned toward the older men who had come out of the workshop to see what was happening. Inwardly, she was appreciative of the momentary distraction that would allow her a few moments to consider her words before she would answer the Oakwood messengers. She asked Bill to explain. The teacher in Bill took over, and he gave a brief summary of how the small economic and political units that came into being as they struggled to survive the Roman Empire's disintegration evolved into larger and larger political units in the face of threats from others.

"Interesting," replied Maggie, "But where is our threat?"

"Begging your pardon, Chief Maggie," interrupted the messenger, "The Council, and Mayor Peterson before he died, talked about how they were concerned that Stone Creek and Princeton would cause us problems. Their idea was that we all would be stronger, if we were one unit, rather than just allies."

Maggie gave an air of thoughtful consideration before she replied, "Go back and tell the Council that I am favorably inclined to what they say, but that first I need to talk this over with my council of advisors."

"Yes, ma'am."

"Oh, and please communicate our sadness and condolences. We will send an official delegation soon, but Oakwood should know that we mourn with them."

After the messengers turned and departed down the driveway, Maggie turned to Bill and Geoff.

"This is a great opportunity, isn't it guys?"

"That it is," replied Bill.

Geoff asked, "But what about the logistics of it? From the Rudd farm north of Oakwood to the furthest of our control is in the range of 15 to 20 miles. That seems like a large territory administer."

Bill mused, "You know, that's about the size and boundaries of the former Oakwood school district."

Maggie smiled, "Yes, it is. And Oakwood was a school district even before the internet age. If that was a manageable administrative unit back then, then perhaps we can manage it, even given your logistics concerns, Geoff."

Bill asked, "So is it a go, then, Clan Chief?"

Maggie grinned. She knew every time that Bill used a more formal title for her in front of others it was a way that he reinforced her authority.

"Not officially, Bill. I do like the idea, but I still want to talk this through with the whole group of advisors. There may be issues that we haven't considered. Would you please send word to any of my council members who are in the valley today, that I'd like to have them come to the main lodge as soon as possible. We have some planning to do."

"Most of them are here, but Jack is over at the western farm exploring the logistics of expanding security operations there."

"We'll meet without him. I think we need to send our response to Oakwood as soon as possible."

Maggie looked away from her conversation with Bill and saw a couple of the young workers walking toward her. They were walking barefoot and carrying their shoes. Maggie frowned. It had been a hard winter on footwear. Shoes wear out, and with the hard physical labor that was now required of most people, shoes were wearing faster. During the last couple of days, it had seemed that an inordinate number of her people had found their shoes to be simply falling apart. She had attributed it to the hard work and harsh conditions, but these shoes looked to be almost new athletic shoes. She looked down at her own feet and saw her scuffed and worn old leather work boots. They had seen a lot of wear this past year, yet they were still holding up. Then it hit her. Synthetics! For the last several days, her people had been experiencing the breakdown of clothing and other items made from synthetic fibers. These athletic shoes, even the best of them, were made almost entirely from synthetic materials. She sighed deeply. This was going to be another huge problem.

By this time Bill had stepped to the side to send messengers to the other advisors, and Geoff had come to stand by her side.

"Yep," Geoff said calmly, "I can see you recognize the problem. You know what the scary thing is?"

"No," she replied apprehensively, "what is it?"

"A lot of those shoes we think of as leather, really aren't. You see, much of the uppers are leather, but many of the soles are synthetic. They won't last much longer. We need to start tanning leather, and we need to figure out how to cobble shoes."

"Oh, no."

"Yep. But don't worry Chief, Bill and I have been researching it. We could do it the Native American way, but if we want a larger scale industrial operation, we'll need a place with a water supply to do the tanning - and it should be downstream from here - so we're looking at a place on the river past the valley and county forest, southwest of the old Arnold farm. That's where Jack and Mandy are right now. They're checking out how safe and defensible that area would be for such an operation and the expansion of farming."

"As long as you guys are on top of it, I won't worry too much." She stopped. A thought had obviously struck her. "We may want to reconsider the placement of that tanning industry. If we are going to join Oakwood, which now includes the Rudd bison farm outpost, then we may want to locate the tannery there."

Geoff mused, "Hmmm, that would be upstream from us, but it is something to consider."

Chapter 55 - Arnold Farm

At the old Arnold farm to the west, Jack and Mandy were leading a scout team. Mandy was in the second trimester of her pregnancy, but she wasn't about to let that slow her down, and she insisted that she be allowed to join the scouting team. The other two members were Megan and Caleb Henderson, whose family home had been near this farm. The team was intentionally checking out the farm and surrounding area as a possible site for a leather tanning operation and for expansion of the community's farming operation. With the size of Spring Hill's growing population, the limited acreage of the valley was a concern. It was an excellent defensive site, but the valley's size limited how many people and livestock could be sheltered there. The advantage of raising some livestock at this farm is that any raiders from the Millers of Stone Creek would have to pass by Spring Hill to get here.

The house, barn, and outlying farm buildings had held up well, despite being deserted for nearly a year. When the Arnolds left the farm to move to Spring Hill almost a year ago, they had brought all their 4-H animals and pets along with them. However, the barn and pens were in good shape. This had been a century farm before the family had stopped farming and it appeared it would be a good place to build a livestock compound. If they had enough livestock, it would be good to have another one east of the southern ridge road, outside the gates towards the Crossroads Outpost. That would have the advantage of being closer to the valley itself.

As far as a location for a tannery, it would be a good location. The water supply would be sufficient, and it was downstream from Oakwood and Spring Hill. The only question in Jack's mind was that of defense. Their excursion to the northwest toward Sunset Lake for the steam engine had left Jack thinking that there was little danger from there, and from Eagle Grove beyond. However, he was unsure of what threats might emanate from the southwest. Bill had told him about the town of Galena, located fifteen miles or so, amid hills and valleys southwest of where they stood now. If a population of people had survived the first year of the aurora there, then they could pose a threat to Spring Hill. Or, they might be valuable trading partners and allies.

Jack summarized his observations with his team and then instructed Mandy and Megan to return to Spring Hill with an initial report. He would take Caleb and carefully scout several miles to the southwest to see if there was any sign of human activity. It was the case that most of the people scattered about the countryside had either joined larger communities like Spring Hill during the past year or died off during the winter. It was a harsh new world, and the truth of the matter was that few individuals had the survival skills to make it on their own. However, there were still scattered pockets of individuals and small groups that roamed the countryside. It would be good to know if there were any in this area.

At first, Mandy objected, declaring she was as fit as anyone to help him. Jack agreed with her about her abilities but insisted that she and Megan return.

"It will be better if Caleb and I do this task. We are going to be trying to move undetected. I respect your skills, Mandy, but both of us know that Caleb is one of our best hunters. I need him with me."

Mandy frowned and sighed, "Alright. But don't you go doing anything to get yourself into trouble. When should we look for you to return?"

Jack glanced skyward to see the position of the sun. "We'll plan on getting back to the valley before it gets dark. But don't worry if we don't get back tonight. If need be, we can find a place to shelter overnight. We'll definitely do our best to get back early enough in the morning to celebrate with the community."

"If you don't get back before nightfall, Aurora will be upset - with the both of you! You know the festivities will start during the night."

The men nodded in understanding. The women departed eastward up the gravel road that ran along the river toward Spring Hill, and the men turned and went to the west.

Chapter 56 - Barefoot

Lacy and Lisa were walking barefoot by the time they reached Jack's deserted car on the county road. Both pairs of shoes had fallen apart at virtually the same time, almost as if in unison. Lacy lamented that they didn't have any duct tape with them. A couple of good wraps of the tape would have helped hold the shoes together for a few more miles, maybe several, but they carried none in their packs. They searched Jack's car in the hope of finding something that might help, but the car had obviously been ransacked by previous travelers and little of value could be found.

Then it was as if a light bulb went on in Lisa's head and she suggested, "What if we take our extra pairs of cotton socks and pull them on over our shoes. That should at least hold them on our feet until the socks wear through."

"That might work," Lacy added. Then an idea struck her. "And what if we rip some wiring from the car and wrap it around the socks and shoes?"

Lisa quickly accepted the idea and they went to work. Several minutes later they had reshod their feet with the shoes held in place by socks and wire. They agreed that it wasn't the prettiest sight, but it was functional. At least temporarily.

They continued on their way, pulling the travois with their gear piled upon it. By noon they had reached the old Grady place. There they were met by a couple of sentries posted by the Spring Hill Guard. The sentries included Dylan Grady and three of his former high school friends. It was obvious that Dylan and his buddies were charmed by the college-age women. The sentries questioned the women briefly and then offered to share their lunch with them. They determined that the new arrivals posed no threat and directed them to the Crossroads Outpost, where they would again be questioned and then redirected to head to Spring Hill Valley. Dylan Grady handed them a handwritten note that they were to give the crossroads guards when they met them.

The Grady farm disappeared behind them as they dragged their travois on the road to the Crossroads outpost. Their shoes had temporarily been repaired, yet they were uncomfortable on their feet. Still, they continued. As they rounded a corner and saw the Crossroads in the distance, Lisa hesitantly offered her thoughts.

"Lacy, what if Spring Hill is a nicer place?"

"What do you mean?"

"I mean, what if we get to Spring Hill, and they take us in as we planned, and then we find out that we like it there? That it is really a better place than Bluffton?"

Lacy was quiet for several steps before replying.

"I don't know. We'll just have to wait and see. Our first task is to get there and get in."

"Okay, I'm just thinking that Bluffton was good in some ways, but in other ways, it wasn't. Maybe this place will be better. And if it is? What do we do then?"

Lacy sighed, "I don't know. I guess that, as the old saying goes, we'll just have to cross that bridge when we get to it."

They fell silent as they continued to walk toward the crossroads. They were met there by the posted sentries who read the note from Dylan and then sent them down the gravel road to Spring Valley.

They started down the road, but soon stopped because the bottoms of the cotton socks that they had pulled over their disintegrating shoes were completely worn through. Only the wires they had stripped from Jack's car held their shoes in place. Their walking became increasingly uncomfortable. Then some of the thin wires snapped through from the wear and stress. Finally, about a mile from the valley entrance, they decided to stop and walk barefoot the rest of the way.

Walking slowly and stepping carefully, they made their way down the gravel road. They rounded the final corner and saw the bridge that crossed the Strange River.

Lisa commented whimsically, "It looks like it's time to cross that bridge."

"Very funny," replied Lacy, "at least you still have a sense of humor."

The gate on the bridge was open, but there was a sentry posted there. They were stopped at the bridge gate by the sentry. The numbers of refugees had slowed as the months had gone by. The last large group had been the one that consisted of the exiles from Bluffton. The sentry looked over the note from Dylan and asked them where they were from, and if they were sick or had been around anyone who was.

Lacy smiled and replied, "We are exiles from Bluffton. Other than sick and tired of walking, we're fine. But we're both hungry."

The sentry smirked back, "Probably footsore, too - being barefoot like that."

"Yeah, our shoes just fell apart. We had no choice but to go barefoot."

"Well then, head up the driveway to your right. The dogs will announce your presence." Lisa looked worried, so he quickly added, "But don't worry, they won't hurt you unless you attack. And they'll have food for you too. Supper isn't far off. Later, unless they kick you out," he joked, "you'll be able to enjoy the festivities."

"Festivities?"

"Aurora Eve?"

"What?"

"We're holding a celebration of the anniversary of the night of the first aurora! Oh, sure, we're also remembering those who disappeared that night. But the major point of it is to celebrate our survival. One year, and still here!"

"That's nice," said Lacy. She was going to say more, but at that moment she noticed two women approaching from the river road from the west. The sentry waved an arm in recognition and greeting. Both women carried walking staffs and wore daggers on their belts. The women carried themselves with an air of confidence, and Lacy could see that they were evaluating Lisa and her from afar. The women may not have had the look of King John's Attendants, but they appeared formidable in their own way.

Lacy and Lisa walked through the open bridge gate and took a couple of steps forward to where the driveway branched off the main road, and there they waited for the other two women to join them.

"Ah, new arrivals, I see," the taller one said as she walked up. She seemed familiar to Lacy, but Lacy couldn't identify what it was. The woman went on, "Walking barefoot on a gravel road, that takes guts."

Then it hit Lacy. She recognized her. They had competed against each other on sports teams between their high schools.

"Amanda? Amanda Grady? Is that, you?"

Mandy didn't answer immediately. She squinted her eyes slightly and looked intently at Lacy. Then Mandy recalled the girl from Sandstone that she used to compete against.

"Lacy Millbanks! What the heck are you doing here?" Mandy asked in wonderment, and then immediately she turned suspicious and added, "Did you come here from Sandstone or Stone Creek?"

"No. We were in Bluffton when the world changed. We've been there ever since, well, we were until two days ago when they kicked us out."

Mandy appraised the two carefully, looking them up and

273

down.

"Why did they kick you out? You look healthy enough?"

Lisa answered, "They said I didn't look white enough. They accused me of being Asian and said they didn't want my kind there."

Megan, standing next to Mandy, said to Lisa, "Well, you do look like you could be a little bit Asian. But that should be no reason to chase you away." She turned to Lacy, "What about you? You're from Sandstone. Why should they kick you out?"

Lacy sighed and gave a shy and furtive, yet noticeable, glance toward Lisa.

"Yes, I'm originally from Sandstone, but ..." she hesitated, reached out and took Lisa by the hand, and then went on, "when they ordered Lisa into exile, I had to go with her. She is my closest friend. We love each other. I couldn't let her leave alone."

Mandy, still suspicious, queried, "Why didn't you go back to Sandstone? You'd have family and friends there."

"I didn't think they would understand our relationship. Besides Krystal Miller's family is running the show in Sandstone and Stone Creek, and she went along with kicking us out. I doubt they'd want us."

Megan turned to Mandy and said, "That meshes with what the Bluffton exiles told us this winter when they came. Let's take them up the hill. Chief Maggie will decide what to do with them."

Mandy nodded her agreement. In short order, the two Spring Hill women led the exiles pulling their travois through the open gate and up the driveway to the main encampment. They were greeted by a chorus of barking dogs as well as the stares and greetings of the community members.

Chapter 57 - Aurora Eve

Early May nights in the north-central part of what used to be the United States are often quite cool. The night of the Aurora Eve celebration was on the higher end of average for the time of year, and on this night there was no fear of frost. It was not as warm as the night of the first aurora a year ago, but it was still a pleasant Spring evening.

Lacy and Lisa had been accepted by Maggie, who asked Holly to find a place for them to bunk. After settling into a section of the newest longhouse, they were escorted to the cookfire where they were each given a bowl of the "eternal stew" that was kept cooking at all times. There they encountered several of the other Bluffton exiles. A few of the exiles questioned them as to how things were going in Bluffton, but all of them seemed to accept the account of Lisa's exile and Lacy's accompanying her.

After supper, they were directed to go to the old farmhouse where Doctor Julie Westin had set up a clinic for the community. The aurora may have sent human society back to a technological level of the Middle Ages, but Doctor Westin was determined to use modern medical knowledge to keep her charges as healthy as possible. It had been a severe winter, and there had been several deaths in the community because of the lack of "modern" medicines, but she was doing the best she could.

The doctor examined them in private, and when she saw the brand that marked Lacy's upper breast, she asked Lacy about it. Lacy knew that eventually someone would see the brand and ask about it, so she had considered what her response should be. Knowing that there were other exiles from Bluffton in the community informed her decision to be as truthful as possible. Other exiles would understand what it meant. So she told her the story of how she acquired it, except, of course, the part about

Krystal's comment and threat. She also stressed how Krystal had been angry at her when learning about Lacy's relationship with Lisa, and of how Krystal was glad to see her leave Bluffton.

Dr. Westin listened carefully but made no comment on her story. She gave both of them a clean bill of health at the end of their examinations and sent them on their way to join in the festivities. Meanwhile, she departed to the Hall to give her report on the new arrivals to Maggie.

Lacy and Lisa walked to what had developed as the center courtyard of the community. It was actually the circular turnaround of the old driveway, but since no vehicles were driven upon it, it had transformed into the communities outdoor assembly area.

There was a large pile of logs in the center of the courtyard. They had been carefully stacked to make a grand bonfire, but they had yet to be lit. The sun had not yet set, but already torches had been lit around the perimeter of the courtyard.

Once the sun set, they still waited to light the bonfire. They had hoped that the skies would be clear so that they could see the northern lights pulsing throughout the sky, and they were not disappointed. As the fading remnants of sunlight vanished, the lights of the aurora took over the sky. The nightly light show had seemed to diminish during the course of the year, but tonight it blazed again with the intensity of its first appearance.

Formal festivities started with readings by members of the community. Several people volunteered to read selections from literature that helped them remember and honor their loved ones who disappeared with the arrival of the aurora. Then a list was read of those who had died in the community during the past year. One of the young men, who still had his trumpet from his high school band days played "Taps."

This was followed by an address given by the man many of them considered to be their "philosopher-in-residence" - Bill Hempstead.

"As we gather tonight, we look for meaning under the swirling lights. This is a time for reflection - we hope that yearly it shall be so. Living - we struggle to understand and to go on. Our world has changed. One year ago, living flesh vanished from before our eyes. One year ago, the power we drew from technologically advanced devices simply disappeared. Even today, products fashioned by that technology continue to dissolve."

"Questions abound for us. Some of us wonder: What caused some people to vanish, yet others to remain? Was it a totally random chance? Could it have been the act of some deity? Do we remain here as a punishment, as a reward, or as an opportunity? Is there some scientific explanation that eludes us?"

"We haven't answered those questions, however, we are rebuilding human society. The question we can answer and respond to is: how shall we do so?"

"This community has pledged itself to live out the ideals of care and compassion, to understanding and cooperation, to human advancement for all our people, to live in ways in which we use our environment while still protecting it."

"So tonight we will light this fire and celebrate the end of our first year, and the beginning of our second year of this new era. We remember, we struggle, and we hope."

The gathered crowd applauded Bill's words, for they summarized the feelings of many of them. Then Clan Chief Maggie stepped forward to say a few words and light the fire. She could see that the children in the crowd were getting antsy in anxious anticipation of the bonfire, so she wanted to keep her words to a minimum, but she had much she wanted to say.

"Greetings, citizens of Spring Hill. Today marks an important milestone in our life together. We have survived, and I would say, even prospered during the first year of the Aurora Era! Tonight and tomorrow we celebrate that. We also celebrate the news that we will be changing our alliance with Oakwood into a stronger union. Let us continue to live in peace and harmony. We light this fire to symbolize life! Let's celebrate!"

Maggie took one of the torches and held it high in front of her. Other members of the clan extinguished the surrounding torches. Only the clan chief's flame now flickered under the undulating skies of the aurora. With a wave and a flourish, she plunged the torch into the waiting kindling of the bonfire. It ignited and within moments the bonfire roared to life. The crowd cheered and roared in response.

Mike pulled out his fiddle and began playing one of the traditional Irish jigs that he knew and had entertained the people with during their long winter nights. Immediately some of the folk started dancing. Maggie was one of the first. As a former dance instructor, she had coached some of the younger members of the community when they were her students in high school. Harkening back to their training those of her former students who were present pulled out the young and old alike from the crowd to dance with them around the bonfire.

Even the newest members of the community, Lacy and Lisa, were among the dancers. No longer barefoot, for they had been given moccasins for their feet, they danced as joyfully as the rest. With instrumental music, singing, dancing, the celebration went long into the night. What could only be called a banquet, given their careful conserving of food during the winter months, was planned for the next day.

With increasing frequency, Mandy shot glances down the driveway hoping to see Jack and Cody striding into view. Finally, they appeared. No dogs barked, or alarm was sounded because these were two of the most well-known members of the community. But a welcoming cheer went up from the crowd as they were recognized. Mandy ran to Jack and threw her arms around him, as Cody lifted Aurora in an embrace.

The women pulled their men to the bonfire to join in the festivities. The men laid their gear to the side and began dancing with their partners. Their official report to Maggie and her advisors could wait until the following day.

A few dances later, Jack escorted Mandy to the edge of the crowd where the more sedate members of the community sat and enjoyed conversation with each other as they watched the frolicking crowd. The couple found a place to sit and talk. Jack whispered a few comments into Mandy's ear and as he did so he eyes roamed over the crowd. His scanning stopped when his eyes came to where Lisa and Lacy were sitting with a group of people. The two young ladies were unfamiliar, yet there was something about Lisa that struck some cord in his memory. Then it hit him. It was Lisa Peele.

Mandy noticed his sudden change in demeanor. "What is it, Jack? Who are you looking at?" She followed where his eyes were looking. "The new girls? They got here the same time Megan and I got back this afternoon."

"That makes sense. I thought they were new here."

"The brunette is Lacy Millbanks. She's my age. We played sports against each other in high school. She went to Sandstone High School. The other one is Lisa . . . I forget her last name. They came together from Bluffton. Exiled because Lisa is Asian. They're lovers."

Jack wrinkled his brow in thought.

"What?" Mandy asked. "Why the worried look?"

Jack hesitated before responding. "Nothing." Then after a moment, he added, "Are we sure they aren't spies? After what the earlier exiles from Bluffton said, I don't think that their King

John will be our friend."

"They seemed legit to me. No one else voiced concern."

"Okay. Say, would you wait here. I'll be right back, but I want to go bounce a couple of ideas off of Bill. Get him thinking about something. I promise I'll be back in a few minutes."

She agreed and watched him walk around from the bonfire toward where Bill and a few others were sitting on the far side of the fire. Then she turned and started taking with those seated near her.

Jack found Bill sitting with Geoff and Julie and motioned for him to come with him. Bill got up and followed Jack away from the bonfire. They talked for a few minutes and then Jack started making his way through the crowd toward Mandy. Suddenly someone bumped into to him. He looked to his side and saw Lisa Peele. She looked up at him and held her a finger over her mouth warning him to be quiet.

She leaned up and whispered, loud enough for him to hear, but soft enough so no one else could hear over the music, "We don't know each other, please." Then she quickly stepped aside and melted back into the crowd.

Jack pursed his lips briefly and then muttered to himself, "Then that's the way we will play it." He shook his head slightly, forced a smile onto his face, and walked the rest of the way back to Mandy.

When the fire tenders stopped adding wood to the fire, and it began to die down, Jack and Mandy did what several of the couples did. They grabbed a blanket and went to find a somewhat secluded spot to lie together under the Northern Lights. Mandy was pregnant, and they were both tired from their long day of activity, but it was a memorable night under the stars and the aurora.

Chapter 58 - Aurora Morn

Aurora and Cody followed the example of the other couples, trysting under the lights of the nocturnal sky. They were still lying under the stars when the eastern horizon began to brighten softly with the promise of the new day. Cody had fallen asleep, but Aurora lay awake thinking about what it meant to be living in the second year of the new era. It was a bittersweet time. She had miscarried in her first trimester. Doctor Westin had tried to reassure her that it wasn't Aurora's fault and that in the "old modern world" ten to fifteen percent of women miscarried in the first trimester, but she still questioned herself. She pondered what living in these times meant for her.

Bad things happened, but so did much good. Women and men made love and built families. Children played. People worked hard and played in their free time. There remained good and bad people in this world. Some people schemed and were self-centered. But, by and large, the goodness of humanity shown through. Life went on. Sure, ultimate questions were pondered upon - but when wasn't that the case. They had survived the early days and months following the change. Now they must live the best they could. As it had always been. Or perhaps, now they had the chance to live - better than they had before. Only the coming years would tell.

The sky brightened and the aurora faded behind the veil of daylight. The new day began.

Watch for book 2 in the series:

UNRAPTURED: THE ALCHEMIST

The Alchemist is a practitioner of alchemy - which means nothing unless one has an understanding of the history of the practice. Since ancient times, men and women of knowledge have studied ways of mixing metals and elements. Often times this was done in the hope of transmuting common metals into more valuable ones, such as gold. One branch of alchemists, called apothecarists, focused their efforts of mixing naturally occurring ingredients to formulate elixirs that might poison or cure. Because of their arcane knowledge and potions, some people considered them to be wizards. With the development of scientific theory and technological advancements, such practitioners of alchemy became modern day scientists, chemists, and pharmacists.

Now, the changes wrought by the aurora have forced modern scientists to return from the technology of the space age to the technology of previous eras. Scientific methodology and knowledge are still available to them, but as their tools shift, so do their resources, instruments, efforts, and results. They become again - alchemists.

Chapter 1

Tom adjusted his protective goggles as he leaned over the steaming kettle, which simmered over the small brazier in his workshop. He was about to pour a cloudy liquid from a test tube into the kettle of boiling green fluid when a knock on the door halted him. He sputtered invectives about always being interrupted in the middle of his work, and then shouted, "Come in!"

He set the test tube carefully into a rack on the work bench as the door swung inward and a delegation of people filed in. He recognized a couple of his "guards" as well as the boss of the town. The two other men were strangers to him. He wasn't surprised, for there was very little that surprised him anymore. He cared little for who the people were, other than for the fact that they had interrupted him.

Tom had survived the changes following the first two years of the Aurora Era, but it had been fraught with difficulties. He had managed to deal with the physical deprivations of the changed world and to navigate the human machinations that swirled around him. The evening of the first aurora had found him umpiring a high school baseball game in the town of Galena. After the game, he had stayed to drink a few beers with some of his teaching acquaintances. However, when the northern lights flared and everything electrical was fried, he became stranded in Galena. For a short time he had enjoyed the time of camaraderie with his friends, but soon enough the time came when he wanted more...

Other works by Joel Kreger:

Thin Times and Thin Places: Life Lessons from the Labyrinth

CHRONICLES OF EIRGALON
Land Beyond the Sunset
Search for the Loon's Necklace
Brigit's Bow

Amazon Author Page: amazon.com/author/joelkreger